Cape May

Cape May

Chip Cheek

CELADON
BOOKS

NEW YORK

CAPE MAY. Copyright © 2019 by Chip Cheek. All rights reserved. Printed in the United States of America. For information, address Celadon Books, a Division of Macmillan Publishers, 120 Broadway, New York, NY 10271.

www.celadonbooks.com

Library of Congress Control Number: 201861341

ISBN 978-1-250-29715-0 (hardcover)
ISBN 978-1-250-23110-9 (international, sold outside the U.S., subject to rights availability)
ISBN 978-1-250-29716-7 (ebook)

ISBN 978-1-250-29746-4 (trade paperback)

Our books may be purchased in bulk for promotional, educational, or business use. Please contact your local bookseller or the Macmillan Corporate and Premium Sales Department at 1-800-221-7945, extension 5442, or by email at MacmillanSpecialMarkets@macmillan.com.

First Celadon Books Paperback Edition: 2020

10 9 8 7 6 5 4 3 2 1

For Katie

From the time that their love is avowed, neither sees the other but in a mask; and the cheat is often managed on both sides with so much art, and discovered afterwards with so much abruptness, that each has reason to suspect that some transformation has happened on the wedding-night, and that by a strange imposture, as in the case of Jacob, one has been courted and another married.

—DR. SAMUEL JOHNSON, *THE RAMBLER*, NO. 45

One

The beaches were empty, the stores were closed, and after sunset, all the houses on New Hampshire Avenue stood dark. For months, Effie had been telling him about this place and the many things they would do here, but she had only known it in the summer, and this was the end of September. She had not understood what "off-season" meant. They had come up from Georgia on the overnight train. They were supposed to spend two weeks here, for their honeymoon.

"I love it," Henry said their first evening. "It's like we got the whole place to ourselves."

Effie laughed at that. A minute later, she began to cry.

"It's nothing," she said. "It's nothing, really—don't coo over me. I'm just tired, that's all." She smiled at him. "I'm glad you like it. We're going to have a wonderful time."

Before this trip Henry had never been north of Atlanta, and he had never seen the ocean. He and Effie had grown up in the little town of Signal Creek, half an hour east of Macon, and in the spring they had graduated from high school: Thomas E. Cobb, Class of

1957. He was twenty—like many people from the country, he had started school late—and she was eighteen. They both, as far as Henry knew, had been virgins.

In the taxicab from the depot they'd come out beside a harbor teeming with masts, and the sea beyond it was roiling, immense, speckled with whitecaps. From the harbor they turned into a residential area shaded with elm trees, and here were the grand Victorian houses Effie had told him about: bright colors, slate gables and conical towers, widows' walks with wrought-iron railings, porches trimmed in elaborate woodwork, trellises opening onto the sidewalks, chrysanthemums in bloom. On New Hampshire Avenue the houses were more plain—one- and two-story cottages that wouldn't have looked out of place in Signal Creek, aside from the colors. Aunt Lizzie's place was one of these: pale pink, two stories, with a deep front porch above a dead flower garden. It was disappointing. But when he stepped out of the cab and heard the ocean three blocks away, a hushed, deep roar, it seemed to him that his true life was just beginning, and that every possible door was open to him now. He scooped Effie up into his arms—she shrieked and laughed—and carried her across the threshold.

The house looked different, she said when he set her down. She hadn't seen it in three years, since the summer before her aunt Lizzie passed away. The wicker furniture was new. The gas stove, the refrigerator and freezer: none of these conveniences had existed. They seemed to trouble her. There were four bedrooms on the second floor—these looked different too—but Effie insisted they sleep in the attic room, where she had slept as a child. At the top of the stairs she slid a heavy glass door open and they stepped inside. This room, happily, had not changed a bit. The walls slanted sharply, bare wooden beams. A single bed stood in the middle of the room, a chest of drawers, a dusty vanity table and mirror. In a corner stood a small, dead Christmas tree, threads of tinsel still caught in the branches. That had been there too. She knelt down to the floor-level windows and cracked them open. From here you could see the ocean over the houses across the street; Henry crouched down for a look.

"I know it's a little peculiar," Effie said, "but you can humor me, can't you? Just for a night?"

He could humor her for the rest of his life, he wanted to say, but Effie laughed at expressions of deep feeling; she had been on the verge of laughing all through their wedding ceremony. He kissed her instead, and put his hand on her thigh, his body humming. All these months of anticipation, and here they were. They had known each other since they were children, from church and from school, though for most of that time they had not thought much of each other. He could see her standing at the blackboard in Mrs. Mobley's fourth-grade classroom, in her Mary Janes and white stockings, copying out a line from the Psalms: Mayor Tarleton's snotty little daughter. And he, one of the boys from *out there*, beyond the town line. Now they were here, together and alone. In New Jersey, of all places.

She laid her hand over his. "Let me take a bath first," she said.

It happened not in the attic room, which was too full of memories, but in one of the redecorated bedrooms on the second floor. They chose the one with the rose-patterned wallpaper. He drew the curtains closed. She'd just taken her bath, and while she stood still he undid the loose belt at her waist and slipped her robe off her shoulders. Until now, what little they had done had come in stolen moments back home: an afternoon at the bend in the creek, when he'd pulled the straps of her bathing suit down and seen her breasts for the first time; the night, shortly after they got engaged, in the backseat of her Buick, when he'd reached up her dress and she'd let him—the soft skin above her stockings, the elastic of her underwear, the scent that had lingered on his fingers—and every detail was burned into his memory but at the same time unreal, as if he'd dreamt it. Now, in this dim room, early on a Sunday afternoon, when they would normally be in their church clothes having dinner with their families, Effie lay naked on the rose-patterned duvet. She looked away while he unbuckled his trousers and let them fall to the floor, and after hesitating a moment, he pulled down his BVDs and got into the bed beside her. They kissed for a minute, skin against skin, smooth and cool and then warm, before he got on top of her, where he couldn't quite see what he was doing. He hovered over her, fumbling between her legs, until she looked down, took his penis lightly between her fingertips, set it in the right spot—and there she was: their intimacy deepened in an instant. His breath caught. She lay still. In a few seconds, it was over.

Afterward they lay beside each other looking at the ceiling tiles. He wondered whether he felt irreversibly changed.

"Well," Effie said. "I guess we've done it, then."

Later, as they walked down to the beach in the early evening, they held hands and had little to say to each other. What was there to say? They knew each other now, in the biblical sense. He smiled at her; she smiled back. The dress she was wearing was one she'd worn often to school, before the thought of dating her had ever entered his mind, and the familiar sight of it made her strange: she was both the girl he knew then, in the hallways of Thomas E. Cobb, and the girl he knew now, far more intimately, in Cape May, New Jersey. His wife. With whom he had already shared an indignity: they'd made a mess on the rose-patterned duvet. But Effie, bless her, had been sporting enough to laugh about it, and asked him to run and fetch her a towel. He was grateful for her.

Down at the promenade they stood for a while and looked at the sea. The waves curled over and crashed, one after another, an endless succession. All that water: it was a wonder it didn't swallow them up. The day was overcast and the wind had a bite to it. Seagulls hovered overhead, shrieking.

"It's so weird," Effie said. "In the summer this place is *teeming*."

She pointed to a pier that jutted out from the promenade, at the end of which stood an arcade where there had been games and music, she said, where she and her friends would spend entire afternoons, until the lights came on. Acrobats and strongmen performed on the promenade, there were stands of cotton candy and saltwater taffy, and boys surfed in the waves.

"We'll just have to come back in the summer, then," Henry said.

She took his hand again and they continued on down the promenade toward town. All along Beach Avenue, to their right, the shops were shuttered and dark, signs posted in the windows: CLOSED FOR THE SEASON. SEE YOU IN MAY!

At last they found a diner that was open and sat at a booth by the window. Their waiter was a boy with the kind of accent Henry had only ever heard on the radio. He wondered if he could tell that they'd recently had sex.

"If you're from all the way down there," the boy said, "why didn't you just go to Florida?"

"Because it's beautiful *here*," Effie said.

Henry ordered the meat loaf, she ordered the fish and chips, and as the boy slipped his notepad into his back pocket he said, "Well, if you came to get away from it all, you came to the right place."

They ate in silence. "I'm so glad to be here," Henry said.

That evening, they called it an early night and went up to the attic room. It was not quite eight o'clock.

She prayed the way his grandmother did: on her knees beside the bed, hands clasped, muttering to herself. Henry looked away. She wore a nightgown and her breasts were loose inside of it, but after her praying, a pious aura surrounded her that stunted his arousal. She kissed him and said, "Is it all right if we just go to sleep now?" The look of pity on her face was annoying.

"Yes," he said. "That's all I want to do too."

In the dark he clasped his hands over his chest and prayed silently.

He thanked God for the day. He prayed for their happiness and future. He prayed that he would be a good husband. Then he lay rigid on his side of the bed, listening to the wind and the waves through the open windows—feeling gassy, worrying he'd pass it in the night, wishing he could be alone for a little while.

The next day was better. It was raining, but they were starving and there was no food in the house, so they had to go outside. They were soaked by the time they found the grocer's in town.

There was life here, as it turned out. Weathered men in pea coats— fishermen, maybe. A group of Coast Guard cadets, from the train- ing station north of town. A few men and women running errands under umbrellas. They passed a grammar school, and at least one of the windows was lighted, though they didn't see any children any- where. In the central part of town, several blocks inland, a candy shop was open, a dry goods store, the grocer's on Washington Street, and beside it a hardware store and a liquor store. The old clerk at the grocer's seemed as happy to see them as they were to see him, and Effie called out orders as if she were preparing for a banquet: a pork loin, a pound of haddock, a loaf of bread, a pound of butter, sliced ham and cheese, potatoes, eggs, peach preserves, plums, apples, strawberries—she would fill the kitchen with abundance. On the way back to the cottage the rain became a downpour and they started running, each of them hugging a bag of groceries, the paper turning soft and dark in their arms. They arrived winded, doubling over with laughter. They put the groceries away and then, up in the attic room, peeled their wet clothes off and made love, memories be damned, over a beach towel spread under them on the bed.

Afterward she lay naked against him—so casual, like it was noth- ing already. "I'm sorry I was so gloomy yesterday," she said.

"You weren't, Eff," he said. His penis lay tipped against her thigh. He liked how it looked there. "You were tired. We're settled in now."

She nodded, her head moving against his shoulder. He couldn't see her face. "It just feels so weird to be back here. It's not like I remember it."

He kissed the top of her head—her hair was still damp—and gave her bare behind a squeeze. "Hey, so what. We're making new memories now."

She looked up at him and smiled. "You're such a sweet boy, Henry." She kissed him soft and slow, and in a minute he was up again, and though she resisted, playfully—"I *told* you, Henry, I'm *starving*"—with a nudge she got on top of him and they found each other without trying.

After lunch they sat out on the front porch and watched the rain, which was cool and fragrant, and she pointed out houses on the street and told him about the people who had lived in them during the summers. There were the Woods, in the cottage across from them, whose daughter, Betsy, used to babysit her sometimes. Next door to the Woods, in the large house with the barn-shaped roof, lived her friend Vivian Healy, whose older brother, Charles, had died in Korea. A few houses down, on this side of the street, in the big purple Victorian, lived an older couple who always kept to themselves. She never knew their names. "You'd just see them walking hand in hand down the sidewalk, and they'd smile at you and say hello, but that was all. There was never anyone else there, no children or grandchildren. Just the two of them."

"That'll be us someday," Henry said.

Effie laughed. "Don't say that. It's too sad."

"How is it sad? It sounds sweet to me."

She shook her head. "No," she said. "You and me—there'll be no peace for us, I'm afraid. We're going to have us a *roost*."

"God help me," Henry said. She'd made it clear to him that she wanted five children at least, all boys if she had her way, that she wanted a house that never rested, that she and Henry, into old age, would be at the center of a maelstrom of life (she wanted dogs too), and though he didn't care one way or another about children, or dogs—in fact her idea of the future had alarmed him when he really thought about it, in the weeks before their marriage—now it made him feel light and for a brief moment radiantly happy. They were going to be all right.

"What are you smiling at?" she said.

"You," he said.

"Quit it," she said, and she kissed him before he could say anything more.

They drank some of Uncle George's brandy. In the house instructions he'd left for them on the dining room table he told them they could help themselves to his liquor cabinet, but if they drank more than half of any bottle he expected them to replace it, and he provided them with the address of the liquor store on Washington Street. "We should leave exactly half of every bottle," Henry said, and Effie laughed. This Uncle George, Aunt Lizzie's widower, lived in Philadelphia and wasn't a blood relation. Effie had never had much to say about him, aside from the logistics of the trip and when the cottage would be available. Henry had the sense she didn't like him very much.

She made the haddock for supper—it stuck to the pan and crumbled to pieces, but it was good—and afterward they turned the radio on, found a hits station that wasn't too fuzzy with static, and danced in the den to "Chances Are." They played a game of checkers, which Effie won handily. They passed the halfway mark on the bottle of brandy.

"What's he going to do, bill us?" Henry said.

"To hell with King George," Effie said. "Bottoms up."

On Tuesday the sun came out and the streets and squares in town were spangled with light. They walked out to see the lighthouse, which stood near the point, on the other side of a wetland. This spot, according to Henry's understanding of the town, marked the southernmost tip of New Jersey. Ahead of them lay open ocean, to the left of them lay open ocean, and off to the right somewhere, on the other side of the peninsula, lay Delaware Bay. Now that the sun was out, the sea was royal blue. "Just think," he said, pointing to the horizon ahead, "about ten thousand miles down that way is Antarctica, or South Africa, or something. We could just swim and swim and never see the end of all that water."

When she didn't answer he looked at her and saw that she was frowning. She'd been grumpy that morning. They'd both had too much to drink. "That's not right," she said. "That way's west."

He felt a prick of annoyance. He'd only been trying to put a little wonder into things. "How is that way west? It's ocean as far as you can see."

"No, it's Delaware," she said. "You can see it with binoculars— I'll show you a map when we get back to the house." She pointed off to the left of where they were standing. "*That* way's south. If you swam *that* way, you'd run into Antarctica or South Africa or what-have-you. Actually, I think you'd run into Venezuela first."

Never mind. He wrapped his arms around her and kissed the top of her head. "Fine, Rand McNally, south is west and east is north," and she pushed him away, smiling.

*T*hey made love every morning, before they got out of bed, and again in the late afternoon. They were gentle and considerate with each other. He caressed her between her legs, shy of looking too closely at it. He kissed her breasts, her soft, plump belly, her impressive nest of pubic hair, which smelled of linen, but he went no further, afraid of offending her, afraid that she would recoil or laugh or call him a pervert. How could he ask what she wanted? How could he tell her what he wanted? Sometimes she held his penis lightly and he lifted his hips to encourage her—he wanted her to hold it more firmly (but not too firmly), he wanted her, in his dreams, to put it into her mouth—but she shied away, afraid of hurting it, or else wary of it, or revolted. He didn't know. But they made love, no words necessary, and it seemed to go a little more naturally each time. He took it slow and easy, holding back the tide for as long as possible. The headboard tapped the wall. She breathed close to his ear, her fingers in his hair.

Later, while they ate breakfast or tried a new route through the town, her expression would grow distant, and they might go half an hour without saying a word. He had to remind himself that these silences weren't necessarily awkward, that in fact it was a sign of intimacy that they didn't have to be speaking all the time. But even so, he couldn't help thinking that if he'd been a brighter person, less quiet and inward—more funny and gregarious like his best friend, Hoke, whom Effie adored—then maybe she would be happier.

The days were long. There was little to do. She took naps in the afternoons, and Henry coveted the time alone. He'd been constipated since before their wedding, and only when she was asleep did he feel comfortable enough to try to go to the bathroom—far away from her, in the lavatory off the kitchen. The results were always unsatisfying. Afterward, feeling bloated, he'd sit in the den with the windows open or out on the back porch, where the birch trees made a calming sound.

He was reading Boswell's *The Life of Samuel Johnson,* which his uncle Carswall had given him as a wedding present. Carswall had read it when he was a young man, and it had been a good guide to him, he said. "You're always going to be at work on yourself, son, and it's always going to be a struggle. But it's the struggle that'll make you a good man." Henry liked the ideas; he had a vision of the kind of man he wanted to be—virtuous, humble, strong, and bold, full of good cheer but in healthy moderation—and he was eager to learn. But the book, so far, was a thumping bore, and he couldn't read more than a few sentences before his mind began to wander.

Thursday morning they walked out to the marina to look at the boats. At the end of a pier stood an octagonal building with large windows on all sides. Effie thought she remembered going to parties there. The entrance was padlocked, but beside it a fresh-looking poster of a jack-o'-lantern in a sailor's cap advertised a dance for Friday, October 11. "Is that tomorrow?" Henry asked, but Effie said no, that was next Friday.

"Hey," he said, "that's our last night here." He took her hand. "Our last night, there's going to be a *dance* here. How about that?"

She didn't seem to share his excitement. She touched her fingertips to the poster. "My God," she said. "I can't believe we're going to be here that long."

They went down to the beach and walked along the edge of the surf with their shoes in their hands.

"You know," she said after a long silence, "we don't have to stay the whole two weeks. We could take the train out on Sunday and be home by Monday morning."

"You want to leave?" he asked.

"Maybe?" she said.

From here Cape May really was beautiful. The edge of the ocean stretched off into the distance ahead of them, on one side the beach and the tall grasses and, farther off, the big Victorian hotels, the columns and striped awnings. Signal Creek seemed so dreary in comparison. Pine woods, fields of cotton and peanuts, the Courthouse Square, the toffee-colored creek itself. Carswall and Henry's mother were having an annex of the house—what they grandly called "the

Old Wing"—remodeled for them. A living room with a potbelly stove, a bedroom, a lavatory, a tiny hopeful room for the future baby. The thought of settling into their lives there—so soon, anyway—depressed him. "*I* don't want to leave," he said. "I could stay here forever."

Effie smiled at him. "I'm glad you feel that way." She stopped to pick up a shell from the flat, wet sand at their feet and turned it over in her hand. "It just feels so sad here, Henry. Sad and—I don't know." She looked past him. "Dull, I guess."

It stung, and he opened his mouth to speak, but she kept on, oblivious: "Aunt Lizzie's dead and gone. None of my old friends are here. Uncle George . . . Did you know he wanted to charge us for the cottage, and Mama had to talk him out of it? She had to remind him we were still technically his family. She was so embarrassed." Henry didn't see what that had to do with anything, but he said nothing. "I don't know what I was thinking. That boy at the diner was right: we should have gone to Florida."

"Eff," he said, collecting himself, "we can't go home early."

"Oh, Henry . . ."

"No, listen," he said, but he wasn't sure how to say what he wanted to say. How humiliating it would be. How everyone would detect failure, even if it wasn't really there: they would think it and it would burrow in and eventually become true. "Think of your mama," he said. "*My* mama. What are they going to say?"

It seemed to have an effect on her. She nodded, and tossed the shell away. They continued walking, and Henry thought he had won the point, although what good was it if she was just going to be sad and bored the rest of the time? But after a few minutes she said, "I don't care what people say, Henry. I just want to go home."

So they would leave Sunday afternoon. At least they would have the weekend. Henry felt hurt and angry at first—it was rotten of her to

be sad, to say things were dull after what they had shared—but soon
he felt as though a pall had risen from them, now that their honeymoon was ruined. After supper—the pork loin, which was delicious—
they opened Uncle George's brandy again and the evening took on a
valedictory air. They took the bottle out to the front porch and
watched the light fade from the elm trees. They told stories. How
Betty Moody wanted Maynard Givens's babies. How Suzie Blanchard
could let the farts rip when it was just the girls. The time Hoke had
tried to jump Lord's Gully on his bike. Henry loved the rare occasions when he could make Effie laugh, when she briefly lost her cool
and the whole top half of her body bounced. "Stop it, stop it," she
said, "you're going to make me wet myself." They finished the brandy
and opened a bottle of scotch. They couldn't pronounce the name.
"I bet it's expensive," he said, and they said cheers and clinked their
glasses. It was dark out now, and they'd turned the radio on, and soft,
airy music was coming out to them on the front porch. They were in
a lull—a comfortable silence this time, drunk and content—when
Henry noticed the lights down at the end of the street.

He stood up and went to the railing to get a better look. There
were lights in the windows of the house on the corner—three houses
down, on the other side of the street, where New Hampshire Avenue
intersected with Madison Avenue. He called Effie over to see.

"Well, I'll be damned," she said.

They weren't alone anymore.

"You never said anything about that house," he said. "Do you remember who lived there?"

She thought about it. "I don't know," she said. "It's been so long."

With their drinks in hand they walked down the sidewalk until
they stood directly across from the house. Most of it was invisible in
the dark, but the downstairs windows were bright. They watched and
listened for signs of life, but nothing moved behind the curtains, and
all they could hear was the surf and the wind in the trees.

"Should we go say hello?" Henry said.

Effie reached up to pat her hair. "No—Lord, no. It's late." She held up her drink. "We'd look like a couple of drunks, wouldn't we?"

"Maybe tomorrow, then."

She nodded. They stood watching a few minutes longer, until Effie pointed out that they were acting like creeps, and they turned back to the cottage.

*T*he next morning, on their way down to the beach—it was a balmy day, finally, and Effie thought they might be able to get into the water—they passed the house on the corner and saw three automobiles crowded in the driveway: a little red sports car, a baby-blue Cadillac convertible, and what looked to Henry like a Rolls-Royce, though he'd never seen one in real life. They were rich, these people. Except that the lawn, more than the others on the street, was overgrown with weeds, and the house, set back in the gloom of the trees, had a condemned look to it.

The water was too rough for swimming, so they climbed up onto one of the tall lifeguards' chairs and looked out over the surf. Effie was trying to remember who had lived at the house. She held the wide brim of her hat with both hands so it wouldn't fly off. "It could have been the Richardses, I guess. They had a daughter, Mattie, who was a few years older than me—but they might have lived over on Maryland Avenue, I don't know. It's probably no one. A lot of these places turn over."

When they passed the house again on their way back, two more cars had parked along the curb—a long, shiny Buick and another Cadillac. "It must be a party," Henry said.

"Or a family thing. It might be rude to crash it."

"Who said anything about crashing? We can just say hello."

*T*hey decided they would do it at five, which was early enough, Effie thought, that they wouldn't interrupt the newcomers' supper. "We'll just stop by," she said. "If they invite us in, fine. If not—well, we'll just see if there's any life in this town on a Friday."

They were nervous, for some reason; he could tell that she was too. Maybe it was the Rolls-Royce in the driveway. Maybe, absurdly, it was that they were expecting some kind of rescue and didn't want to bungle it. Henry wore his good trousers and shoes and a gray blazer. Effie wore her navy-blue dress with the white collar and white belt cinched tightly around her waist. She'd bundled her hair up and looked pretty, especially in the late-afternoon light, but not as though she'd dressed up for a party, which might come off as presumptuous.

Another car had parked by the curb. That made six in all. They walked up the gravel drive and found the path, almost completely obscured by weeds, that led to the front door.

The front door was open, and through the screen door they could see to the back windows, but they couldn't see anyone inside. Effie pulled a rope hanging by the door and a bell clanged inside. They waited. After a minute she pulled the rope again, and finally a voice came from deep within the house—"Coming!"—and soon a handsome woman with blond, elegantly coiffed hair and a white halter-top dress pushed the screen door open. "Hello!" she cried, looking at Henry, whose eyes dropped involuntarily to her breasts. "You must be . . ." And she seemed to search for the right name, ready to be utterly delighted, whoever it was.

"We're just staying down the street," Effie said. "We were on our way to supper and saw the cars down here and figured we'd introduce ourselves. We don't want to bother you."

While Effie spoke, the delight in the woman's face faded, and she leaned forward to get a closer look. "No," she said. "No, it can't be— it just *can't* be. Is that my little belle?"

Effie glanced at Henry, as if he would know the answer.

"My God!" the woman cried. "It *is* you. You're the little Southern girl from down the street! My God—I could faint!" The woman wrapped her arms around Effie and squeezed her, and Effie tipped her head up as if for air. She seemed alarmed. Finally the woman let her go and said, "Don't you remember me? You're going to break my heart if you don't remember me."

And now something seemed to dawn on Effie. "Clara?" she said. "Clara Strauss?"

"Yes!" the woman cried, clapping her hands together.

And though Effie was smiling broadly, Henry knew her well enough to know better: she was sorry they had come.

Two

"*Come in, come in —Jesus!*" *the woman demanded, as if to scold* them for not arriving sooner, and led them across a wide foyer into a bright living area that looked out through a bank of windows onto a lush patio and swimming pool. The shadowy look of the house from the outside was a disguise for the brightness inside. It seemed to Henry like an enchantment.

"We can only stay a minute," Effie said. "We were just on our way to dinner."

"I can't *believe* it's you," Clara said, stopping to appraise her. "How long has it been? Five, six years? A lifetime? Who is this?" She placed her hand at the small of Henry's back. When Effie told her he was her husband, the woman gasped—she had never heard of anything so marvelous—and gripped his hand firmly, painfully. "My God, how do you do? I'm Clara—Clara!"

"I'm Henry!"

"Yes!"

Effie explained that Clara had been her older cousin Holly's friend back in the day. On occasion Effie would have to go along with them to the beach or into town, if there wasn't anyone else to watch her.

"*Holly's friend.*" Clara put her hands on her hips. "What a cold bitch you are. I adored this creature," she said to Henry, and to Effie: "Don't you remember how much fun we had? But you were so young and impressionable then. And look at you now: a beauty! Married to William Holden, no less!" She laughed, and took hold of Henry's forearm, and Henry smiled back at her like a fool. "Oh, my belle," she said, and in a voice like Scarlett O'Hara: "My Effie Mae. That's what I called you, do you remember?"

"Yes," Effie said evenly.

"Those were good times, weren't they? But the years do pass. Sit, sit!"

She directed them to a sofa that faced the back windows and a large fireplace made of slate and what appeared to be loose rocks. It didn't look stable. The ceiling was open rafters, very high, and two frosted windows in the roof let in more light, and over the foyer, behind them now, an upstairs balcony ran the length of the living area. It was a much larger house than Aunt Lizzie's, but it felt scattered and haphazard—and at the moment, empty of people.

"What can I get you to drink?" Clara said.

"Oh, we're fine," Effie said. "Really, we can't stay for long."

"Nonsense. It is cocktail o'clock. You *have* to stay for a little while. I haven't seen you in so long, and here you are, like magic, back in this godforsaken place." She looked at Henry. "What will *you* have?"

He waited for a cue from Effie, but she only stared at him helplessly. For his part, he was content to stay. "I'll take anything," he said.

"Gin and tonic it is!" she cried. "The only suitable drink before dinner." She swept over to the minibar, and Effie closed her eyes and laid her head back on the sofa. "My God! Effie Moore, right here in Cape May, after all these years."

"Effie Tarleton," Effie said.

"That's right! Oh, it's all coming back to me now."

She was a whirlwind, this woman. Henry had never met anyone like her. She was in her early thirties, he guessed, and big, not just physically big but aura big, the way Jayne Mansfield would be big if she could step out of the screen at the drive-in. She was at least as tall as he was, with a strong jaw and broad shoulders, and her breasts seemed always on the verge of falling out of her top. It was an effort not to stare at them.

"But what are you doing here this time of year?" she asked, taking two tall glasses down from a shelf behind the minibar.

Effie lifted her head and reported, as if with regret, that they were on their honeymoon.

"No!" Clara slammed the glasses down, and for a moment Henry thought she was actually angry at them. "You mean you're *newlyweds*? You mean you're on your honeymoon *right now*?" She turned away from them and shouted, "Mrs. Pavich!"

From an archway that led off the den a voice came back to them, thickly accented and dripping with ennui: "Yes, Mrs. Kirschbaum."

"I have changed my mind. We *will* have the carrot cake." She turned back to Henry and Effie. "But of *course* you're newlyweds. You're *glowing*—I can see it now."

Henry smiled at Effie, but Effie kept her eyes fixed on Clara, a taut, neutral expression on her face.

"Well, that settles it: you're staying for dinner. I can't imagine where you were thinking of going; it can't be better than what old Mrs. Pavich is cooking up. Everyone's down at the beach right now— well, not Richard, of course—but we're having a party, and you two are going to stay and celebrate with us."

In his confusion Henry said, "You're throwing us a party?" and Effie looked at him like he was an idiot indeed.

"Oh, I love him!" Clara said.

"I wish we could stay," Effie said. "But we're not here much longer, and we really wanted to see a little more of the town, you know—have dinner, see a movie . . ."

But Clara was rummaging behind the bar. "I hope Mrs. Pavich hasn't forgotten the ice. We will need a lot of ice." She stood up straight. "You two just sit there and look perfect and I'll be back in thirty seconds. I can't *wait* to catch up." She dashed off toward the archway, shouting "Mrs. Pavich!" again.

"Wow," Henry said. "She's something else, isn't she?"

"We're leaving," Effie said.

She stood up from the sofa, but Henry took hold of her wrist. "Why? What's wrong?"

"The *one* person we run into, and it's got to be Clara Strauss. Or whatever her name is. She must have snagged a husband."

"What's wrong with her?"

She brushed his hand away and looked toward the archway, from which they could hear Clara gleefully lecturing Mrs. Pavich: "*This* one is for the hollandaise, dear, and *this* one is for the pepper sauce. Do you see the difference in the spouts?"

"She's a snot-nosed bully and a harlot," Effie said. "She's not a good person."

Henry laughed. "Come on. Sit down. We're not just going to walk out on her, I don't care who she is."

Effie sat down. "Of all the people—I mean, really. It never occurred to me. She wasn't here the past couple of times, not since Holly married." Clara was her cousin Holly's friend, she explained again. Holly was Uncle George's eldest daughter from a previous marriage. She was more than a dozen years older than Effie and never took to Aunt Lizzie or to the rest of her new family from Georgia, who were nothing but rubes, as far as she was concerned. The two of them, Holly and Clara, teased and tormented Effie, made fun of her accent, asked where her *mammy* was, made references to things she couldn't possibly have understood—she was, what, eight years old?—and laughed at her ignorance. . . .

"What kinds of things?" Henry asked.

She seemed to struggle to find the words. "Like—I don't know. Like they'd always be drinking and smoking around me, or they'd take boys under the promenade and leave me there on the beach to play with myself."

"It sounds fun."

"I was a *child,* for heaven's sake."

Henry smiled. "Well, you're grown-up and married now. And so is Clara. She seems like she worships you."

Effie cocked her head and felt the tiny mole behind her ear, a reflex when she was piqued in a certain way. "People don't change so much."

He knew that wasn't true. There was a time when he could have called Effie a bully—like when she'd fed Betty Moody's hair into the gears of the pencil sharpener in Mrs. Jackson's class—and look at her now: his lovely wife. But he only shrugged and let it go.

A violent chopping sound came from the archway; they listened to it. A minute later Clara swept back into the room with a bucket of ice, her movements so smooth she might have been roller-skating. "I'm sorry to keep you waiting so long. Look at you two! I love the old dear, but if I'm not there to look over her shoulder every second . . . Well, you know how it is." She was at the bar now, dropping ice into the glasses.

"What are you doing here?" Effie asked.

"We're just here for the weekend. It's my brother's birthday. You remember Scott, of course," she said, smiling meaningfully, but Effie didn't. "Effie, you're joking! You had such a crush on him!"

"I did?"

"God, yes! You were smitten with him. You used to hug him around the waist and he'd have to pry you off. You were a determined little girl. Is she still that way, Henry?"

Henry didn't know what to say. He laughed.

"You're thinking of someone else," Effie said.

"Don't worry, Henry," Clara said, "Scott's married now. To a little cunt, if you want to know the truth, but married nonetheless. You're far more handsome, anyway."

He wasn't sure he'd heard her correctly; she couldn't have said what he thought she'd said. He beamed at her and remembered Reverend Miller once saying in a sermon that Satan appeared in beautiful guises, singing praises and charms. He could listen to her talk all day. While she fixed the drinks she explained that Scott was turning twenty-five—next week, technically—and they were going to have a bash, and all his friends from Princeton and the army and the junior associates at the law firm were coming down, people from Philadelphia and D.C. and New York and as far away as Boston. Where they would sleep, she had no idea. "On top of each other, I suppose!" She crossed over from the bar and handed them their drinks and sat with her own drink in an armchair by the sofa.

"Well, it sounds like a personal thing," Effie began, but Clara cut her off.

"Stop it right there. You will *not* be intruding, I promise you. It's a party! Mother and Father aren't even here, they're staying in Philly." Clara leaned forward and put her hand on the arm of the sofa. "My belle, I'm begging you to stay. I'll hardly know a soul. You'll be doing me a favor—really."

It would be rude, Henry thought, to refuse at this point. He took Effie's hand. "We can stay a little while," he said, and when Effie said, "I mean . . ." Clara cried, "Oh, joy!" and held up her glass. "To long-lost friendships," she said. "And to new ones too."

The drink was delicious. He'd never had gin before, and the piney taste of it went perfectly with the airy room, the big windows, and the verdant backyard shimmering in the breeze. Before he knew it, he'd had half of it.

Clara grilled Effie about her life, but before Effie could fully answer anything she would interject with a story of her own, or a reminiscence about people they'd both known or things they'd done in Cape May. Like the time Clara and Holly had broken into the lighthouse and flashed their tits at the summer regatta, in the full light of day, while Effie sulked below because she was too scared to join them. (Effie had no memory of this.) Or the game of hide-and-seek, which Effie had begged them to play, when Clara and Holly and some other girl they were with had managed to elude her for nearly an hour, until Effie was sobbing in the street, in a part of town she didn't know, and had to ask a stranger how to get back to New Hampshire Avenue. (This Effie remembered. "It was horrible," she said, unamused, and Clara, stifling her laughter, said, "It *was* horrible, wasn't it? Oh, darling! We were little beasts. I'm sorry.") Occasionally she would ask Henry something—"Have you just been in love with her your *entire* life?"—and he would answer sheepishly, smiling like a fool. But mostly he just listened, or half listened, distracted by the sparkly sensation of the drink going down and the glowing light coming into the house. The gin was working; his body felt effervescent. Clara crossed her legs and displayed a lovely foot in high-heeled sandals, her skin tanned and gleaming, her toenails glossy white. She was the most glamorous person he had ever met. She lived in Manhattan, and she was married to a man named Richard, who ran a bank and whose family, Henry gathered, was extremely wealthy. There was no mention of children. Clara came from Philadelphia, from a more modest family of lawyers, and this place in Cape May was her parents' summer getaway. "This old shack," she called it. She and Richard had a place on Nantucket that she liked much more—but this was Scott's weekend, and it was what he wanted.

Henry and Effie finished their drinks at the same time, and when Clara heard the clink of ice in their glasses she leapt up and took them and went back to the bar, talking all the while. When their drinks

were refreshed, she glided over to the record player on the other side
of the den and put on something smooth and Latin—or maybe Ital-
ian, because she started talking about her own honeymoon in Italy:
Naples and Rome, a week each. The spring of '54. It had been a
dream, she said, but a very fleeting dream. (With small movements,
she was doing a sort of cha-cha back to her chair.) "Richard was about
to lose his mind by the time we got to Rome. Relaxation makes him
anxious, you know. So I mostly walked around the city by myself. I
had to have strangers take my picture. There's me on the Spanish
Steps. There's me at Caffè Greco. I pretended I was a runaway princess, like Audrey Hepburn." She sighed wistfully and sat down. "Ah,
love! Hold on to it, darlings, for as long as you can. But you two must
be in the *throes* of it."

They looked at each other. Effie seemed more relaxed now. Her
cheeks were pink, a wan smile played on her face.

"But why Cape May of all places?"

"I don't know," Effie said. "We thought about a few places"—that
wasn't true at all—"but then we've got the house up here, I guess,
and I hadn't been back here in so long."

"Nostalgia, yes. I am the exact same way."

"Mostly we wanted to keep it simple and easy. We could have gone
anywhere in the world, I suppose, but we've got time enough for that."

"Hear, hear," Clara said.

All of this was news to Henry, but somehow, just now, it felt true.

Clara held her glass up to them. "You've got your lives ahead of
you," she said. "Right now, all that matters is love." She gave them a
smile that seemed pained. "Oh, you darlings. I just want to eat the
two of you alive."

Soon a stout, middle-aged woman appeared at the archway, scowling at Clara. "Mrs. Kirschbaum, the food is ready."

"That's wonderful, Mrs. Pavich. Will you go out and ring the bell?
They won't hear it, but who knows? The wind may be in our favor."

The woman shuffled back through the archway, and a moment later a loud bell rang outside—there must have been a bell tower out there—and it rang, and rang, until Clara shouted, "That will be enough, Mrs. Pavich!"

*T*he bell worked, or else it was a coincidence: not five minutes later a crowd of young people burst into the den from the backyard, looking flushed and windblown, wearing shorts and linen shirts and light dresses, all of them talking at once: "God help us!" "But I was turned the other way!" "It's a wonder Dottie isn't blind!" "But I was turned the *other* way!" "Hello, hello!" Clara made a flurry of introductions. There were seven or eight of them in all, and their names—Dottie and James, Alma and Roland and Max, Karen, and Betsy—were lost to Henry the moment he heard them, except for Scott, Effie's old crush, who was handsome like his sister, and whose unbuttoned shirt showed off a well-tended chest and stomach. "You don't say!" he said when Clara told him who Effie was, but Henry could tell he didn't remember. Even so, he wrapped her in a hug and pressed her cheek to his bare chest, and Henry felt a prick of jealousy. Who were these people? They were weirdly, effusively nice: "Fabulous to meet you!" "Georgia, you say?" "Congratulations!" "Hank, you're the luckiest man in the world." This last came from a shirtless man with the stocky build of a boxer. When Henry said, "I know, believe me," the man laughed and clapped him so hard on the back that Henry spilled part of his drink out onto the rug.

"I'm sorry," Henry said, meeting Clara's eyes. "I'll clean it up."

"Don't even think of it," Clara said. She came over and laid her hand on the boxer's bicep. "My darling, you don't know your own strength."

"Sorry, Hank," the man said, and struck him again, more gently, on the shoulder. Clara's hand lingered at his back. Was this possibly

Richard? He seemed too young for her. He was handsome, but shorter than Clara by several inches.

The crowd swarmed the bar. Ice rang in their glasses. One empty gin bottle was discarded with a crash, another one opened. Henry and Effie stayed close together, but when the group returned with their drinks they brought a whirlwind of merry chatter that radiated outward and broke them apart. They all seemed to know one another intimately, but it could have been an illusion; they made you feel like you were in on the conversation, even if you had no idea what they were talking about, and they were given to strange gestures of confidentiality—leaning in close, clutching your forearm, only to disclose some little trifle: "I hear there may be bourbon tarts on the dessert menu!" Henry smiled and nodded; a few feet away, Effie was doing the same. The talk was hard to follow, names and places and references that eluded him but that sent sparks through his imagination: Gabby and Sophie and Anders; Marblehead, the Berkshires, Palermo; the Fourth of July party with the Great Dane; Lorenzo's hyacinths; the place setting that caught fire. Clara weaved among them all, holding a gin bottle in one hand and the tonic in the other, their host but—as Henry imagined—more than that: their sorceress, the one who was setting them spinning.

Mrs. Pavich appeared in the archway again. "Mrs. Kirschbaum," she said, drawing everyone's attention. "The food is getting cold."

But then the doorbell clanged and more guests arrived, and the merry band rushed to see who it was. Cheers and greetings rang from the foyer.

Henry and Effie were reunited. "Do you want to go?" he asked.

She couldn't seem to settle her eyes on any one place. "I mean— we're *here*. We might as well stay for supper." She caught herself and looked at him. "Do *you* want to go?"

"No," he said. "I'm fine staying. If you are."

"*I'm* fine."

"Then we'll stay. A little while."

"If that's what you want to do."

Their number had doubled. The newcomers were in two groups, as far as Henry could tell: one of them very fine, as if they had just arrived from Hollywood—two couples in light blazers and sparkling dresses that revealed a great deal of skin—and the other appeared to be beatniks—a bearded man in glasses, and three women who wore their hair long and had thick eyeliner. One of the women wore nothing more than a slip and heels. If she'd been out on the street in Signal Creek, she'd have been arrested.

Eventually they all gathered, in twos and threes, around a large table outside, in a covered section of the patio bordered by hedges and vines. A giant platter of what looked to be gumbo lay in the center. Around it, bowls of soup and sauce, plates of greens and olives and bread, and three carafes of red wine. It all looked vaguely foreign. There weren't nearly enough places at the table, and people were dragging chairs in from the poolside or were content to stand, but no one would take Henry's seat when he offered it—in fact, they laughed at him: "No, really! I'm fine! Stay, stay!"—and he had the feeling that he was acting too formally, too politely for this crowd. He was the only person wearing a tie; he took it off and stuffed it in his jacket pocket. Clara sat across from him and commanded everyone to dig in, though she ignored her own plate. Beside her sat the boxer, who had still not put his shirt on. Henry's mother would have had something to say about that. Likely Effie would have too, if she weren't dazzled, as he was, by the drinks and the chatter and the motley party gathering around them. Everyone was talking at once. Here and there, peals of laughter. A woman reached over him, pressing her breast against his shoulder, and her skin grazed his cheek and the tip of his nose; he caught the scent of strawberries.

The sun was setting. A soft, golden light lingered in the treetops. On the table, votive candles flickered among the settings. Everyone looked beautiful.

He was more comfortable out here than he had been inside. The gathering dusk enveloped him, and all he had to do was eat and drink and listen, catching one thread of conversation over here, another over there. Scott sat at the head of the table, beside a pretty blonde who must have been his wife—*the little cunt*. Most of the talk was impenetrable to him, about people and places and events he had no connection or access to, but some of it excited him: talk of art and gallery openings, of bebop records and clubs in Harlem, of cases before the Supreme Court, which some of the crowd seemed to know intimately, of the integration of the schools—vis-à-vis the tensions in Little Rock—which everyone seemed to support without question. It was thrilling to think of what Uncle Carswall or his mother would have said to all this, how disgusted they would be with these people, and Henry found himself nodding eagerly about opinions he'd never spent much time thinking about one way or another. The gumbo was delicious, rice and potatoes and sausage, a good bit of spice in it too, and he was pretty sure there were cashews in it, if that was possible, and crunchy disks of some kind of root vegetable—he didn't care, he was shoveling it in. He said this to Effie: "Boy, I'm just shoveling this in! It's outstanding, isn't it?" But she only gave him a generic nod, distracted by someone on the other side of her, and that was all right, he had finished his third gin and tonic and had poured himself some wine, and he was feeling thoroughly, pleasantly drunk. Effie was too, he could tell: she had become chatty. The woman she was talking to, who appeared to be Mexican or Arabian or maybe just Jewish, was continuing the conversation about the integration of the schools, soliciting Effie's opinion as if she were an eyewitness in a war: "But do you see much trouble where you are?" she asked, and Effie said, "Oh, no, no, no, not one bit, really, that's just stuff in the news—I mean it's *there*, you know, it's obviously an issue, you understand, but it's not the day-to-day, or rather, we *live* the day-to-day, so it's quite different . . ." It might have been the alcohol changing her, or affecting his own ears, but Effie's voice didn't sound like her own: she sounded faintly aristocratic, a little like Clara imitating Scarlett O'Hara. She described how close her family was to her cook's family, how they exchanged gifts at Christmastime; she explained how her father was the mayor of the town where they lived (this impressed the woman very much), how he owned a farm-supply store too, and gave money to charity. It was strange to hear Effie talk about Signal Creek to someone who knew nothing about it, and for a moment he felt a powerful kinship to her, of a sort he would never have felt back home. When the woman, seeing Henry listening in, asked about his family, Effie spoke for him, calling Uncle Carswall's property an "estate" and saying he had nearly a thousand acres of land. She wasn't lying, exactly, but it gave the impression that he lived on a big antebellum plantation instead of the plain old ugly country outside of Signal Creek. He didn't mind, though. He could play the part. "How lovely it must be!" the woman said, and Henry cleared his voice and said it was, it was indeed.

An elderly man in a sweater and blazer came out onto the patio. He surveyed the crowd and, seeing Clara at the table, came over behind her and set his big veiny hands on her shoulders. To Henry's shock, she said, "Richard, dear!" and reached up to squeeze his forearms.

The man couldn't have been younger than sixty. He had a long, solemn face and unruly white eyebrows. He would have made a good schoolmaster. "I see the party is under way."

"Sit, darling, sit," Clara said. "How wonderful you've decided to join the living. Max, dear, would you mind?"

The boxer bowed and got up from the table with his plate, and Richard took his place and waited while Clara piled a heap of gumbo for him. Henry squeezed Effie's knee under the table, to get her attention and point out what was happening, but she was too absorbed in her conversation to notice. If Clara was going to make introductions, she never got a chance, because another group of people came out onto the patio, and when she saw them she cried, "Helen Crabtree, you horrible bitch!" and bolted up from the table to give the woman in question a hug. Poor Richard was left to himself, but he didn't seem to mind; his attention was directed at his plate, and steadily he made his way through the gumbo and a side of greens, pausing only once to pour himself an austere amount of wine.

Through the big windowpanes, now that the inside was brighter than the outside, Henry could see more people gathering in the den, big groups of them, laughing, sipping from martini glasses, smoking cigarettes. He saw the beatnik in the slip take her shoes off and hand them to a man who placed them into a potted plant. He saw a naked toddler run screaming from the archway. He saw an Oriental woman with a complicated bun and silvery eye shadow. He saw a man with circular sunglasses and a shaved head under a beret. Who were these people? Where had they come from? They had materialized out of the enveloping dark. Most of them seemed to be young, Scott's or Clara's ages, but there was a group of older men too, in tuxedos—family friends, maybe, or Richard's friends, or people from Scott's law firm, or professors at Princeton. Who could say? The record player had been turned up and something hopping, with horns and a drumbeat, was coming through the open French doors. For the past week he'd felt isolated from the world, and now the world was upon him, or some strange version of it.

A chill had set in. Through a part in the trees that bordered the yard Henry saw billows of fog drifting past the streetlight. The patio was clearing. The gumbo was gone. Richard remained, chatting with a couple of the older men. From time to time Mrs. Pavich would stomp out and silently gather a stack of empty dishes. The boxer—

Max—had replaced the woman next to Effie. He was still in his trunks, but he'd put on an Oxford shirt and at first Henry didn't recognize him. He was saying something to her, and she was chuckling, shaking her head, until he paused and said, "Three times!" and she burst into laughter, snorted, put her hand to her mouth, and twisted to hide her face against Henry's chest. She must have been drowned; Henry had never made her laugh like that.

"What's the good word, Hank?" Max said over Effie's back.

"The good word?" The question confused him. It sounded like something a Bible salesman would say.

"Oh, Henry," Effie said, sitting up and recovering herself. "Heaven help me, I'm not in my right mind."

"Another drink would set your mind right," Max said.

"I don't think so," Henry said. He wasn't sure he cared for this Max very much.

"You," Effie said, pointing at Max, letting the word hang there a moment. "You do not have my best interests at heart."

Max laughed. "What do you say we dance instead? You dance, Hank?"

"Oh, *does* he," Effie said, and she turned and smiled at him. "He was the best damn dancer at the Spring Fling. Wasn't I proud, baby?"

"The Spring Fling," Max said, grinning, and Henry felt a flush of embarrassment. What was the Spring Fling to these people?

"Look at him," Effie said, "he's so modest."

"Come on, Hank." Max pushed his chair back and stood up. "Why don't you show us the stuff?"

Henry demurred—he didn't see anyone dancing inside—but Effie was getting to her feet too, taking the hand Max offered, and he didn't have a choice. He followed them inside. He took Effie's hand and slowed his pace so she would let go of Max.

The large airy room they'd been sitting in earlier was close and smoky and loud now, and the music was jumping, infectious—a

heavy drumbeat, saxophone and piano—and over by the record
player a crowd of people was dancing, doing some kind of impro-
vised bop, shaking and twisting and flailing their arms. Scott was in
the crowd, and there was Clara too, shaking her hips in the middle
of a cluster of Coast Guard cadets. What were *they* doing here? Had
they heard the music from their cutters and leapt ashore?

"God, Louis Prima," Max said, raising his voice over the music.
"How I hate this sock-hop shit. I should have brought my Bird
records."

They joined the dancing, the crowd pressing them close, the air
warm and humid. Henry's normal reserve disappeared whenever
there was music. He maneuvered himself between Effie and Max and
let himself go. He danced and danced. The woman in the slip was
hopping in place, her breasts bouncing wildly. A few feet away, one
of the cadets was nuzzling Clara's hair. A spray of something, Champagne or beer, fell on the crowd near Henry and they answered it
with a cheer. What a party! The music let loose and went wild. He
elbowed a woman in the back of the head, but before he could apol-
ogize she laughed and threw her arms around him and kissed him
on the cheek. "Hey!" Effie cried, pulling him away. "Hands off, you
hussy!"—and Henry gripped her hips to still her, but she was only
playing: she got up on her tiptoes and kissed him, her tongue grazing his lips.

"I can't take you anywhere!" he cried.

"But you have to take me *everywhere*—I'm your wife!"

One song ended with a cry of saxophones, the crowd cheered, and
right away another tempo began, piano and drums, low but tense
with suppressed energy. Henry didn't know this record—Louis
Prima?—but he was loving it.

Now Clara wedged herself into their midst. "My little darlings!"
She hooked her arms over Henry's and Effie's shoulders, smelling of
Chanel No. 5 and radiating heat. "I thought I'd never escape."

"This is some party," Effie said. "I'll give you that, Clara Strauss."

"Did you see that boy trying to get his hooks into me?" Clara said. Henry said he had, but she was talking to Max, who was suddenly frowning. He had his chin up, trying to see over the crowd. He wasn't very tall. "Max," Clara tried again, "you may need to defend my honor before the night's over."

Max didn't hear her, and Clara leaned in and repeated herself, and he laughed and said, "Anytime, my lady"—but then he excused himself and made his way through the crowd. Clara watched him go, and for a moment Henry thought he really was going to defend her honor: he approached one of the cadets, who was kissing a girl's neck, but instead of pushing the boy away he grabbed the girl's wrist and dragged her to the edge of the crowd, toward a corner of the den that led off into a hallway. She was one of the merry band who had burst into the den from the beach earlier in the evening. She wore a long, drab cardigan over a white bathing suit and shorts, and her hair was tied up carelessly, strands falling all about her face. She stumbled after Max, looking not so much angry as bored.

"You know what?" Effie said, speaking more loudly than necessary. "I'm glad I ran into you, Clara Strauss, or whatever your name is. I was not glad at first, if I am to be one-hundred-percent honest, but I am glad now."

Clara looked away from the hallway where Max and the girl had disappeared. "What are you talking about, my belle?"

"She's a little soused," Henry said, putting his hand to Effie's back.

"I'm as soused as I ought to be. It's a party, isn't it?"

Clara laughed. "It certainly is!"

The beat let loose again and they were jostled but Effie cried over the music: "I used to think you were an awful person!"

Clara laughed again and cried, "What?"

"You and Holly," Effie said, bobbing her shoulders to her own beat. "I used to think you were terrible! Well—you *were* terrible! I used to pray for your souls, but I didn't mean it. I'd say, 'Lord, please don't send Holly and Clara to hell on *my* account, I'm *sure* they don't know any better.'"

Clara stopped dancing and looked down at her incredulously. "Effie Mae, are you trying to tell me a joke?"

Henry took Effie's arm and told her to stop it, but she jerked away. "Quit clutching me, Henry—damn! I'm not saying anything bad. I am building up to a compliment, in fact."

"What a relief," Clara said.

"I'm talking to *Clara* anyhow. As a matter of fact," Effie said, placing her hand on Henry's chest, "why don't you go fix yourself a drink and let us two have some girl time?"

Clara looked at him and shrugged; she seemed content to hear whatever Effie had to say. And what did he care? He didn't know these people. He left Effie to do what she would—to put her foot in her mouth, if that's what she wanted. To hell with it.

Behind the bar, he made his best guess at a gin and tonic. He poured it half and half over the last fistful of ice from the bucket, and the first swallow seared his throat. Never mind: it would be a sipping drink. He was in a state of inebriation in which he felt in full possession of himself and at the same time in complete control of the room, free to wander anywhere, drop in on any conversation, or just stand and watch people without feeling self-conscious. He saw Scott dancing with a woman who wasn't his wife—as far as Henry understood—and his hands were lost up the back of her skirt. *For shame,* he thought, and laughed. Elsewhere a group of young men was huddled close together near the foyer, around a small table on which sat a transistor radio, talking excitedly about something to do with the Soviets, and when one of them looked at him warily he had the thrilling idea that they might be covert Communists, of the sort that had supposedly infiltrated the upper echelons of American society—here, it was possible!—and quickly he left them to their business.

He wandered the perimeter. There wasn't much to see, as far as photographs and decorations. A few paintings of sailboats and lighthouses. A picture of what must have been Clara's family standing around the helm of a boat, holding sailboat-shaped trophies. A sepia portrait of a couple in Bavarian costumes. Near the record player he tapped the keys of an upright piano, but it was inaudible under the music, which had changed into a kind of honking, arrhythmic jazz that Henry found disorienting, and the dance floor had cleared up a bit as a result. The people who remained, he didn't recognize. There'd been a slippage in time. Clara and Effie were nowhere to be seen. Neither was Max, or the girl he'd stolen away. At one point Mrs. Pavich muscled herself into the room and, without any announcement, giving everyone around her a withering look, dropped a carrot cake down on the coffee table and stomped away. The sight comforted him; he remembered, dimly, that the cake had been made for them, him and Effie, in celebration of their marriage. He went over to it and ran his finger along the side and tasted the frosting. It was perfect: smooth and buttery.

He thought he might dance some more, in spite of the music. One of the beatnik girls was dancing by herself and he swore she'd caught his eye and smiled at him. But first he had to relieve himself. It was, suddenly, an urgent matter. He hadn't gone all evening.

Instead of navigating the crowd and trying to find the lavatory, he wandered outside onto the patio, where the air was cool and thick with fog, and the relative quiet was soothing. By the pool a group of men was looking up at the sky. He made out Richard among them, and one of the young Communists. Henry followed their line of sight but there was nothing to see through the haze. Maybe they were inspecting the fog itself. He walked away from them, along the side of the house, into the darkness of the yard. The grass was damp and overgrown. He ran into a bush near the back corner of the house and stepped around it to a hedge. The glare of a streetlight on Madison Avenue came through the trees. He was surprised to find that his glass was almost empty. He downed the rest of it, dropped it into the grass, unzipped his trousers, and let go—at last!—into the hedge.

What a night! He smiled up at the streetlight. It seemed to be telling him that his life was going to be brilliant. And it really was, it was really going to be brilliant. This was a party he would remember for the rest of his life—because it would mark the true beginning of his life. Yes. He would apply for that scholarship again. Forget Emory, he could go to Princeton. Marblehead, Nantucket: they would be places in his life. He and Effie would not speak often of their honeymoon, but when they did, they would say, Do you remember that party at Clara's? Do you remember how we *were*? How you told Clara she was an awful person? And they would laugh about it, and they would have no memory of the first few days. God was pleased with them—he was thankful for that.

He shook himself and zipped up and was about to make the trek back inside when he heard something, so close he thought it might be coming from the other side of the hedge: a woman breathing. Under that, a steady rhythm that at first he couldn't make sense of, until the woman cried, "Oh!" and again, "Oh! Oh!"

The cries were coming from a dark, open window of the house, just a few feet away from him. He had never actually heard a woman make that sound before—Effie hadn't made it—but it was so precisely how his friends had made it for laughs that he wondered if someone were playing a joke on him. But there was a man in there too; he could hear his grunting. Henry held as still as he could, swaying, making an effort to keep his balance. "Oh!" the woman cried, and it seemed that she would never stop. The man was a Titan. Henry felt an acute pang of longing and envy. He stood transfixed, unable to pull himself away, until at last the man made a strained sound, the woman sighed, and they both fell silent. Henry waited a moment before he crept away from the window and around the bush, and he made his way back to the patio through the fog. He felt an urgent need to find his wife. The ground tilted under his feet.

The group of men outside had dispersed. Inside he saw one of them, an elderly man, slow dancing with an elderly woman who may or may not have been his wife. Who knew with these people? The party had changed again: the music was drowsy, people were mostly in pairs. Soon they would slip away together, he thought, into dark rooms.

Effie stood by the sofa holding her pocketbook. She looked lost and confused and he felt a rush of tenderness for her.

"Where have you been?" she asked.

"I was just outside—I'm sorry. I needed some air." He put his arms around her.

"We need to go," she said. He smelled peppermint on her breath.

"What's wrong?"

"I was just sick in the bathroom."

"Oh God."

Outside, the fog was so thick they couldn't see the houses on the other side of the street. Madison Avenue was lighted but New Hampshire wasn't, so they walked into a thick darkness where, somewhere, Aunt Lizzie's cottage lay. They stumbled over the ruts in the street. They passed the cottage without realizing it and turned back when they saw the big Victorian looming out of the fog, but eventually they found it.

Effie tripped on the top step and fell onto her hands and knees. To Henry's relief, she started laughing. "For heaven's sake," she said, "I'm *screwed*."

He helped her up and asked if she had scraped anything.

"Nah," she said. But she had dropped her pocketbook and lost a shoe. He bent down to pick them up. She kicked the other shoe off and he bent down for it too.

Inside, he nearly knocked over the end-table lamp trying to find the switch. When he found it, and clicked the light on, she was leaning back against the doorjamb, grinning at him. Her eye makeup had faded into dark coronas, there was a run in her stockings, and she looked dissolute and utterly ravishing. He wanted to bend her over the sofa and violate her. But then she hiccuped, and put her hand to her mouth, and for a moment he thought she was going to throw up again.

"Come on," he said, when the danger seemed to have passed. He took her arm. "Let's get you into bed."

Three

If they were leaving Sunday, they had done nothing to prepare
for it: no washing of sheets, no cleaning the kitchen, no packing.
They had not even called their families to let them know they were
returning early. Effie shuffled over to the kitchen counter and looked
at the "Before You Leave" list Uncle George had made for them—it
was long—and hung her head in despair. She'd woken up in the night
and was sick again, and Henry had found her, just before noon, asleep
in her bathrobe on the sofa downstairs.

"The time is ours," Henry said. "We can leave Monday, or Tuesday. We don't have to leave tomorrow. Can't we give ourselves a day?"

She considered this, and after a moment said he was right. The
decision seemed to cheer her. Tomorrow they would get ready to leave,
maybe go to church in the morning. Today they would rest. "As God
as my witness," she said, raising her fist to the ceiling, "I will never
drink again."

He didn't understand at first that she was trying to be funny,
mocking Scarlett O'Hara. He laughed a beat too late, and she told
him to shut up.

———————

After she'd had a bath, he made buttered toast and they ate it out on the back porch, at a frosted-glass table he'd wiped clean of twigs and leaves. She was wearing her bathrobe, her feet propped up on his chair, her cheeks resting on her knees. He was wearing only his pajama bottoms, the fabric luxurious at his groin. It was a beautiful afternoon, cool and breezy, but his hangover made his skin warm. A line of beech trees bordered one side of the yard, and overnight, it seemed, they had turned brilliant yellow.

"I made a complete fool of myself last night," Effie said.

"Baby, no. You were charming." He rubbed her leg, felt the prickly hairs on her calf.

"I feel sordid," she said, and he laughed, and she lifted her head to glare at him. "Don't belittle me."

"I'm not belittling you."

She was being playful, miserable though she was. She narrowed her eyes at him.

"Come on," he said. "It was fun, wasn't it?"

She put her head in the crook of her arm. "It was *kind of* fun, I suppose."

They talked about it, describing the things they had seen. He asked if she'd seen Richard, Clara's husband. She hadn't, and when he described him she perked up and put her hand to her mouth and laughed maliciously. "Oh, Clara, Clara," she said. "Clara Strauss—I mean Kirkbaum, or whatever the hell. She married for the money."

"It could be love."

"Oh, stop it."

She remembered having a heart-to-heart with her, but she couldn't remember a word they'd said. They'd been interrupted by a man trying to tell them a joke about a cow. "He kept saying, 'Moo! Moo!' but we weren't getting it."

Henry said he thought he saw Communists scheming. Effie said she wouldn't doubt it with that crew. "They may be well-to-do, but that doesn't mean they're good people."

"Maybe," Henry said. "But I'd do it again."

"God," Effie said. "Once was enough."

She went upstairs for a nap and came down in the early evening, dressed and made-up, her sandals dangling from her fingers. "I think I'm coming around," she said. "How're you feeling?"

"I'm alive." He rubbed his eyes. He'd been trying to read Boswell in the den, images from last night overtaking the words, and fallen fast asleep. She asked if he wanted to take a walk—she needed to move around a bit—and he said sure.

He put his loafers on, and they went out.

The Cadillac convertible and the Rolls-Royce were still parked down at Clara's, and from the open windows came the sound of someone repeating an intricate line of music on the piano—skillfully, Henry thought. He didn't know the piece, but it was lovely. It reminded him of the stone Jesus in his aunt Lily's flower garden, the lichen growing in the folds of its robe, which made it look like an ancient ruin.

"It must be awful over there," Effie said. "I feel for Mrs. Pavich."

They walked down to the promenade, where the lights had come on. The sea was soft and calm. *The gloaming,* Henry thought—a word he enjoyed. He took Effie's hand. There were people out: three or four of them, a family maybe, far ahead of them on the promenade, an old couple down on the beach, a pack of Coast Guard cadets going purposefully down Beach Avenue. Henry had an urge to follow them. Saturday evening: the place was stirring, a little. The storefronts were still dark, but from somewhere deeper in the town came music—jazz, something lively, but very faint, like an echo of the party last night.

They came to the end of the promenade, where the horizon was still bright, and Venus hung like a diamond partway up the sky. Henry suggested they sit at one of the benches and watch the light fade, but the wind coming off the water was too chilly, so they turned back.

For supper she fried up some ham and boiled a few small potatoes, which was the last of their food, aside from what they'd saved for breakfast tomorrow. He tried the radio, but on every station it was the news, something the Soviets were doing. Always there was something about the Soviets. Korea, outer space, the threat of nuclear war. He tended to avoid the news. He put on a Glenn Miller record instead, the best thing he could find in Uncle George's collection, and sat down to say grace.

"I'll say it," Effie said. "You don't put enough feeling into it."

"You want me to say it like Uncle Carswall?"

"God no, we don't need a sermon. It's just—you have to mean what you say. You have to be *conscious* of it."

"It's grace," Henry said. "It's 'Good bread, good meat; good Lord, let's eat.'"

But she insisted, and Henry said fine, clasped his hands together, and closed his eyes. "Dear Lord," she said, "thank you for this food we are about to receive, and thank you for this week that Henry and I have shared together, which is the first week of our marriage."

He opened his eyes. "Today is our one-week anniversary."

She smiled at him. "Don't interrupt me." He closed his eyes again, and she continued: "Thank you for this week, dear Lord, and thank you for bringing us together, and for sending me such a fine and thoughtful husband, who I know will be a support to his family. Please bless us, dear Lord, with healthy children, and be with us as we raise them to be good and sensible people. Bless us with wealth and happiness, dear Lord, inasmuch as you see fit, and please forgive us for all our sins, for we try to be good, and we ask in your name—amen."

How he loved her. He took up his fork and knife and told her that was very nice.

"You just have to say things you mean," she said.

*E*ffie went up to bed early. Henry poured himself some of Uncle George's scotch and went out onto the front porch, feeling aroused. It wasn't yet nine. Down at Clara's the windows were aglow, and the sky overhead was full of trembling stars. Over there, the night would just be beginning.

Sometime later, when he'd begun to doze off, the sound of breaking glass startled him. It had come from Clara's. He sat up to look, but couldn't see anything. Now a car door slammed, an engine started, the red glow of taillights appeared. Then the car swung out of the drive, skidded to a stop, accelerated around the corner, and was gone.

It had been the Rolls-Royce. He'd seen it in a flash, under the streetlights on Madison.

Soon the downstairs lights went out, and a light in a window upstairs appeared. Henry looked at it for a long time until it too went out, and all the house was dark.

*E*ffie woke the next morning in a playful mood, nuzzling and tickling him, laughing at his morning erection, which tented his pajama bottoms—but she was adamant about going to church. When he reached for her she rolled away and got out of bed, declaring that they would be late if they didn't hurry.

"The Good Lord gives a pass for holidays, doesn't he?" he asked.

"If you don't want to go, don't go," she said, pulling her slip off over her head. Her breasts lit the room. "You're an adult, I can't force you."

Outside it was warm, and a few other people were strolling about, including a young couple—like them, but in comfortable linens—who smiled and nodded as they passed. A trio of young boys ran by wearing swim trunks, and Henry desperately wanted to go wherever they were going. Instead, they entered the gloom of Cape May United Methodist Church.

The preacher was already speaking. They took a seat in the last pew, and Henry waited for his eyes to adjust. The congregation consisted of no more than a dozen people, and most of them sat apart from one another, as if they were strangers. On the walls between the stained-glass windows were plaques filled with names—sailors lost at sea, Henry imagined.

The sermon had to do with the woes of the Pharisees. All worldly concerns were worthless. The only thing of value was the soul, which was a candle in a vast dark. The preacher, a slight, balding man in a white alb, was not a gifted speaker. Not like Reverend Miller back home, who preached like he was sharing an amusing story, who made Jesus an amiable friend. This preacher intoned, the sound of his voice like an omen of doom.

"Ye are like unto whited sepulchers," he read, "which indeed appear beautiful outward, but are within full of dead men's bones, and of all uncleanness." Then he stared into the space above the congregation. "Your bodies are naught but walking coffins."

They bolted as soon as the sermon was over.

"Do you feel better?" Henry asked outside.

"God," Effie said. "If I had to listen to that man every Sunday, I think I'd slit my wrists."

They found an ice-cream shop that was open—a miracle—and bought cones of Neapolitan and walked with them through the town, making a lazy circuit past closed storefronts and houses, through deserted but sunny squares. They could go to the grocer's while they were out, Effie suggested, and stock up on a few provisions, and then they could go to the beach later and try to swim—for once. "Does that mean you want to stay a little longer?" Henry asked, and she looked up at the sky and said, "If it'll be like this."

They passed a fence overflowing with bougainvillea, bright pink and violet, and below it fragrant lavender. Reverend Miller had once said that all we see of life on earth is a brief flourish of the elements. God breathes life into the seed and the seed rises, it turns the crude matter of the earth into a flourish of color and shape, scent and sound. How the world flaunted itself. Effie's skirt swished about her knees. She was wearing her prim white stockings. When they got back to the cottage he would pluck the garter straps off one by one, place his nose and lips to the tender skin there, breathe in the faint scent of talcum powder.

At the grocer's they bought enough food for two or three meals, plus cuts for sandwiches and a bundle of oranges, and they started back, Henry carrying the bag. They turned down Madison in the direction of the sea—and just before they came to New Hampshire he spotted Clara, down at the house on the corner, sweeping the flagstone patio in a lustrous blue robe, a pattern of giant, overlapping flowers.

"Oh, hell," Effie said.

Henry laughed. "Do you want to hide?"

Clara saw them, tossed her broom aside, and cried, "Hallo!" They waved back.

"What about your heart-to-heart?" Henry asked. "Aren't you friends now?"

"I have no idea."

They crossed the street to meet Clara at the end of the drive. Only the baby-blue Cadillac remained, its top down. "Dear friends!" she said. "You're still here."

"So are you," Effie said.

"It's so great to see you again," Henry said.

She took their shoulders and kissed the air by their cheeks, smell-ing of coconut. "Look at you two, you're all dressed up," she said. "Wait—it's Sunday, isn't it? You've been to church, haven't you?" She laughed, and before she could say anything more about it Effie asked if she was still cleaning up from the party. "God!" she cried, looking back at the house and wiping her brow as if she were sweating. It had been a nightmare, she said, but she'd sent the last of the riffraff home last night, thank God. "You should have seen it. I felt like I was running an orphanage."

"It was some party," Henry said.

"I hope I didn't embarrass myself too much," Effie said.

"Of course not!"

"I never, ever drink like that. I know I said some things . . ."

"You were a perfect lady," Clara said. "You didn't display your tits like Vera Watts, did you? God! Truth or Dare, among adults, *really*. But you were gone by then. I was sure you'd skipped town. How long are you staying?"

Henry felt a pang. He didn't know who Vera Watts was, but he wished he'd seen her tits.

"I don't know," Effie said. She looked at Henry. "A couple more days?"

"Me too!" Clara said.

It had been a last-minute decision, she explained. Her old friend Max—they remembered Max, didn't they?—he'd proposed the idea of staying on for a few days, when everyone else was leaving, because what was the rush? He was a writer, and Cape May seemed condu-cive to productivity. And Clara had thought, why not? The city was so depressing in the fall. The ocean air agreed with her. She hadn't seen Max in ages.

"Is your husband staying too?" Effie asked.

"Richard?" Clara laughed. "Oh no, darling, Richard was the first to leave, thank God. It's just us kids now." Effie laughed uncertainly, glancing at Henry, and Clara rushed to continue: "I only mean, the poor man. He's such an introvert, you know, and so devoted to his work . . ." She stopped herself. "But what are you doing today?"

Henry shifted the grocery bag in his arms, and Effie looked at him and said, "We were just coming back from the store. We thought we might go to the beach later, or . . ."

"We're taking Papa's boat out today," Clara said. "Do you want to come?"

She must have seen the joy light up in Henry's face, because she made a little hop and continued: "Please come. It's a perfect day for sailing. It's just Maxie and me. And his little sister, Alma, sadly. A dear girl, but useless. We could use the extra crew."

"Do you want to?" he said to Effie, and Effie, looking cornered, said, "I mean . . ."

*N*ow their honeymoon had begun, Henry thought. Now the clouds had parted and the bright days were upon them.

Back at the cottage they put the groceries away and went up into the attic room to change into their bathing suits. He had an erection again, and when he was naked he put his hands on his hips and waited for Effie to admire it. "Jesus!" she cried. She stood by the vanity table in her underwear. "On the Lord's day?"

"The Lord is pleased with us," he said, and dragged her down onto the bed.

She made a show of giving in—sighing, lying flat on her back, arms flung out: "Just do what you got to do, heathen, I won't help you"—and so he pulled her underwear off her hips and pressed his nose in, breathed in deeply the close, pleasant smell of her hair. He gave it a lingering kiss. She got up on her elbows then, alert, as if to say, *What do you think you're doing, sir?* And in answer he freed her from her underwear, spread her legs, and opened her with his tongue: a soft, soft bursting, warm and smoothly wet, like olive oil. The baffling folds of skin. A scent, mostly, of Dial soap.

"Hello," she said, and held very still, until a car horn down in the street interrupted them, and they leapt out of bed—flushed, laughing, saying nothing—and hurried into their clothes.

Four

The baby-blue Cadillac idled at the curb. Max was behind the wheel, Clara was in the passenger seat in a headscarf and sunglasses, and in the back sat a girl in a light-green dress.

"Katie Scarlett, Hank," Max called to them as they came down the porch steps. "We meet again." He leapt out and pulled the seat forward to let them in, bowing grandly, wearing the same red trunks and Oxford shirt he'd been wearing Friday night. Like a gentleman, he took Effie's bag, where she'd stuffed their towels and tanning oil, and Henry remembered he didn't particularly like this man.

"You know Max," Clara said. "And this is Alma. You met her the other night."

The girl gave them the thinnest of smiles and moved over to make room for them. She was the one Max had pulled away from the Coast Guard cadet—his sister. She had long, light-brown hair bundled carelessly on her head, and a scatter of freckles on either side of her nose. If Max was in his twenties, she might have been eighteen—Effie's age, maybe younger. She sank low in her seat, impenetrable behind her sunglasses, and looked away from them.

Max tossed their bag into the trunk, and with no further preliminaries he got back in the car and put it in gear, and they lurched forward and flew down New Hampshire Avenue. Clara whooped and raised her hands. In a few minutes they pulled into the empty parking lot by the marina and got out at the gate. Henry helped Max unload a large cooler and picnic basket from the trunk. Clara unlocked the gate, and they followed her down a dock crowded on both sides with sailboats, their masts gently bobbing and clinking.

Effie's hair was wild; she'd neglected to bring a scarf. "It's awfully windy today, isn't it?" Out in the cove beyond the marina the water was choppy. "You're sure it's safe?"

"Of course it's safe," Clara said. "I told you, it's a perfect day."

Theirs was a large boat—a sloop, Clara called it—near the end, with a white hull, a deck of stained wood, and a single mast. It was named *The Mistral,* after a Mediterranean wind, but Clara's papa called it his mistress. She wasn't technically allowed to sail it, but not to worry: she'd done so many times and was an expert. She gave orders, and Henry leapt aboard after Max to remove the canvas shroud over the cockpit while Effie and Alma waited on the dock. Clara opened the hatch, releasing a musty odor from within, and Henry followed her below, where there was a galley, a head, and a stateroom. On a sailboat, Clara said, everyday things had new and interesting names. He helped her bring up the jib sail, as she called it, and he and Max, who had made it known that he was an expert sailor himself, started hooking it up while Clara busied herself back at the wheel. Effie stepped gingerly aboard and stood as if uncertain what to do. Alma got in, dropped her bag to the floor, lay back by the stern, and tilted her face up to the sun.

"I used to race boats with my grandfather when I was a boy," Max explained to Henry up at the bow as they clipped the jib to the front stay. Up close Henry noticed his delicate fingers—he was no boxer— and his face, with its bright blue eyes, could almost be called pretty, except for the long scar on his chin. "Catamarans mostly, nothing like this old clunker. But I know my way around any boat. You ever sail?"

"My friend Hoke's got a bass boat," Henry said, and Max laughed.

They finished with the sail, and after some effort Clara got the engine going. A cloud of pungent smoke rose from the stern. Max jumped out to untie the ropes and give them a push, and soon they were motoring slowly across the cove, bobbing over the wavelets, toward a point of land beyond which lay the open sea. In her blue robe Clara stood at the wheel, their captain. At the mouth of the cove she cut the engine, and together Henry and Max hoisted the sails, which flapped violently in the wind until Clara turned the wheel and they caught and went silent and ballooned out, and the boat suddenly pitched to the side. Effie shrieked and held on to a stay. Something tumbled and banged below, but Clara said not to worry, she'd secured the gin.

They cleared the point and angled toward the open horizon, cutting through the water. All around them the sea shimmered. A couple hundred yards to their right—to starboard, as Clara had taught them—lay the promenade. Henry picked out the pink motel that stood at the end of Madison Avenue, and the stretch of beach where he and Effie had walked only three days ago, when she had told him she wanted to go home. They would have been on a train by now, making their way back to their familiar lives.

Clara offered him the wheel. He declined adamantly. She insisted, and so he made his way over to her and she gave him a quick lesson— pointed out the wind vane at the top of the mast, assured him they wouldn't capsize, warned him about the boom, said she and Max would take care of the jib ("Right, Maxie? If you *do* know what you're doing")—and with that, left him to it.

The wheel tugged against his grip. A few yards to port, a seagull hovered over the water, following along with them. Ahead, nothing but the horizon and a bank of clouds like chalky cliffs suspended in the sky. This, he thought, may have been the happiest moment in his life thus far. Clara told him when it was time to tack, and he turned the wheel and the boom swung smoothly over, and the boat tilted to the other side. They sailed on, and no one spoke, except to comment on the splendor of the day, the wind, the condition of the water, until gradually Cape May turned gauzy behind them, and in front of them, clearly visible now, was land—the coast of Delaware, just as Effie had said.

Clara took the wheel back and turned the boat to. The sails flapped angrily again. Henry and Max let loose the halyards and lowered them, and everything went quiet. The waves that had struck the bow now gently patted the hull, and the boat lazily bobbed and pitched.

"Who wants a gin and tonic?" Clara said. She'd slipped her robe off. Beneath it she wore a blue bathing suit, and her hips were bare and generous. You could sink in between them and disappear.

Max wanted one. Henry, looking at Effie, said he'd have one too, and Effie, forgetting her vow, said sure—sure, why not?

Alma, who had stepped up onto the deck, said she'd just have ice water, and as Clara went below to fix the drinks, she spread a towel out next to the mast, pulled the green dress off over her head—she wore a white bathing suit underneath—and lay down on her back, away from them.

They all stripped to their trunks and bathing suits. Unlike Henry, whose skin retained a negative image of his shirt, and Effie, who was so pale she seemed bluish in the sun, Max and his sister were golden brown all over. Alma lay half hidden behind the mast and the bunched-up jib, but he could see the curve of her hips, her long, smooth legs, her feet at the edge of the bulkhead. What lives these people must have led. Effie retrieved the tanning oil from their bag and asked Henry to do the little patch on her back that she couldn't reach. Her swimsuit was chaste compared to Clara's and Alma's, but she was pretty in it. They were all beautiful, Henry thought, and in the fullness of his mood he included himself. He squeezed the oil onto his fingers and rubbed it into Effie's skin, smelling the warm, summery coconut.

Clara returned with their drinks and handed them around. Alma sat up to take her ice water.

"It's nice, isn't it, little belle?" Clara said. She sat over by Max, perpendicular to him, and stretched her legs out in front of her, her toes nearly touching him. "Do you feel relaxed now?"

Effie smiled and nodded. Copying Clara, she stretched her legs out too, laying her feet in Henry's lap, and looked at the sea around her. She seemed wary of it. "I've never done this before."

"You can trust me, you see. I'm not such a . . . what was it? A harpy? A brazen slut?"

Max laughed. Effie looked mortified. "Did I call you that?"

"It's all right, dear." Clara slipped her sunglasses down and looked at her over the rim, smiling. "You meant it kindly. You meant that I'd changed."

Effie seemed flustered and uncertain how to respond. Up on the deck, Alma, who'd been grinning down at them during this exchange, took a sip of her water and resumed gazing at the horizon.

Henry asked how they all knew one another, and Clara explained that Scott and Max had roomed together their first year at Princeton. For a couple of years, she said, before Scott was drafted, the two of them had been best friends.

"He invited me to spend Thanksgiving with him in Philadelphia," Max said. "I'd only known him for a couple of months at that point, but I jumped at it. I was going to spend the weekend on campus, by myself."

"Poor Maxie," Clara said.

He set his hand on her foot and rubbed his thumb over the tips of her toes. "I fell in love with the Strausses," he said. "All you big, brash Teutons."

Clara drew her knees up to her chest and asked if she could have a cigarette, and while Max retrieved his pack and lighter from his bundled-up shirt, she explained that this was before she'd married Richard and moved to New York, when she was still living with her parents, trying to decide if she should go to secretarial school.

"Secretarial school?" Max muttered, two cigarettes in his mouth.

"I was almost a spinster."

He lit both cigarettes and handed her one. "I thought you were squarely on the Kirschbaum ticket by then."

"We were separated," she said. "Don't you remember? That weekend before Christmas, when we were at Sardi's. We saw Elmer Rice, the playwright, and he complimented my pearls, and you said he looked like a toad."

"Ah," Max said, smiling. "My God, has it really been seven years?"

He offered cigarettes to Henry and Effie. Effie refused, but Henry reached across to take one and accept a light, and for the next half hour they listened as Max and Clara quibbled over dates, recalled occasions, made references to people they had known in common. They were addressing themselves to Henry and Effie, explaining things to them, making them feel included, but they were talking to each other, Max leaning back, his legs spread, Clara bunched up tight, her attention fixed on him, lips parted, as if he might perform a magic trick. Most of what they were talking about meant nothing to Henry, although the details dazzled him. He caught a few things. That Max had dropped out of Princeton and moved to Hawaii of all places, where he had lived for more than a year, going from island to island—doing what for a living, Henry could only guess. That Clara had gotten pregnant and married Richard, in that order, then lost the baby. ("Oh, Clara, I'm sorry," Effie said, but Clara waved it away.) That Max had moved back to the mainland after his father died and settled in the

East Village, where he'd started writing seriously, at least until his sister had moved in with him. (Up on the deck Alma rolled over onto her stomach and buried her face in the crook of her arm.) That Scott had returned from Korea to finish his degree, go to law school, and get married, and that he no longer took Max seriously.

"That's not true," Clara said. "You were his best man."

"He knew I'd give the most colorful speech."

Mournfully Clara jiggled the ice in her glass. "Can that really be the last time I saw you? Scott's wedding? That was two years ago."

"So it was," Max said. He tugged at the hem of his trunks and looked down at his feet.

They were quiet then. The gin was working. Overhead, the sky remained clear, but the bank of clouds over Delaware no longer seemed benign. The land below it had disappeared in a dark blue band, and the sun was beginning to descend toward the cloud tops. Max offered to make another round of drinks.

"Shouldn't we start back?" Effie said. Like Henry, she was looking at the clouds.

"Those won't hurt us, dear," Clara said. "They are moving laterally." She slurred the last word, and quickly shook her head. "My God! I never ate lunch."

Max said he'd bring up the picnic basket, and a minute later he passed around sandwiches made with baguettes, some kind of honey sauce, slices of pear, and ham. They were good, although the baguette was a little tough for Henry's taste. Alma sat up Indian-style to eat her sandwich. The drinks came next, and when Max had settled himself beside Clara again he said, "I'm sure you've heard enough about us. What about you?"

Effie laughed, and looked at Henry. "What about us?"

He asked how they'd met, but Effie brushed the question away.

"We've known each other as long as I can remember. We grew up together. It's not very interesting."

"So then how did you . . ." He brought his palms together, and she smiled in a way that seemed uncharacteristically shy.

"I don't know. It was just a gradual thing," she said. "We weren't really ever friends or anything. We didn't run in the same circle. But we were in the same grade, so we were always in the same classroom. And I always thought highly of his family." She looked at Henry. They had never had to tell their story before. Until now, Henry had never thought of it as a story, it was just things that had happened, things everyone knew already. "He started mooning over my friend Ida June."

"Ida June!" Clara said. "What a perfect name!"

"Ida June Garnett," Effie went on. "Her family was kind of trash, actually. Her daddy did odd jobs around town; her brothers were in prison for armed robbery. But she and I were friends. She was pretty, I guess, if you didn't mind the freckles. She wanted to step up in life and I respected that. Henry had a crush on her, it was so obvious."

He felt his cheeks growing hot, and looked down at his drink, making an effort to keep a smile on his lips. The last person he wanted to think about right now was Ida June Garnett. He remembered her long hair, the color of cinnamon hard candies, the freckles that covered her nape. He'd had a sexual dream about her one night and woken up in love, simple as that. He'd been fifteen, she'd been thirteen.

"He worked up the courage, finally, to ask her out to some mixer or other," Effie was saying, "and they went with each other for a little while, and that's how I got to know him. I was going with this other boy then, but I thought Henry was sweet. We'd go as a group to the movies every Saturday."

"And so you stole him away," Max said, lighting another cigarette.

Effie shook her head, taking a swallow of her drink. "No," she said, "Ida June showed her true colors eventually and got herself knocked up by this man Rupe who worked for the power company, and she dropped out of school and married him. It's a shame. She wasn't seventeen. That was just the year before last, wasn't it?"

"Tough blow," Max said. He was holding a cigarette out to Henry, and Henry, affecting nonchalance, shrugged and accepted it. It was all supremely embarrassing. That, not the brief heartbreak, was what remained of Ida June. How he'd hold her hand until their palms were slick with sweat. How they'd kiss in the woods behind her place until his lips and chin were raw. When he'd confronted her, after the news got out, she'd told him he was boring.

"You should have seen him," Effie said. "He was a wounded bird."

"I was not," Henry said, low.

"You came to his rescue," Clara said.

Effie laid her hand on his leg. She could tell he was suffering. "No, it wasn't like that. Henry and I just started hanging around together, just the two of us. He asked me to homecoming, and we kissed out by the baseball diamond, down in the dugout. Remember?" She looked at him fondly, and he put his hand over hers. He remembered the dark dugout, how she'd pressed his hand to her breast. Only then had he understood that she liked him, and what he'd felt in the moment was the thrill of an open door, an invitation he hadn't expected. "I told you it wasn't interesting," she said, "but then a big thing like that ought not to be too interesting. He asked me to marry him at Mrs. Pritchett's New Year's Eve party. I nearly cried, it was so sweet. He had his grandmother's sapphire ring. I asked him if he'd talked with my daddy yet, and he hadn't, so I said, 'You clear it with him first,' and he did, the very next day. He promised Daddy he'd provide for me. And when he asked me again, I said yes."

Max and Clara laughed, but kindly. "How sweet," Clara said. Henry cleared his throat and said, "Felt like a stroke of genius or something. There she was in front of me the whole time," and Clara pouted.

"So what is it you do, Hank?" Max said. A folksy drawl had entered his voice, lifted, probably, from Effie. "Now you've got a wife to provide for."

"He helps his uncle manage his properties," Effie said.

"His land, yes," Henry said. "For the time being."

"What kind of properties?" Max asked.

"Cotton, peanuts, grain," Henry said. "Some orchards too, depending on the season."

"Ah—farming," Max said.

"Honest work," Clara said to Max, as if to explain it to him.

"And soon, a great deal of development," Effie said. "That's the important thing. The city of Macon's going to swallow us up soon, and that land's going to be worth a fortune."

This was one of Effie's favorite subjects, and before she could get too warmed up to it, he said, "I'm hoping to go to school, at Emory next fall." He didn't have to look at Effie to know her eyes had glazed over. Max asked what he wanted to study, and Henry blushed. He'd never been certain of the answer, and he had the faint suspicion that Max understood this somehow and was amused. "History, maybe," he said. "Or English literature."

Clara nodded eagerly, as if to encourage him to go on, but Effie said, "Those clouds are getting closer, aren't they?"

They all turned to look. She was right: the dark blue band over Delaware was larger, it had moved out into the bay, and the white tops of the clouds were on the verge of covering the sun. The wind had picked up.

"We'll be fine," Clara said. "But we should start back."

For a time it seemed the rain would certainly envelop them, but it stayed behind and to the side of them. Overhead the sky turned gray, and the day took on a twilight gloom. The temperature was dropping. It was just after five. Henry made out the flash of the lighthouse. Soon they passed it, and turned up the coast, and there again were the hotels and storefronts of Beach Avenue. At last they entered the little cove. Henry and Max lowered the sails, and Clara motored them into the marina.

On land, when the wind wasn't blowing, the air wasn't so cold, but a chill had entered their bones and they were all shivering. Max put the top of the Cadillac up—he'd left it down the whole time—and they climbed inside.

"Lord, turn on the heat," Effie said.

"How does whiskey and a fire sound to everyone?" Max said, cranking the engine.

"Divine," Clara said.

"Katie Scarlett? Hank? You'll join us, I hope?"

To Henry's surprise, Effie, rubbing her hands together for warmth, said without pause, "We would love to."

Max built up the fire and Clara made whiskey sodas. She asked for Effie's help ransacking the kitchen. Mrs. Pavich was gone, she said, but there was plenty to eat, and they returned a few minutes later with a platter of sliced sausages, cheeses, bread and olives, and dips of various kinds: olive oil mixed with pepper and Parmesan, something like honey but with flecks of red pepper in it, a green paste Henry couldn't identify. Clara put the platter on the coffee table and they settled around it, Henry and Effie on the couch, Clara in the armchair beside it, Max in a straight-back chair next to hers, his feet up on the coffee table. They were castaways, Henry imagined—they had that look about them: windblown and sun-kissed, in their bathing suits and loose linens. Effie and Henry shared an afghan; Clara spread a sweater over her legs.

Only Alma had changed out of her bathing suit. She'd put on a brown dress with little white polka dots, and she lay apart from them, on the rug near the fire, reading a book, her bare feet bobbing in the air.

The warmth was rejuvenating. The big open room, where they'd danced on Friday, felt close now, and as the evening darkened outside, the fire and the two lamps on either end of the couch made a circle that separated them from the rest of the world, and most of the living room—the foyer, the staircase, the little bar, the archway that led back to the kitchen—lay in shadow.

As on the boat, Max and Clara led the conversation. They seemed used to being in charge of a social setting, though Clara was prone to defer to Max, and when he cut her off, as he did fairly often, rather than get annoyed she'd look at him with a kind of delighted shock and then slowly her mouth would close and she'd seem to be lost in whatever he was saying, until she caught an edge and jumped back in. She was dramatic but gullible—or pretended to be, Henry suspected, for Max's sake.

Max was also dramatic, but everything he said was laced with irony. He was good at imitations. He told stories about his old friends at Exeter, the prep school he'd attended in New Hampshire; about bar fights he'd gotten into in the Village; about girls who wore knee-length skirts without underwear. The stories were long and skillfully told—rehearsed, Henry thought—and Clara and Effie and even Henry laughed until their stomachs hurt.

"You haven't heard this one, I know you haven't," he said to Clara at one point, and launched into a story about an old prep-school teacher of his, whom he and his friend Oliver had run into in New York, and the long night that followed, which had ended in a whorehouse in Little Italy. It was a shockingly vulgar story, involving the teacher's "cock" and a dessert called "tres leches," but something about Max's charm made it not entirely distasteful, and soon the four of them were doubling over with laughter, holding their stomachs—

especially Effie, who seemed to have lost control of herself, until everyone began to laugh anew, now at her. Even Alma looked over her shoulder, amused.

"I'm sorry," Effie cried, wiping the tears from her face. "I'm sorry, y'all. That is just so awful. That is the most awful story I have ever heard."

They refreshed their drinks. In the harsh light of the downstairs bathroom Henry saw his face in the oval mirror over the toilet. His eyes were dilated; he was smiling broadly. He looked strange to himself, and was glad to return to the relative dimness of the living room, their little circle by the fire.

Occasionally Clara made the mistake of trying to tell a story of her own in Max's way, about her old girlfriends in Philadelphia, or her failure to impress Richard's business partners, and the laughter would be forced, but then Max always came to her rescue, making a joke of it that was his own triumph but that also saved Clara's story. She was her best with a bon mot, her quick asides to Henry and Effie, or else when she was passionately, self-consciously earnest—when she described a book she'd read or a movie she admired or music she'd heard for the first time. "My God, Iris Murdoch makes me *mad* with joy. She's just so—*potent!*" She was a writer herself, she admitted. She'd published a few stories in little magazines ("You're joking," Effie said flatly), and she was at work on a play. She wouldn't discuss what it was about, not even a hint, and she wasn't being coy: when Effie pressed, Clara cried "No!" and laughed almost hysterically, shooting a glance at Max, and got up to fix herself another drink.

On the few occasions when Effie told a story, the room quieted— the fire popped, the trees outside the windows sighed—and Max and Clara listened carefully. She told the story about their fifth-grade teacher, Mrs. Hughes, and the bottle of Elmer's glue, and when she got to the part where the cap popped open, Max clapped his hands together, fell back in his chair, and laughed in an exaggerated way that bothered Henry—as if Max felt the need to bestow his approval. The story wasn't *that* funny. But most of the time Effie was just an audience, as Henry was, an audience Max clearly relished, which Effie satisfied by sitting on the edge of the couch cushion, smiling, her cheeks flushed bright red.

Henry himself had little to say. The few times he was asked a question, or when Effie asked him to fill in some little detail of a story, he replied with a curt bashfulness that pleased his own ears. Without quite realizing it, he was conjuring his uncle Red, the old Southern Railway engineer who in retirement sat permanently perched on his armchair with a slightly ironic grin on his face while the ladies chattered. He seemed to amuse Clara and Max. He could say something as simple as "Yep," or, "Hell, *I* don't know, Effie," and both of them would laugh. But it pleased him; it wasn't like they were making fun of him. He would be a man of few words.

Once they'd finished the platter and Henry had lost count of the number of whiskey sodas he'd had, Clara, in a lull, said, "It feels so late, doesn't it? Is it late?"

Effie slapped her thighs. "We should go."

"No," Clara said. "That's not what I meant. Stay as long as you like. Stay all night if you want to."

"Yes, please," Max put in.

"Our house is just across the way," Effie said.

"I know where your house *is*, darling. I just meant, stay as long as you like. Come and go, even—I'm serious. For as long as you're here. Think of it as one house. Your wing, our wing. We never lock the doors."

The idea made Henry happy. He said, "Our windows are always open, I can tell you that. She can't sleep without the windows open," and Effie shoved him playfully.

"Oh, good," Clara said. "We'll slip in and surprise you sometime."

"All of these houses are ours for the taking," Max declared. "These past few nights, I haven't seen a single light in any of them—except for yours. Haven't you noticed? No one's here, and no one will be until May."

Clara laughed. "Don't instigate." She put her hand on Max's forearm and, leaving it there, said to Effie, "He's been talking about breaking and entering all weekend. You'd better watch out for your belongings."

"I've just been making the observation. We could easily walk into any house on this street. Half the people who summer here don't lock their doors for the winter, and the ones that do don't lock their windows."

"What do you know?" Clara said, taking her hand away. "I know the people who live here. I grew up with them."

"Then prove me wrong," Max said.

"Not tonight, not tonight. My God"—Clara yawned dramatically— "I *am* exhausted."

But she didn't move to get up, and no one said anything for a while. The fire had subsided to a dull glow, two or three little spears of flame. Clara's feet were propped up on the coffee table beside Max's, and their toes were lightly touching. Whatever they said, Henry thought, these two wanted to be alone.

Down on the rug, on her back now, Alma turned a page of her book.

"What is it you're so engrossed in down there?" Effie said.

Alma raised the book and looked down her nose at Effie, and when she saw that Effie was talking to her, she sat up and flipped the spine around as if to remind herself. "*The Call of Cthulhu*," she said. "By H. P. Lovecraft."

"You didn't find that here, did you?" Clara asked.

Alma smiled. "Actually, I did." She had beautiful teeth: very white but irregular, one canine more prominent than the other; it caught on her bottom lip.

"I don't believe it," Clara said. "Here—hand it over."

With a sigh Alma scooched a few inches across the rug, lay on her side, and stretched her arm as if she could go no further. Clara had to lean forward to reach the book.

"I bet it's Uncle Otto's," Clara said, looking at the cover, which was red and unmarked as far as Henry could see. "He goes in for this pulp-horror shit. It's about monsters or something."

"A giant sea monster," Alma said, sitting up again and leaning on her hand. "And the secret cult that worships it. It's sort of appropriate. It was up in my bedroom."

It was the most she had said all day. Her voice was clear and light and assured, a very fine and precise line of sound. There was the hint of an accent, maybe French.

"It must be pretty good," Effie said. "You've had your head buried in it all night."

"I guess I go in for the pulp shit too."

"Let me see it," Max said, and he took it from Clara. He flipped a few pages and, in a baritone and English-accented voice, read: "'I know not why my dreams were so wild that night, but ere the waning and fantastically gibbous moon . . .'"

Alma rolled slowly onto her knees and with a show of effort got to her feet. "All right," she said. "I'm going for a walk."

"A walk?" Max said, closing the book. "What are you talking about? What time is it?"

"It's not late," Alma said. She stepped into her deck shoes, which she'd left by the fireplace, and lifted each foot in turn to pull the heels on.

"It's dark out," Max said.

"So? There's nobody here—like you said. I'm just going down to the beach."

"Alma," Max said. "You're not going to the beach."

"But I am." She was walking toward the foyer now, smiling at Max in what seemed to be a loving way. "See? I already am."

When the front door closed behind her, Henry was sad to see her go. She'd pointedly ignored them all day, but her rudeness had a magnetism to it. Probably she knew this. All night, barely conscious of it, he'd been unable to keep himself from glancing at her legs, her bare feet bobbing rhythmically while she read, the lovely curve of her behind.

"Is she all right?" Effie asked.

Max shook his head. "She's fine."

They left soon after. A quiet had fallen over Clara, and when Henry saw Max running the backs of his fingers up and down the side of her armchair, he told Effie they'd better go. She agreed. They stood up before Max or Clara could protest.

"Come back in the morning," Clara said. "Ten o'clock? We'll make mimosas. It'll take the edge off."

The night was not as cold as they'd expected it to be. An almost full moon stood high in the sky, and all the houses of the street were clearly visible. Back at Clara's, the lights had gone out already. The thought that she and Max were at that moment rushing to bed together gave him a pang—of excitement, or jealousy, he wasn't sure.

"Those two are having an affair," Effie said, and the coolness of her tone surprised him.

"Do you think so?" he said, playing dumb.

"Oh, please." She stumbled over a rut in the road and clung to him. "Now I see how her marriage works. Clara, Clara . . ."

It was only a little past ten. Despite all the drinks, Henry felt wide-awake, and he wanted to go where Alma presumably was right then: down on the beach, watching the silvery waves crash. He asked Effie if she felt like going.

"I just feel like going home," she said, taking his hand, but before his disappointment could register she said, "King George has a full bottle of gin, doesn't he?"

The night wasn't over. "I believe he does. I don't remember any tonic water."

"There's vermouth or something. We'll manage."

At the cottage they made their drinks and took them out onto the back porch, and within a few minutes they'd stripped their clothes off, flinging their shirts and shorts and bathing suits onto the deck, and made love—much too quickly, and awkwardly, Effie straddling him—on one of the deck chairs. Afterward she stood naked against the porch railing, looking out at the yard, while in the afterglow Henry lay back admiring her, trying to tamp down the feeling that he was inadequate. She looked like a marble statue in the moonlight. "The air feels amazing," she said. "Doesn't it feel amazing?"

On her request he went inside to put ice into their glasses, to temper the nearly undrinkable mixture of gin and dry vermouth they'd made, and he liked the feel of his nakedness, his half-erect penis hanging in the open air, while he went about this little domestic task—opening the freezer, chipping a few shards off the block, dropping them into their drinks, swirling the ice around.

When he went back outside, Effie was no longer on the porch. He whispered her name, and her voice came back from far away: "Out here."

She was a white ghost down on the lawn. Henry laughed. "What do you think you're doing?"

"Come down here," she said. "It's exciting."

He walked down the porch steps and across the lawn to join her, the grass and fallen leaves soft on his feet, the cool air thrilling against his skin. In the moonlight Effie was vividly naked: the glowing white skin, the black patch between her legs, the black coins of her nipples. "You're crazy," he said, handing her drink to her.

"Who cares, if no one's here to see us?"

He put his arms around her and pressed her body to his and kissed her neck. They were covered in goose bumps, they were laughing and shivering—an electric current was running through them. He took her hand and they made a circle around the yard. The tool shed lay mysterious in a dark bed of ivy. The line of silvery beech trees on one side of the yard, an old picket fence in need of repair on the other. In the neighboring yard stood a swing set, the rusty hinges singing, and the yard beyond it was crowded with thick trees. Against the light grass the shrubs and fence posts and lawn chairs became presences; he felt eyes upon him.

"Let's walk around a little," Effie whispered.

"Walk around?"

But she had already turned away from him, and he followed her pale behind into the deep gloom at the side of the house. They were infected with laughter—the air was tickling their stomachs. "Effie," he whispered. "Someone's going to *see* us." But she ignored him and continued on, stepping carefully over the taller grass, holding her drink out and high as if she were on a balance beam.

They came out onto the cement sidewalk in front of the house, in the shadow of an elm tree, and looked up and down New Hampshire Avenue. Henry's heart was pounding. Effie dared him to walk up the sidewalk. "That way," she said, pointing to a long stretch of open moonlight in the direction away from Clara's house.

"You do it," Henry said, and Effie said fine and walked out of the safe harbor of the shadow. Laughing, trembling all over, he jogged up to join her, cupping himself pointlessly until, after a moment, he took his hand away.

They sipped their drinks and strolled easily down New Hampshire Avenue, past house after deserted house. Henry had never felt so liberated. Everything was enchanted and strange, and neither of them spoke, as if in respect to something hallowed. The breeze was strong. The trees cast impenetrable shadows, and the houses seemed bathed in silver. Henry's loins tickled him and he kept touching himself.

Now the moon went behind a thin line of clouds and the neighborhood dimmed. Henry pointed out that today marked a week since they'd arrived in Cape May, and what a difference a week made. "Aren't you glad we didn't leave?"

"I'll tell you when it's over," she said.

They were coming within reach of the yellow streetlights on Philadelphia Avenue, but they continued on anyway, until they reached the corner. Another large elm tree sheltered them. Three blocks down, Philadelphia ran into Beach Avenue and the seawall, and beyond the lights of the promenade long pale lines appeared out of the darkness and then faded away, one after another. They stood watching them for a while. Henry, emboldened now, was about to suggest they risk a dash down to the beach, when Effie said, "Look," and pointed with her empty glass.

A lone figure was walking along the promenade. They were too far away to make it out, but Henry thought it must be Alma, still wandering the night. A slender frame, an unhurried pace. The thought of her out there within sight of them thrilled him in a way he couldn't articulate. "I guess we're not *entirely* alone," he said, his voice trembling.

Effie laughed and hugged her shoulders, and Henry rubbed the goose bumps away from her arms. They watched until the figure went out of sight.

"We better head back," Effie said, "before we get thrown into jail."

They started back down the sidewalk, in no hurry. Effie wandered into the middle of the street, and Henry followed, but the street was dirt and gravel and broken seashells, and they retreated after a few yards. Just before they reached Aunt Lizzie's, the moon came out again from behind the clouds and caught them in a bright segment of the sidewalk. Effie had gone a pace ahead. She seemed to give off her own light. Henry reached forward and grabbed her hips and pulled her back against him. He didn't want the night to end. Neither did she. She took his hand and pulled him onto the next-door neighbor's lawn, and they dropped their empty glasses and got to their knees. The grass was dewy and cold, but they wouldn't have to lie in it: he told her to bend over, gently nudging her down, and she complied, and after a little searching, a little adjusting—they'd never done it this way before—he found her.

For a few perfect, suspended minutes Henry was the master of himself. It was the whiskey and gin, it was the quick release on the back porch, it was the strangeness of the evening and the watchful presences all around them. He imagined a ceiling inside of her and aimed for that and thought he could feel himself striking it. The day rose before him: the scent of Dial soap, the taut and shuddering sails, the bank of clouds, the warmth of the fire, Alma's long, slender legs— and now Effie's buttocks spread open at his waist. The best days of his life were upon him. Live wires ran under his skin from every extremity, converging at his groin, and he tried to keep the center warm but not to overheat it. He held her hips to steady himself. But then the scales tipped subtly and Effie wasn't under his control anymore—she was up on her elbows now, pushing back against him, more quickly than he wanted. She had discovered something, an edge of something, and now she was trying to get at it. Henry stopped moving and let her do the work. Their bodies clapped. Her flesh shuddered. He saw the dark cleft between them, where they met in a ring of friction, and the sight brought him to the verge—so he closed his eyes, and imagined her father scowling at him, and then his own mother, and he was so concentrated on the struggle that he didn't realize he was coming until the crest had passed and the wave was already receding—shallow and disappointing. But he would make himself hold on a little longer. Effie had really found something; for the first time she let out a little cry: *"Oh."* She sat up higher, to bring her weight down on it, eyeing him over her shoulder, as if to warn him not to give in now—so he leaned back on his hands, pressing his pelvis up so he wouldn't slip out, and held on until, finally, to his relief, she gave up with a sigh, pulled away from him, and fell over onto the wet grass.

For a long time they lay there, angled apart, and looked up at the moon and the fast-moving clouds. Henry sat up. Effie was embedded in the grass. She was spent, he thought; beyond rescue. He helped her up. They found their empty glasses and went inside through the unlocked front door.

They went to bed naked and woke late. The attic room was hot and bright.

"We were foolish last night," she said from her pillow.

"Are you ashamed?" he asked.

She smiled, and shook her head, and reached for him under the covers.

Five

They spent the early afternoon after breakfast by Clara's pool, drinking Champagne and orange juice. Clouds drifted overhead and the light swelled and faded and swelled again. They lay out on deck chairs in their bathing suits, but the pool was too dirty to swim in. Leaves softly clattered over the patio and into the water.

"We're lovers, you know," Clara said, after Max had shown them his backflip off the diving board and gone upstairs to wash the grime off. "I'm a little tipsy already, so forgive me if I'm being shocking."

Effie laughed. "It's none of my business." But Henry had perked up, wanting to hear more.

"We always had this kind of open thing with each other, whoever else we were with. You're such decent people, maybe it sounds bad to you." She was smiling at Henry, who smiled back, and shook his head.

"Honestly, Clara," Effie began, but Clara went on:

"It's not so unusual. Richard and I, we have an arrangement. I don't mean we actually *talk* about it, you know, but—but of course you don't know, you're so sweet and young. There are different kinds

of marriages. Happy families are *not* all alike. I'm a comfort to him.
And he's a dear, sweet man."

"So long as you're happy," Effie said.

"Oh, I'm happy," Clara said. "Oh, I really am." She sighed and
tilted her face up to the sun, stretching her legs out.

When Alma came down at last, squinting, wearing the same dress
she'd been wearing the night before, they roused themselves and went
out for a walk.

The town seemed to have emptied again after the weekend. They
wandered the deserted streets, no longer alone. If a place was open,
they drifted inside. A malt shop. A curio shop, full of crafts made of
seashells and driftwood and sea glass. Effie was happy and lively. As
they walked she shared facts about the place. It had been the first
beach resort in the country. In 1878 a fire—arson, most likely—had
destroyed most of it, and most of the Victorian architecture dated
from the rebuilding. "Our own little docent," Clara said. There had
been great floods, of course. Some years ago, in the winter, the sea
had surged as far as New Hampshire Avenue, and Clara said she remembered it well: how they'd found the house in ruin, shattered
glass, stains on the walls, a mildewy smell everywhere. They were
coming back along the promenade now in the early evening. The sea
softly roared to their right. Henry imagined a wall of water rising up,
curling a hundred feet overhead, consuming the promenade, smash-
ing into the hotels beyond, rushing up the avenues. At any time, he
thought, it could happen again. The danger was exhilarating.

"Some kind of monster washed up on the shore here this summer," Alma said. She'd been trailing behind, and now they stopped
and turned to her. She pulled her cardigan close. "No one knows what
it was. Some species of squid, maybe. It had tentacles, but it had rows

of teeth too, like a shark. It was big. One of the Coast Guard boys told me about it. He said the smell was all over town."

"Charming," Max said.

Clara laughed. "Did you get that from H. P. Lovecraft?"

"No, like I said, it was one of the Coast Guard boys."

"Well, it's interesting," Clara said. "Who knows what terrible things are out there." She gave the sea a glance, turned and took Max's arm, and they continued on. Alma fell behind again. Henry had gathered by now that she and Clara didn't like each other, although for Max's benefit Clara only spoke kindly of her, calling her "dear," worrying for her safety, commenting on how pretty she was, or could be if she'd put the effort in. She was Max's half sister, as it turned out. She'd grown up with their mother in Los Angeles, under squalid conditions, apparently. (Clara had told them this, while Max had been busy making omelets in the kitchen.) The mother had died not long ago, and now Max looked after her. They lived off the money, a generous sum of money, his father had left him. He was a Hewitt— as in Hewitt-Rowe, the shipping company.

"You mean he doesn't have a job?" Effie had asked, and the disdain in her voice had pleased Henry. If there was one thing that turned Effie off, it was a man who was not gainfully employed.

"No, the poor soul," Clara had said. "Aside from his writing. I feel for him deeply. You wouldn't guess it to meet him, but he's a lost child, really."

"But—I mean—he can *get* a job," Effie had said.

Back at Clara's they made gin and tonics and warmed up the pot roast Mrs. Pavich had made on Saturday. They settled around the coffee table with their plates. Clara lit candles. All the doors and windows were open, and everything in the den was fluttering and alive.

Leaves had begun to gather in the corners. A small bird—no, a bat, Effie cried—flitted in from the kitchen and turned sharply out to the patio.

Clara suggested they play a game of charades. There'd be no need to keep score, it was just for fun, but Effie didn't see the point of a game if you didn't keep score. She and Henry made one team, Clara and Max the other. Alma, who had built an unnecessary fire, sat on the rug near the hearth reading her book.

Effie held the stopwatch, and Clara drew the first slip of paper from the sun hat. She signaled that it was a person, and held her arms out to indicate a big belly, doing a little bounce. "Santa Claus," Max said. "Jackie Gleason," and Clara laughed and shook her head. Then she said, "Ah!" and looked above her in terror, holding her fingers to her cheeks. She dashed across the den, pointed at the radio, then up to the ceiling, and with twenty seconds to go Max cried, "Orson Welles," and she shrieked and jumped and clapped her hands.

"That's a lot of racket for one point," Effie said, standing and handing the stopwatch to Max. She was all business when it came to games. She drew a slip of paper, frowned a moment, indicated that it was another person—and transformed herself: swaying her hips, batting her eyelashes at Henry, biting the tip of her finger in a perfect impersonation of Marilyn Monroe, which had been one of his contributions to the hat. When he guessed it she said, "Very good," sat down, and recorded their point.

Max made the sign for book. And then stood still for several long seconds. Clara laughed. "Darling, *do* something." So he halfheartedly mimed rifle fire, then seemed to run away from it, then repeated the sequence. "Do something else, Maxie, I'm not getting it." But he was stuck on the move. For someone so sure and confident—someone who could execute a perfect backflip off the diving board—he seemed strangely self-conscious now. The poor lost soul. He was beginning to grow on Henry.

"Time," Effie declared. The book had been *The Red Badge of Courage*.

"Oh, but that's a hard one, darling," Clara said.

"No, it's not," Effie said. "Point at something red—your trunks—make like you're flipping a badge or something, I don't know. Act courageous."

Everyone laughed—especially Max. "You're merciless, Katie Scarlett," he said.

When Henry stood up for his turn, he pulled *The Birth of a Nation*, in a barely legible scratch that wasn't Effie's. Clara was sitting across Max's lap in the armchair, which distracted him for a moment. He knew that it was a movie and had something to do with the KKK, but that was all. He made the sign for movie, and then, like Max, did nothing.

"How many words," Effie said.

Four—no, five, he indicated, then held up two fingers for the second word. Unlike Max, Henry, who was shy around small groups of people, was not shy when he was performing, and though he could have mimed "birth" in any number of less dramatic ways, he chose to lie down on the rug, inches from Alma's feet, lift and spread his knees, and with his hands make a kind of gushing motion from his crotch. Max and Clara howled with laughter. Effie, not laughing, focused on guessing the word. "Baby," she said. He shook his hand: *Sort of.* He made as if to wrangle a baby from between his legs, grimacing in pain, and when she got it he said, "Yes," and leapt to his feet—hopping, into it now. Clara had fallen from Max's lap onto the floor. Fifth word. Hand to his chest, back rigid. "Flag," Effie said. "Allegiance." No, forget that. He paced. He indicated a cone growing up from his head, looked stern, made a whipping motion, all of which only confused Effie, who muttered, "A birth . . . Birth allegiance . . ." until she got it—*"Birth of a Nation!"*—just as Max called time.

"We get the point, right?" Effie said.

"You get the point," Max assured her.

"That was simply amazing," Clara said, leaning back against Max's knees. "Henry, you surprise me."

Henry sat back down beside Effie and hugged her shoulders. Across the way he saw Alma watching him. When he caught her gaze she held it, and he gave her a thumbs-up—lamely. She laughed, and returned it.

They played four more rounds, until there were no more papers in the hat, though by the third round it would have been mathematically impossible for Clara and Max to win, as Effie pointed out twice. "Fourteen to six," she declared at the end, and Max said, "There's no need to rub it in."

They made more drinks and settled in. Effie, thrilled with victory, rested her legs over Henry's lap and pulled an afghan over them. Once again Alma put on her shoes, bid them all good night, and slipped out the front door. Max stoked the fire.

"Where do you think she goes?" Effie asked.

Max shrugged, not looking away from the fire. "She's an adult, she can take care of herself."

"Clara says you're her guardian," Effie said, and Max looked at her in surprise. Her cheeks were flushed. She was getting forward. But before Max could answer, Clara said, "I was telling her what a good brother you've been."

He put the poker back in its stand. "I don't know about that."

Clara had moved to the smaller sofa perpendicular to the main one, and she'd drawn her legs up, obviously making a space for Max. But he remained standing. Effie watched him, waiting for him to go on.

"I'm all she has," he said, "for better or worse." He took his cigarettes out of his pocket and tapped one on his wrist. "Her mother died last year. Our mother, I should say. I didn't know her, aside from the letters. She left when I was a baby. I don't think she took very good care of herself, or of Alma for that matter. She died of heart failure." He lit a cigarette and settled in the armchair near Effie, on the opposite side of the coffee table from Clara.

"You so rarely speak of your family," Clara said.

"There's not much to speak of."

"He says humbly. Your family built the third-largest shipping company in the world."

Max put his feet up. "My father was a miserable old man," he said to Effie, "and my mother was a failed starlet. The rest of my family were teetotalers, descended from Quakers, like Ahab. They're all dead now, the ones I cared about."

"How sad," Effie said.

"Yes," Max said, simply, and the silence that followed was awkward. Henry broke it by jiggling the ice in his glass, and Max got up to take it, and Effie's as well, and went over to the bar. Another drink was going to put Henry over the edge—but no matter. The day shimmered in his head.

"Oh, Maxie, let's just go to Hawaii," Clara said. It seemed to be a continuation of some other conversation. "I mean really, why not?"

"I told you," Max said, dropping fresh ice into their glasses. "*I* would go."

"Hawaii—yes," Henry said emphatically, and Effie laughed and said, "Are you drunk?"

"Of course he's drunk," Max said. "Bravo. So am I."

"You could come with us if you wanted," Clara said, to Henry and Effie. "The more, the merrier. There's nude beaches. We could lie out in the sun as nature intended."

"We'd make a handsome set," Max said.

Henry imagined the four of them lying naked on the beach before a vast turquoise sea, while Alma played out in the waves ahead of them.

"God knows I'd love to spend my life loafing around," Effie said dryly, tilting her head back to see Max. "But alas."

Her tone was an act. Under the afghan Henry had pushed his finger past the elastic hem of her bathing suit, and she'd opened her legs a bit so he could reach her. She was wet. The muscles in her groin tensed.

They were no longer shy of each other. They slept naked. In the morning she greeted his erection with a kiss, tickling it with her tongue, until he said he was going to die if she didn't do it. So she did it, for the first time, and he lay back groaning, holding as still as he could, afraid of choking her. When he was about to come he said, *Okay, okay,* and she left off, and watched it leap out onto his stomach. It smelled like starch, she said. She reached down by the side of the bed to retrieve a towel for him and mooned him spectacularly. He laughed: now he had seen everything. She threw the towel at him. He apologized, laid her back, and repaid the favor, and she drew her knees up and sighed. *That's nice. That's very nice.* They rolled around on the bed. They made a sixty-nine. Angels averted their eyes. When he was up again she straddled him, which was how she liked it best.

They took the boat out again in the late afternoon. A film seemed to lie over Henry's senses, and through it everything seemed soft and sweet and desirable. He felt open and unbounded. He relished every scent, every touch, every taste. How the world flaunted itself. At the marina he pointed to the octagonal building out on the pier and told everyone there was going to be a dance there on Friday night.

"The Historical Society fete," Clara said. "I heard about it the other night."

"We could crash it," Max said.

"We don't have to crash it," Clara said. "It's open to everyone. Except I don't have anything to wear."

"That's our last day here," Effie said, taking Henry's hand.

"That's too sad," Clara said. Henry couldn't tell if she was being sincere. "What day's today?"

"It's Tuesday," Effie said. "It's still days and days away."

The sea was calm this time, deep blue in the late-afternoon sun. They sailed straight toward a ghostly tanker in the distance, until Cape May was nothing but a line of fiery orange and yellow land behind them. After they'd dropped the sails and made a round of drinks and drifted for a while, Alma stood up without a word and dove into the water.

Max leapt to his feet. When she came up for air she made a shriek and said, "It's freezing!"

"It's October," Max called out to her. "It's the North Atlantic. You're an idiot."

"It's the *Mid*-Atlantic," she called back.

"Stay close, dear," Clara said. "We're not anchored."

Henry wanted to join her. His muscles twitched with intention. How would the others have reacted if he had? What would Effie have done? But he was afraid. And now Effie was saying, "Aunt Lizzie used to tell me, 'This isn't the creek, girl. If you're in the water up past your knees, you're fair game for the sharks.'"

They let Alma be. She dove and splashed in the water, and a few minutes later climbed out, up the ladder at the stern, her hair slicked back, water streaming off her body, glistening in the low, red sun like a white-and-gold seal.

That evening, after dinner, after several drinks, they decided it was time to explore the other houses on the street. They would test Max's theory. Everyone was in agreement. Especially Alma, who brightened when Max suggested it.

They went out.

The moon was still low in the sky, and New Hampshire Avenue lay mostly hidden in the dark. The excitement stimulated Henry's bowels, and occasionally a cramp would nearly paralyze him, but then it would pass. Alma led the way—first to the house across the street, where the front door and windows were locked, and then to the house next door to it, which was locked up as well. "We tried," Clara said, but Alma ignored her. They crossed the street again, not back to Clara's, but to the house next door. The Healys' place, Effie said, and Clara said, "Yes. Mrs. Healy made my birthday cakes. I can't do it." She stopped on the lawn. "I'll stay out here." But it didn't matter, the house was locked. So they tried the one next door, which was the house directly across from Aunt Lizzie's. The Woods' place, where Effie's babysitter Betsy had lived. She had never been inside. The house lay in a sliver of moonlight. The front door was locked, but when Alma tried the tall window beside it, it lifted open.

"*Et voilà,*" she said, and ducked down and stepped inside. Henry went in after her, and the others followed.

It was nothing special inside, what little they could make out. A sparely furnished den, an oval rug, a bookcase full of portraits, the faces indistinct and ghostly, and hanging on the wall above it, a long paddle. But to Henry, the simple thrill of being inside a stranger's house at night, uninvited, was almost unbearable. Another cramp seized him, and he was glad for the dark. Every half-visible object seemed charged with secret meaning. There was a clicking sound, and Alma announced that the electricity was off, and Clara said, "Well, Jesus, we don't want to turn the *lights* on, do we?" They found their way into the kitchen, which was a little brighter, from a bay window at one end, and Alma rifled through the drawers until she said, "There we are," and a blinding light startled them. She'd found a flashlight. She held it to her chin and made herself ghoulish.

They went upstairs, into what must have been the master bedroom. Shag carpet on the floor, a queen-size bed with a multicolored quilt. On the dresser stood a photograph of a middle-aged man and woman, the man bloated and self-important, the woman with thick, horn-rimmed glasses. Was that the Woods? Henry asked, and Effie said she wasn't sure. Clara hung around the doorway, her arms crossed as if afraid to leave any fingerprints. Alma and Max were in the attached bathroom, looking through the medicine cabinet and under the sink, but they found nothing interesting, or embarrassing for the Woods—or whoever these people were—aside from a stack of used menthol camphor tins.

Max declared that he knew all he needed to know about the Woods. "Their children are grown and don't care about the beach house anymore. The mister is retired. He was a home-appliance salesman. He and the missus still come out here, but without the children, they bore each other to tears. They'll likely sell the place soon."

They made their way back outside. "That was fun," Clara said, but Alma, who had kept the Woods' flashlight, was making her way to the next lawn, and they followed. That house was locked, but the one next to it was wide open: they walked in through the front door.

Effie didn't know these people. Neither did Clara. The den was garishly nautical. Model ships lined the mantel. A ship's wheel hung over a leather sofa, and a giant painting of a World War II battleship firing all of its guns hung opposite. In a corner stood a small armchair with white-lace arm covers. "He voted for Eisenhower," Max said, "and she voted for Stevenson, twice, though she will never admit it to him."

After they'd wandered upstairs Effie said, "No, he's a bachelor." In one room was a metal-framed bed and bare walls, in another a workbench of some kind and a strong smell of varnish, and in an-other a small four-poster bed with a plush quilt. "His mother comes to visit sometimes."

Quietly Alma inspected every piece of furniture, every decoration and trinket, as if searching for something in particular. Back down in the den she stood in the middle of the room and turned slowly in a circle, her eyes closed, while Clara led the others back outside. Henry hung back. "What are you doing?"

She opened her eyes, holding the flashlight aloft. "Just imagining them here." She smiled at him. "I don't think I'd like them very much."

Outside, the night was warm and still. "Can we go back now, friends?" Clara said. "I'm afraid the gin is wearing off."

But Alma said, "Just one more," and pointed to the big Victorian house diagonally across the street, three houses down from Aunt Lizzie's. It was the only house like it on the street—purple in the daylight, now a looming black mass, only part of its slate roof, its widow's walk, its lone tower exposed to the moonlight. It looked like a haunted castle.

"That's where that old couple lived," Effie said to Henry, "the one I told you about."

"The Bishops," Clara said. "That's the Bishops' house. Edith and—I don't remember the man's name."

"Do you know them?"

"They're old friends of my mother's. I remember them from parties."

Alma had started across the street already. They followed.

Wraparound porches surrounded the first and second floors, deep and impenetrably dark. They stepped carefully, blind, up the front steps. The door was locked, Alma announced. They felt around for the windows and tried them, but they were all locked too. Alma said she might have seen another way in, and they followed her back down the steps and around the side of the house, where, in the open moon-light, a metal staircase led up to the second-story porch. Alma climbed it and a moment later called down to them: "It's open."

They found her in a spacious, brightly lit room at the end of a narrow hallway. "The electricity's working," she said, and Clara cried, "Have you gone mad? Turn the lights out!" But Alma ignored her.

It looked to be a den or game room. A billiards table stood in one corner, but it was piled with mounds of colorful fabric. Overhead a dangerous-looking wrought-iron light fixture hung from the exposed roof beams. The walls were crowded with masks—ceremonial masks, Henry thought: horrible frowning mouths, furious eyes, wild tufts of hair. Some of them appeared to be Japanese, others from some kind of island culture—New Guinea, maybe. At the back were three large stained-glass windows with Gothic arches, and before these a low plat-form that looked to be a stage, at the back of which, propped be-tween two of the windows, stood a long, stained-wood plank with strings stretched along the length of it, some kind of musical instru-ment. Along the front of the room, facing the street, was a row of glass doors that led out to the second-story porch, presumably; the blinds on them were shut, and tied up between each of them were heavy blue drapes. The furniture in the center of the room was leather, the lamp shades colorful glass. On the rug before the stage, pillows were scattered everywhere, strewn with colorful beads and shiny objects Henry couldn't make sense of at a glance.

"They're explorers," Max said. "Anthropologists."

"Traveling minstrels, maybe," Effie said.

"It's a gold mine," Alma said.

Three different hallways led away from the den, and they went exploring, going their separate ways. Henry followed Alma, and when he looked behind him, expecting Effie to be there, he saw that he was alone with her. She pointed her flashlight ahead. The layout seemed needlessly complicated. There were half floors, doorways un-evenly spaced apart, circular windows nestled into alcoves, a stair-case that spiraled sharply up to a trapdoor. They looked into a lushly furnished bedroom, all of it decorated in various shades of rich blue. Across from it was a room crowded with bellhops' carts full of costumes—old-fashioned ballroom dresses, hoop skirts, harlequin suits, a bear costume. Alma stopped short and he bumped into her and caught a whiff of unwashed hair. "This is so wild," he said, because they had not said anything since separating from the others, but she didn't seem to hear him.

She aimed her flashlight into the next room over, stepped inside, and found the light switch. It was completely empty. The closet door stood open. Silently they looked at it, Henry frozen at the entrance, trying to make sense of it, until they heard Clara's voice from some-where else in the house: "Hey, come look."

They went down a connecting passageway and came to a lighted door, and inside stood Clara, staring at shelves upon shelves of face-less heads supporting wigs of every conceivable variety. "Just *look* at this," she said.

The shelves covered every wall, save for a space for a window at the back. In the center of the room sat a plush circular ottoman, and in a corner an oval mirror. There were men's and women's wigs, some natural-looking, others from history—Roman centurions, seventeenth-century courtesans—and others that seemed to be alien, in shimmer-ing blue and green.

Max appeared at the door, Effie just behind him. "Wow," she said.

"They're theatre people," Max said.

Effie came over to Henry's side. "There's a room full of fake clouds and trees and swords and all. You wouldn't have known it to see them going down the sidewalk."

"You can never know people," Max said.

With a practiced movement Alma bundled her hair atop her head so it stayed there on its own, selected a glittery, ruby-red flapper's wig with a severe cut at the jawline, and put it on in front of the mirror, tucking the loose strands away. She turned around, transformed, and because they were closest to her, she posed for Henry and Effie, hands on her hips, and Henry said, "Beautiful."

"What do you think, Maximilian?"

"That you look like a cheap prostitute," he said.

"Perfect," she said.

Max selected a long barrister's wig, but Alma said that was dull because it was *meant* to be a wig and there was no illusion to it, so he replaced it with a frizzed shock of gray hair and a long beard that made him look, Effie said, like Charlton Heston in *The Ten Commandments*. For Henry, Effie chose a great curly mass of Gibson Girl hair, which amused everyone, and for herself she took a bright blond wig that was, Max pointed out, strikingly similar to Clara's hair. "It isn't close," Clara said, and Max said, "Oh, but it is," and with the same skill she'd shown for Marilyn Monroe, with a subtle shift in her posture and the set of her face, Effie transformed herself into Clara. The effect was disconcerting: there was the real Clara, and across from her a short, squat version—his wife. "Oh, Maxie, darling," she said, batting her eyes at Max, and everyone laughed—Clara especially. She found a wig of dark curls that was similar to Effie's hair, and when she put it on and looked at herself in the mirror, she sang, "Well, I declare! Ain't I the cutest thing you ever saw?"

"You're simply delicious, darling," Effie said. "I want to tear you apart into tiny pieces and gobble you up."

"Well, fiddle-dee-dee!"

Max had doubled over laughing, his Moses beard swinging out in front of him. "Wonderful, wonderful," he said. "Please keep them on, I'm begging you."

"No," Henry said, and yanked Effie's wig off. He laughed nervously. It might all have been in good fun, but the look on Effie's face had been turning deadly. "It's giving me the heebie-jeebies," he said.

They replaced their wigs—except for Alma, who kept her glittery red flapper's wig on—and made their way downstairs, where the rooms were more open and identifiable. There was an elegant dining room with a table that could have sat a dozen people, and presiding over it was a large oil painting of a jester playing a lute. The kitchen, when Max found the light, was bright and spacious, with a large island range and dozens of hanging pots and pans, and the walk-in pantry was stocked with nonperishables. Through another passageway they entered a beautifully furnished den that smelled strongly of pipe tobacco. Alma had turned all the lamps on. The walls were dark wood. A stone hearth dominated the room, and over it hung two crossed swords. There was a sprawling couch of brown leather in three sections, an entire wall of books, a grizzly bear standing up on its hind legs, shelves of curios and artifacts, and a bar.

"I need a drink," Clara said.

Max had picked up a picture from an end table, a photograph that seemed to be from the turn of the century, of a young woman lying on a cushion wearing several strings of pearls. "This must be the lady of the house. You kind of looked like her, Hank, with your wig on."

Clara poured bourbon into four expensive-looking highball glasses and passed them around to Max and Effie and Henry. Alma seemed deeply absorbed in the shelves of curios. Max put on a record, over Clara's protestations, and soon a mischievous-sounding aria was playing, a woman's voice singing in French, interrupted occasionally by a loud chorus and a crash of cymbals. According to Max, she was singing, *Love is a rebellious bird, and nothing can tame it.*

The bourbon, like nails going down at first, quickly refreshed Henry's buzz, and soon it seemed to have cast a spell on all of them. Max and Clara waltzed together over the rug. Effie kicked her sandals off and ran, holding her arms out to her sides, in a track that went from the den back through the dining room and kitchen and into the den again on the opposite side. She had never, she announced, run indoors, not since she was a child. Henry chased her on the third lap and caught her in the dark dining room, pressed her against the table, breathing onto her neck, as she caught her breath and seemed to wait for what he was going to do—until Max called from the den: "Hank, where are you? I challenge you to a duel." They found him in front of the hearth holding one of the swords, testing its weight. Henry pulled the other one down from its mount, and in slow motion—the swords were heavy—they clashed them together. "Oh God, I can't look at this," Clara said, and crossed back over to the bar. And sure enough, after a few swings, Max popped Henry on the knuckle, and Henry dropped his sword. "Ah, shit, Hank, I'm sorry," Max said, and Henry laughed and said it was all right. It was a small cut, but the blood appeared immediately. These swords were the real thing. "Well—dumbass," Effie said, coming quickly to him and taking his hand, and to his surprise, she brought it to her mouth and gently sucked at the cut. Henry couldn't have done that. Just the sight of blood made him light-headed. He sat on the rug beside his sword. Max said he'd look for bandages. Clara said she'd refill his glass. True to his word, Max returned a minute later with a bandage—he'd found a lavatory—and Effie affixed it to his knuckle, and kissed it.

They all settled on the floor by the sofa with their refilled drinks. The bourbon was going down easily now. Max had put on a Mozart clarinet concerto. There was an impressive classical collection here, he said. He wondered if they should build a fire, but Clara said she would absolutely forbid it, and besides, it was a warm night.

"They like pillows, don't they?" Effie said. As in the game room upstairs, there were pillows scattered here and there all around the perimeter of the space, on the floor as well as the sofa, and Max said,

"It's for the orgies." Effie laughed, but he pressed on: "It's true. You don't know thespians. It's a free-for-all in that set, God bless them. Isn't that right, Clare?"

"Oh yes." She raised her glass. "That's my tribe."

"No, it's not. The playwrights don't have any fun. It's the players. I bet a whole troupe of them have been here. They have parties and put on plays for themselves, and at the end of the night they lay out on all these pillows and fuck each other. I wonder how many bacchanals have taken place here."

"All this time," Clara said, running her hand up and down her shin. "Mr. and Mrs. Bishop."

Effie asked what Max knew about thespians, and he said his mother had been one. "Actually, 'thespian' is a generous word. She had a bit role on Broadway once. She was a pretty face. Alma could tell you . . ." He craned his neck to look over the sofa for her, but she was no longer in the room.

"Do you remember the night we saw the Persian dancers in the Village?" Clara said to Max, and Max smiled and nodded and looked down into his drink. "Now, that was a bacchanal."

"Oh yeah?" Effie said. She'd slouched to Henry's side, and she straightened herself up now, languidly, to listen.

"Oh yeah," Clara said. "This girl at the after-party—it was an intimate affair, a harem theme—and this girl gave us some kind of potion that made everything . . . What would you say, Maxie? Very focused. And interesting. She had Max and me undress, and she did a kind of ritualistic massage on us, using this aromatic oil, that was supposed to rid us of foul humors or something. And oh my God . . ."

"It was nonsense," Max said. "She was winging an incantation as she went. Ten to one she was from Kansas."

"You say that now," Clara said, "but there is no such thing as a skeptical hard-on."

Effie cried out and hid behind Henry's shoulder, and Henry, as usual, felt a couple of steps behind. It was the bourbon. Now Clara smiled at him wickedly.

"I, for one, had the best orgasm of my life," she said. "Up to that time, I mean. I wish I could remember that girl's name. Do you remember, Maxie? She introduced me to my own body."

"You're embarrassing our friends, Clare," Max said.

"Am I? I don't see how. There's nothing to be ashamed of."

The concerto had long since finished, and Max got up to put on another record, and then a short time later, somehow, it was two in the morning. They pulled themselves to their feet, and Henry and Max took a great deal of time replacing the swords on their mounts. Max called out for Alma, but there was no answer. "We're leaving," he shouted, and Clara said, "She's probably out wandering, Maxie. Don't worry about it."

They turned out the lights and went out the front door. The night air was thick and humid and Henry could feel the earth turning in space. Effie leaned against him and they made a zigzag path down the sidewalk. At their porch, after Max and Clara had said good night, he looked back to the Victorian house and saw a lighted window in the tower. It was Alma, he was sure. They hadn't explored the tower. He wanted to go back, but it was all he could do to get himself and Effie up the porch steps.

Six

They woke to gusts of warm wind through the attic windows, and by early afternoon the light outside had turned lavender. Raindrops the size of quarters began to fall, and in minutes, with the sound of distant approaching thunder, the rain became a deluge.

They could run over to Clara's in their bathing suits, Henry said, but Effie wanted to stay in. She felt like burrowing for a while. It looked dangerous out there. And she worried that Clara would begin to think they were freeloaders—all that food and gin, and they'd contributed nothing. "I'm about one hundred percent positive she doesn't think of us like that," Henry said, and Effie said he was probably right. But they'd barely touched the groceries they'd bought Sunday, and maybe it would be nice to have a day to themselves. This made Henry happy—that she wanted his company. He said it sounded like a fine idea.

She made ham-and-cheese sandwiches and they ate in the living room with the windows open. The white curtains billowed in like ghosts, and outside, the wind ravaged the trees, and for a long while not a minute went by without a flash of lightning, an echoing boom of thunder. Henry loved the rain. The more violent, the better. He loved the sound it made on their aluminum awnings back home. Effie admitted she had an exaggerated fear of bad weather, but she liked to keep the windows open because she'd heard you were supposed to, in case of tornadoes—something about air pressure. "Do you need me to comfort you?" Henry asked, and she said maybe, and soon they were making love on the sofa—a great release, since he'd been near to bursting that morning, thinking of Clara's story. He gripped the backs of her knees. When he was spent, finally, she looked winded and pleased.

They played a game of checkers, eschewing their clothes. "Our own bacchanal," Henry said, and Effie gasped and said, "Oh my God. Could you believe what Clara said? About the harem?"

"I bet she feels mortified today."

"I bet she doesn't." She went back to studying the board. "I think she likes to shock people. She was always that way."

"Do you think it was a story?"

"No," Effie said. "An embellishment, maybe. But she is what she is."

Henry wanted to say he'd liked it, how open and frank she was—how she and Max both were—but he knew that what he liked about it was dangerous. "Man," he said, "if anyone back home said that kind of thing—or did it, God forbid—they'd be tarred and feathered."

"She's of a different world," Effie said. "That is a fact."

After she won, they went upstairs to share a bath, and as soon as they'd settled into the water, the lights went out.

They held still a moment. "Did we do that?" she asked.

"I don't know," he said.

Rain struck the frosted window. They got out of the tub and dried off in the dark. Henry tried the hallway light, but it was no use. The electricity had gone out.

"Well, this is cute," Effie said.

"Maybe it's a circuit breaker or something. Do you know where it is?"

"I haven't the foggiest idea."

The temperature outside the bathroom had dropped, and a draft was coming up the stairwell from the den. Up in the attic room they felt around for their clothes and dressed, and went downstairs to look for candles. But to no avail. There wasn't enough light to see into the closets and drawers, and the windows themselves were barely visible in the darkness. They stepped out onto the porch and looked toward Clara's. Not a light anywhere, save for a faint glow in the distance, from the town center, probably. Even the streetlights down on Madison were out.

"I don't know how I'm going to make supper," Effie said.

"It's probably a downed line somewhere," Henry said. He knew nothing about how utilities worked. "They're probably fixing it already."

With nothing else to do, they went back inside and lay down on the sofa and pulled a quilt over them. Effie insisted they keep the windows open, and they listened to the wind and the rain.

A rapping at the door startled them from a doze, and the porch outside the windows was alight. The wind and rain had not abated. There was another rap, more insistent this time, and Effie said, "Who on earth?" and Henry got up to see who it was. In his confusion he thought it must be the police, come to arrest them for last night, and he was relieved to see that it was Max, holding a flashlight, drenched from head to foot.

"Would you believe this storm?" he said. "I had to wade upstream to get here."

Henry welcomed him inside, and he stood dripping on the tiles in the foyer.

"Oh, Max, look at you," Effie said, getting up from the sofa. "I'll get you a towel."

"There's no need. I wasn't sure I had the right house. Are you just sitting here in the dark?"

"We couldn't find the candles," Henry said.

"Why didn't you come over? Don't you love us anymore?"

Effie was standing at the foyer now, smiling broadly. "We didn't want to—"

Max held up his hand. "I've been sent to collect you, and I've been told that no is not an acceptable answer. Clare's gone stir-crazy and made a cassoulet—or what she's calling a cassoulet. You should have seen her. She looked like she was holding a black Mass. I thought she would blow herself up trying to light the burners."

Effie laughed. There was no question of refusing—they would come. Only, she wasn't sure if they had an umbrella. It didn't matter, Max said, it would be useless in the wind. So they found their shoes—one of Effie's sandals had been hiding by the stairs—and followed Max out the door.

By the time they'd made it the short distance to Clara's, through slashing rain and swift-running, ankle-deep streams of water in the street, they were soaked.

"Success," Max called from the foyer, kicking off his shoes.

The den was aglow. A kerosene lamp stood on the end table by the sofa, candles of different kinds were arrayed here and there, a fire was going in the hearth, and in the wicker armchair beside it, like another source of light, Alma sat reading a magazine and bobbing her legs over the armrest. Her hair had reverted to its natural state, a messy pile atop her head, and she wore the same brown dress she'd been wearing for the past three days. Dripping there in the foyer, Henry smiled at her, and she smiled back at him.

"Darlings, there you are," Clara cried, coming in from the kitchen, bearing a tray stacked with bowls and silverware. She set it down on the coffee table beside a large iron pot, which must have been the cassoulet, whatever that was. The air smelled deliciously of pork.

Max took a votive candle and Henry and Effie followed him up the stairs and across the balcony and down a dark hall, into a large bedroom that faced the back of the house. It was where Clara and Max were staying. Clothes—women's clothes, mainly, dresses and stockings and underwear—were strewn all over the floor and the unmade bed. Henry recognized the white halter-top dress Clara had been wearing the first day, crumpled now by the nightstand. Max showed them a walk-in closet and told them to take whatever they wanted, though there wasn't much—sweatpants, pajamas, robes, one dress shirt. He ducked into the attached bathroom and returned with towels, handed Henry the candle, and left them to it.

They pulled their waterlogged clothes off, even their underwear was wet, and dried themselves off. How strange it was to be in this room, sorting through someone else's clothes. In the closet Effie found satiny blue pajamas and a bathrobe. Henry found a baggy Princeton sweatshirt and pink swim trunks that were a couple sizes too big, but he pulled the string tight and they held to his hips. They laughed at each other. Effie's nipples stood up through the pajamas; she wrapped the bathrobe tightly around her. Henry gathered their wet clothes in a bundle, rolling their underwear in his soaked trousers, and they made their way back downstairs.

"Now you have to stay the night," Clara said.

Henry dropped their clothes behind the sofa, and they settled on the floor around the coffee table. Their drinks had been made already, their bowls had been filled—chunks of pork and white beans in a thick broth—and this was exactly where Henry wanted to be, in this circle by the fire, with these strange people, and a drink that would quickly go to his head.

"You're going to get sick of us," Effie said.

"Impossible," Clara said. "There are six bedrooms in this house.

We could each have our own room if we wanted. Although what would be the fun of that?"

They ate, and listened to the ceaseless wind and rain outside and the crackling of the fire. The windows had been closed, but drafts stole in and made the candles tremble, and their shadows danced monstrously on the walls. Max and Clara seemed more subdued tonight. It had been a rough morning, Max said. "Especially for this one," he whispered, as if in secret, indicating Clara, but Clara said that was an exaggeration—anyway, she had always been able to recover quickly. "But what fun last night was," she said. "It made me feel like I was a little girl again, staying up past my bedtime."

"I'm glad to see *you* made it back," Effie said to Alma, who was sitting next to her. It was usually Effie who tried to make conversation with Alma (Max never did), though Alma barely acknowledged her. Henry had tried once or twice too, but every time he spoke to her he felt dumb and exposed, as he did now.

"We lost you there at the end," he said, and winced at the almost fatherly tone he'd put on it.

"I was looking at dresses," she said simply, ladling more cassoulet into her bowl. "I think I found one for the dance Friday."

"Dresses," Max said. "What are you talking about?"

Clara laughed. "She's going to steal a dress for the dance. From the thespians."

"I'm going to *borrow* a dress."

Max seemed exasperated. She couldn't steal a dress, he told her. Alma repeated that she was only borrowing it, and pointed out—reasonably—that it was all of *them* who had done the stealing, by drinking half a bottle of bourbon.

"For all we know," Max said, "the people who own that house could be there at the dance on Friday. What happens if they recognize it?"

Alma brightened. "That *would* be funny."

Max gave up, waving her off. Clara said she hoped she had a dress herself, or she might have to steal one too—and then, changing tack, she said, "My angels, you're not really leaving Saturday, are you?"

Effie said they were, regrettably. She looked at Henry. "I guess it'll be good to get back and settle into the new place." She began to tell them how Henry's uncle was having a new wing built onto the house, but Clara interrupted her.

"How can I convince you to stay? Just one more week."

Henry smiled. She really wanted them to stay. He wondered why—then batted the thought away. Why not? He and Effie were good company.

"Maybe we could stay another day," Effie said, "but we've got to be out of that house this weekend. It was a whole ordeal getting the two weeks we had."

"Well, if that's all there is to it," Clara said, "then it's settled. You'll stay here. I told you, we've got a million rooms."

"That's a fine idea," Max said.

Effie laughed. "We can't just bum around up here forever."

"Not forever," Clara said. "Just a few more days. You've got your whole lives ahead of you, you darlings—but trust me. This is your honeymoon. Make it last."

Effie looked at Henry and said, "I mean, maybe."

*I*t would be an early night. Alma took a candle and went up to her room. The rest of them, after they'd cleared the coffee table, made drinks and played a game of dice that Max had learned in Montreal, but he had trouble remembering the rules, and soon Clara couldn't control her yawning. It spread to Effie. "I'm depleted," she said finally. They blew the candles out, saving one for Henry and Effie, and Clara led them upstairs, bearing the kerosene lamp, to the most comfortable guest room—where Scott and Betsy stayed, she said. There

was a tall bed with a thick quilt, varnished wood walls, and a deep
bay window. They should make themselves perfectly at home. She
kissed their cheeks—Henry loved that gesture, so European—and
said good night.

Effie cracked a window open, and the rain—its scent, its damp,
its chill—was suddenly present in the room. She blew the candle out
and they got in under the quilt. "Oh, this bed is exquisite," she said.
"I think I might have outgrown that little box spring over there." It
was nice, he agreed, and he pulled her to him and kissed the back of
her neck, held her breast through the silk pajamas, coming alive, but
in a few moments he could hear her little snores. She was fast asleep.
She hadn't even said her prayers.

He lay wide-awake, watching the panes of the bay window separate themselves from the dark. It excited him to lie in this house overnight, Clara and Max at the opposite end of the hallway, Alma even
closer, in the room that opened onto the balcony. He would never be
able to sleep. What he needed, he thought, was another drink.

He rose as quietly as he could, the floorboards creaking under his
feet, found the Princeton sweatshirt on the floor, and crept out of
the room, feeling his way down the hallway to the stairs and down
into the den.

The coals glowed in the fireplace. He put another log on, found
what he thought was his glass on the coffee table, poured himself
some whiskey this time—it would take the chill away—and sat on
the sofa. No one else stirred in the house. He had the whole place to
himself. Softly, aloud, he said, "What a week," and the sound of his
own voice comforted him. "What an amazing week."

The whiskey opened and relaxed him. The night and the days
ahead felt warm with promise. He thought of how he and Effie had
walked naked under the moon, and, glancing around the den, as-
suring himself that no one was there, he pulled the sweatshirt off and
pushed the loose trunks down to his knees. He wanted to be out in

the open. *As nature intended,* Clara had said. Lightly he caressed himself, until his penis stood rigid, angling up to the balcony behind him, the skin drawn taut and shiny in the firelight.

He liked the look of it when it was up, like some kind of tall mushroom. The goose-fleshed testicles sagging below it pleased him too. He'd learned from the dictionary that *testicles* shared the same root as *testify,* and it meant "witness"—as in, to bear witness to a man's virility—and when he'd shared this with Hoke—they'd been in the tenth grade—they'd fallen over laughing and made grandiose claims about the size of their balls. Dick, balls, those few cubic inches of flesh: how many hours of concentration had he put into them over the years? In the locker room at school, or during the couple of times he and Hoke and Maynard had skinny-dipped at the bend in the creek, he'd compare himself to the other boys, all of them looking without appearing to look at one another's endowments, and though he'd fretted about size—Hoke's was in fact larger, Ned Connor's was larger still, Maynard's was a button in a nest—he'd always come to the conclusion that his was respectable. He would pause sometimes before his dresser mirror to admire it. When he was twelve or thirteen, he would occasionally lock himself in the bathroom, sit down on the floor with his legs spread wide, and using an old hand mirror of his mother's, watch himself masturbate, angling the mirror this way and that. By that point he'd made peace with himself and with God about doing it in bed, in the dark of night, but after the mirror he'd feel sick of himself, and hide the mirror in the back of his closet so he wouldn't have to consider the possibility that his mother might use it again. But now he thought, So what? There was no need for shame. He thought of Effie bent over in the grass, unembarrassed.

He spread his legs, the trunks falling to his ankles, made a fist around it, and stroked it steadily, feeling the satisfying bounce of his testicles. He closed his eyes and tipped his head back—until the wire went hot and he left it off. He couldn't finish himself off on the sofa. He reached for his whiskey and took the last sip, sat back and looked at it throbbing there in his lap. He would slip into the downstairs bathroom, do it into the toilet, and pour another drink. He was setting his glass back on the table, about to get up, when one of the patio doors opened—the sound of rain rushed into the room—and he yanked his trunks back up and sat forward, elbows on his knees.

It was Alma, coming inside, shutting the door behind her. He could just see her in the firelight. He said hello, too loudly, but she didn't seem startled by his voice.

She wasn't startled, he thought with horror, because she'd known he was there.

"I was just sneaking one of Maximilian's smokes," she said. "Don't tell. Or do tell, I don't care." She walked over to the fireplace, rubbing her arms. She had her cardigan on but her feet were bare.

"I couldn't sleep," Henry said. "I thought I'd just come down and have a nightcap."

She looked across at him sitting there bare-chested, wearing only the borrowed swim trunks. "Should I leave you alone?" she asked.

"Not at all," he said.

She took up the poker and stoked the fire. She'd come in through the door that led to the covered part of the patio, where they'd sat outside for dinner during the party, and there was a line of sight, he knew, from the outside table to the sofa. She must have seen him. She must have walked in on him on purpose. "A nightcap sounds nice," she said. "Do you mind if I join you?"

"Of course not."

She asked what he was having and he told her, and she told him not to get up, she'd fix them both a round. She took his glass, her fingertips grazing his, and crossed over to the bar. He pulled the afghan over his lap.

"I didn't think you drank," he said. "Or does your brother not let you?"

"He's not my guardian," she said. She flicked open a Zippo and lighted it so she could see the shelf of bottles. "I just don't care to be drunk all day, like they do."

Maybe she hadn't seen him. It would be too horrible if she had. And if she had, she wouldn't be sitting down for a drink with him.

She came back with the glasses, handed him his, and sat in the armchair at the end of the sofa, the one Clara usually took, close enough that their toes would touch if they both rested their feet on the coffee table. He kept his feet planted on the ground. She turned in the chair to face the fire, away from him, her back against the armrest, her legs dangling over the other side. She took a sip of whiskey, and shuddered. "This does warm the soul," she said.

"You must be cold," he said. "How long were you out there?"

"Just a little while," she said. He waited for her to say more, but that was all.

They gazed at the fire and sipped their drinks. Her presence electrified him. He was overly conscious of himself, of how he rested his arms on his lap, of whether or not he should cross his legs. The whiskey helped. After a while he cleared his throat and asked if she had any more of her brother's cigarettes, and she said of course, and reached into the pocket of her cardigan. She handed him one, took one for herself, and lit them both with the Zippo. He moved the ashtray to the edge of the coffee table, where they could both reach.

"How long do you think the lights are going to be out?" she asked.

"Who knows," he said. "Some poor fellow's probably out there now trying to fix it."

"I bet no one is. I bet no one even realizes what's happened until the spring."

"You're probably right."

She took a drag from her cigarette and for a while seemed mesmerized by the fire.

"I can tell you're not having a lot of fun here," he said.

She looked over her shoulder at him, frowning. "Are you telling me I'm a drag?"

He hastened to say no, that wasn't what he meant, but she was only kidding. She had to stretch her arm out and roll to her side to reach the ashtray, and as she did so she struck a flamboyant pose: one leg extended straight over the armrest, toes pointed toward the fire, the other bent in front of her, heel tucked into her groin.

"*You* must be enjoying yourself," she said. "You're on your honeymoon."

She was bobbing her leg and smiling at him. He couldn't look her in the eyes for very long. "We're having a great time."

"You look nice together," she said. "You and your wife."

"We make a pair."

"I loved what you said the other day, on the boat—what was it?" She looked up to the rafters as if to find it written there, and a little ember came alight inside of him.

"What did I say?"

"You said it was like a stroke of genius, when you realized you had feelings for her. Because you'd known her all your life."

He was astonished that she'd been paying attention to him at all, even more that she'd loved something he'd said, and the fond way she was looking at him made him shiver. He thanked her, and she laughed at that, and then she started saying something about music—it was related, somehow, to what he'd said—but he was only partially listening. He nodded agreeably. She was sitting up straight now, facing him, her legs tucked underneath her, and when the topic seemed to have run its course, and her attention began to drift back to the fire, he said, "Truth be told, I didn't really care for Effie growing up."

She laughed, stabbing out her cigarette, and asked what for.

"I used to think she was snotty. She was always popular and well-to-do. She wasn't always kind to people when we were in grammar school."

"I know her well," Alma said.

"I never hated her or anything," he said, worrying he'd been disloyal. "She's always been pretty. I was probably just intimidated." He explained that Effie was a town girl, and more than that, her father had been the mayor for many years. "The mayor, wow," Alma said, though she didn't sound very impressed. It was a small town, he said, but still. The Tarletons were a big deal. He explained how Effie's father owned a farm-supply store and café, how it had always been a gathering spot for the town, and how he'd recently acquired a license to sell John Deere tractors and opened a new showroom, and now people came from all over middle Georgia. She asked if Henry lived in the country, since he'd said Effie was a town girl, and he said yes, he lived about three miles from the high school, on about a thousand acres of land, where his uncle Carswall grew cotton and grain and peanuts. "You live with your uncle?" she asked, and he said, "Well, he's my stepfather," and when she looked confused, he realized that what was a given back home might seem strange elsewhere.

"My daddy died when I was four years old," he said. "He was a brakeman on the Southern Railway, and he was in a head-on collision outside of Hazlehurst, Georgia."

"Wow." Now she did seem interested.

"It was a mixed-up train order—one going north and another going south on the same track. It was in all the newspapers, apparently. I was too young to know what was going on. I remember Mama pacing the house and crying, and I remember crying because *she* was crying. But I don't remember very much of him. The clearest thing is the day he shaved his mustache off, and I wouldn't let him near me because he didn't look familiar."

She smiled. She was resting her head on her hand, her eyes fixed on him.

"We moved in with my uncle Carswall not long after Daddy died. He's Daddy's eldest brother. He and Mama married, and then they had my sister, Emily."

"How scandalous," Alma said, and Henry laughed.

"I guess I never thought of it that way."

"How is that possible?"

"Right," he said. "I mean, I'm not naïve. In fact, I can tell you they were married less than a year after Daddy died, and Emily came along only four months after that."

"Aha."

"But if you knew them. Uncle Carswall's a deacon at the church. And Mama's not exactly . . ." He wanted to say something like she was not given to passion, that she was an unsentimental woman, that he had never seen her hold Carswall's hand, much less kiss him, that she might conceivably have married him purely for practical reasons, but as with most thoughts concerning his mother, it was too big and complicated to articulate succinctly. "I guess they weren't always the way they are now," he said instead. "My aunt Nicky—that's Mama's sister—she once called it an 'Old Testament arrangement.'" To his delight, this made Alma laugh. "But to me, it's just my family. It never seemed strange."

Alma wanted to know more, about his mother and stepfather, his sister, his life in Signal Creek, and her interest in him was intoxicating. The words poured out of him. He told her about the ponds he liked to fish in, about the red color of the High Falls Road, about the old abandoned house where he and Hoke would camp sometimes. He told her about Hoke, who'd been a star pitcher in the farm league, and how, if she ever met him, if she was like other girls, she would fall instantly in love with him. "I don't know," she said. "I never liked watching boys play sports." He told her he'd wanted to play baseball himself, but that he lived too far out to make the practices and work the farm both. He told her Carswall was stern but fair, a good father overall, except that he loved Emily more. Emily was fifteen and a princess. He didn't describe in any detail his home life, though she asked about it—the old house, the paint peeling from the boards, the sagging front porch, the yard that Smokey had trampled to dust— because she wouldn't understand that it wasn't poor, that they were a family of means and he had never wanted for anything except broader horizons. He admitted he'd tried and failed to win a scholarship to Emory, but that he was going to try again in the fall. He didn't want to work on the farm. He said he might go work for the railroad instead, like his father, while he waited for college. He didn't say that Effie was opposed to this idea.

"Do you think you'll stay in Georgia?" she asked. She'd lit another cigarette and given him one too.

"Not if I have anything to say about it," he said. "Not in Signal Creek, anyway." He asked her what Los Angeles was like. "That's something I can't even imagine," he said. "What it must be like to grow up in a place like that, a place you only see in the movies."

She seemed amused. "I don't know what Max has told you. I didn't grow up like he did." She'd grown up in Manhattan Beach, she said, which was just south of L.A. "It was just Mom and me. Or really just me; Mom was always working."

"She was an actress?"

"She was, once. We lived up near Hollywood when I was born, with my father, but they split up when I was still in diapers, and we never heard from him again. He was some kind of technician, a lighting guy or a camera guy, I don't know. I never knew him. She moved us down to Manhattan because it was cheap. She was a bank teller— the kind who takes your check through a pneumatic tube and sends you back a lollipop. We lived in a shitty bungalow. Our neighbors were oil workers. But it was near the beach, and that's where I spent all my time, if I wasn't in school."

"See, I can't imagine that," Henry said. "That sounds like paradise."

She laughed. "It's not. There's refineries up and down the shore. It's not the part they show in the movies. But I did love the water."

There had been no one to look after her when she was a child, she said. Her mom's family was from upstate New York, and she was estranged from them. So Alma roamed the beach alone and mixed herself up with the crowd there—surfers, sunbathers, bums, roughnecks from the refineries. "People are mostly nice," she said. "Some people aren't. I took care of myself, though. I made friends. I had a boyfriend for a long time, this surfer, Sal, before he enlisted. No one messed with me then." She went to the public school but was terrible about cutting classes. She dropped out entirely when her mom got sick. She'd been in the tenth grade. She did odd jobs, sometimes a couple at a time. She worked at an ice-cream stand on the Manhattan Beach Pier. She lied about her age and was a cigarette girl at a nightclub, because she'd heard if you were charming enough the men would give you everything they had. And it was true. She took care of the rent and groceries.

"You're from another world," Henry said. He had to pee, but he didn't want to get up and break the spell. She had slumped down in the chair again, ankle up on her knee, and was idly massaging between her toes. She had long, elegant toes. "Really," he said. "My life is so boring compared to yours."

"It isn't to me," she said.

Halting, uncertain if he was prying, he asked what had happened to her mom—"Max said it was a heart attack?"—and she nodded and answered simply, like it was just a fact in the world. "She had an infection that weakened her heart. Any kind of exertion, I mean like showering, getting dressed, it would wipe her out. It was a nightmare, honestly. She couldn't leave her bed by the end. She had to quit her job. We had insurance, but it wasn't enough for what she needed."

That was when she met Max for the first time, she explained—her half brother, her mother's other child, from another life. She used to imagine what it would be like to grow up a Hewitt in New York City, with enough money to buy the world and never have to work again. She'd even felt angry at her mother, because if she hadn't left, they'd have been rich. She laughed. "Of course, I wouldn't exist, either." The immediate reason for the divorce had been an affair—"Mom had a minor part in *Street Scene,* and she was screwing one of the stagehands"—but apparently Charles Hewitt was a bastard and their lives would have been miserable together anyway. His lawyers were better than hers, and he got custody of Max, who was still a baby. She moved to L.A. to get into the pictures. But she wrote Max letters every holiday and on his birthday, and he sent back polite replies and thank-yous. When she got sick, he flew out to meet her.

"I thought he was such a square," she said. "He had on these dumb plaid shorts and a polo shirt, because he thought that's what people wore in California. I probably wasn't nice to him. But he was nice to us. I think it moved him the way we lived, the shitty bungalow and all the sand on the floor. That's Max. His apartment in the Village is a dump. He stayed with us a few days and slept on the couch. He gave us a lot of money. After—I don't know, it was a few months later—I phoned him to let him know. I guess I was crying. I told him I didn't have anyone left, and he said, 'You have me.' He wired me money for a plane ticket to New York."

"And here you are," Henry said.

"Here I am," she said.

The fire had died down, and he could barely make her face out in the dark. "That wasn't long ago," he said.

"About six months," she said.

"I'm sorry," he said. "About your mom."

She thanked him, and they were quiet for a time.

He couldn't hold it any longer. He told her he had to go to the john, and supposed that would be the end of the night. But instead, she sat up and asked if he wanted another one.

"Sure," he said. "If you're having one."

She lit a candle and took up their glasses, and he got up from the sofa, feeling naked without the afghan. He made his way quickly down the hallway, eager to get back to the den. In the bathroom there was the faintest edge of light from the window, and he could just see his dark form in the mirror over the toilet, and what appeared to be presences behind him. He'd always been afraid of mirrors in the dark, but he could never help peeking.

Why did he feel so thrilled? What did he think was going to happen? Nothing was going to happen.

Back in the den Alma had put another log on the fire and it was burning bright, and she was lying sideways in the armchair again, facing it, bobbing her feet. She asked if everything had come out all right, and he said he might have peed into the tub, he wasn't sure. She laughed. He sat back in his place with his drink and propped his feet up on the coffee table.

"It's nice to have another night owl to sit up with," she said.

"You can always count on me," he said. "I'm like a kid. I don't ever want to go to bed."

"I'll keep that in mind," she said.

He told her how glad he was that he and Effie had met them, how much fun they'd had these past few days. "Honestly, we were starting to feel kind of lonely before you all came along. We were going to cut the trip short, in fact."

"Really," she said.

"We just needed to get used to each other, I think. We'd never spent so much time together all at once. Before this it was just dates, and be back by ten. And suddenly we're sharing a bed, and . . ."

She turned in the chair and placed her feet up on the table too, a couple of inches away from his. "It must be awkward."

"It was, at first, but—you know." He'd wandered into uncomfortable territory. She seemed to understand, and smiled at him, and looked back to the fire.

"I feel like a third wheel," she said after a moment. "A fifth wheel, I guess."

"What do you mean?" he asked, though he felt he understood her exactly. He felt, though he couldn't have said how or why, that he was in the same position.

"If Clara could will me not to exist anymore, she would," she said.

"I'm sure that's not true."

"She's trying to rekindle this old wild flame with Maximilian, but she's going to be disappointed. He doesn't like her the way she likes him. Or maybe I don't know. He doesn't like to talk to me much anymore. Sometimes I feel like I've overstayed my welcome. Sometimes I think I should just strike out on my own."

He asked what she planned to do. She didn't know. She could go back to L.A., but everyone she knew there was a bum, and there was no money. At least here she could meet people, as long as she had Max—although most of the people he knew were bums too, artists of different kinds, hangers-on. She could get a job. She'd tried to be a Kelly girl once but failed the typing test. She'd been a hostess at a cocktail bar for a few weeks, but she'd been fired for slapping one of the patrons. She laughed at that. "Maybe I'll just move somewhere tropical and live off mangoes."

"Now you're talking."

Occasionally the tops of her toes brushed the bottom of his foot, and although he was listening, and looking at the fire, every nerve was concentrated on that spot.

"You'll be fine," he said. "You're young and . . ." He wanted to say beautiful. "You seem like someone who can take care of herself."

She smiled at him. "You're nice."

They watched the fire die down again and listened to the wind outside. The side of her foot lightly rested against his. He held still so as not to draw attention to it, so she wouldn't take it away. Nothing was happening. But if Effie were to get up and find them there, he thought, it wouldn't have looked good.

He finished his drink. He wanted to be the first to say it. "I'd better hit the hay," he said. She said all right. He stood up and picked up his sweatshirt. "It was good talking to you," he said, and she said, "To you too," tipping her glass up in mock formality, and he hesitated a moment, looking down at her—a single beat that, he feared, must have revealed himself completely—before he said good night and went upstairs.

Seven

Effie awoke with a sore throat. She sat up in bed with her hand to her head, and Henry rubbed circles on her back. "I can't tell if I'm hot," she said. "Am I hot?"

He placed his cheek against her forehead, the way his mama used to do. She did feel warm. "Maybe some coffee will make you feel better?" he said, and she nodded.

"My poor peach!" Clara cried when they'd made their way downstairs. She and Max were sitting at the kitchen table, flipping through different sections of the newspaper. "You don't want coffee," she said, getting up. "You want tea with honey. I'll make it for you." She and Max had been up for a while. The power was still out. The remnants of breakfast lay on the table, a few pieces of toast. Max said he could whip them up some omelets, but Effie wasn't hungry—she felt a bit nauseated, actually. Henry took a piece of toast. The newspaper was a *Cape May Gazette,* from June.

Alma had gone down to the beach to look at the waves, Max said. They were probably spectacular today. Beyond the bay windows the trees swayed in the wind, and leaves fell like ticker tape.

They decided they would go to the beach too. The sea air would be restorative, Clara said. Effie said they'd have to run to the cottage to change—their clothes were still wet—but Max said not to bother, and fetched her one of Alma's dresses, as well as a clean T-shirt and shorts for Henry. "We're about the same size, wouldn't you say, Hank?"

They changed upstairs. The dress was the green one Alma had been wearing that first day out on the boat. On Effie it strained at the seams, it pinched her sides and barely contained her breasts. "I look awful in this," she said, examining herself in the mirror.

"You look fine," Henry said.

"Fine," she said, "great," and he pulled her to him and kissed her forehead.

They met Max and Clara down in the foyer and started for the beach. Clara carried a bag full of towels. After the chill of the night, Henry was surprised how warm the day was. An Indian summer. The air smelled richly of the damp earth and leaves. Leaves and small branches were scattered all over the street and sidewalk, and the street was rutted with pale blue mirrors.

They stepped up to the promenade, and ahead of them the ocean seethed, the waves forming perfect pipes before they pounded the beach. After a minute Clara spotted Alma's figure in the distance toward town, lying in the glassy blue sand below the tideline. "Crazy girl," she said. "She's going to get swept out to sea." They took their shoes off and stepped down from the promenade and made their way toward her. Effie held the side of her dress in her fist so it wouldn't blow up.

The waves were astonishing. Henry had never seen anything like it. He imagined they were reaching out to him, trying to get at him.

Beside him, Effie looked pale. He asked how she was holding up, and she said she was fine. She slipped her free hand into his.

Alma didn't get up when she saw them coming, only leaned back on her elbows and bent a knee, as if to relax—or to pose, Henry thought. She wore her white bathing suit and sunglasses. The waves crashed and spread acres of foam, and the leading edge of it came within inches of her feet. Her hair hung wet about her shoulders.

"You didn't go in there, did you?" Max asked when they'd reached her.

"Of course I did," she said.

"You must be freezing, darling," Clara said.

"Is that my dress?" Alma said.

Effie crossed her arms over it as if to shield it from view. "I'm sorry."

"Their clothes were still wet," Max said.

"I don't mind," Alma said. "It looks good on you."

"No, it doesn't," Effie said.

Max went a few yards back from the tideline, to spread his towel where the sand was drier, and Effie and Clara followed him. Henry lingered near Alma, watching the waves.

"It's fantastic, isn't it?" she said.

Henry whistled and nodded. "It is that."

"It's like the waves back home."

He had the feeling that they were in league with each other now, that they shared the same language. From the start he'd thought she was untouchable, but now he knew better. It made the world seem more accessible to him. "Before this trip," he said, "I'd never seen the ocean before."

"You're joking," she said. She pulled her sunglasses down and looked at him over the frames. "Never in your life?"

"Never." His eyes drifted for a moment over her body, to where the fabric of her bathing suit was crimped at her groin.

"Have you been in yet?" she asked.

He shook his head. "It's been too cold."

She sat up, dusted off her hands, and got to her feet.

"You want to go in now?" he asked, alarmed.

She laughed. "We'll just get our feet wet," she said. Wet sand stuck to her bottom and to the backs of her thighs, and she batted it off and reached a finger into the elastic of her bathing suit to pull the wedge out. "Come on," she said, and with the same hand took hold of his forearm and walked him toward the waves. Max hollered something behind them, but Henry couldn't make it out over the roar. The touch of Alma's hand thrilled him. She led him just a few yards before she stopped, and the sea was still a ways off. But then another wave crested, curled over, and crashed, and though it had seemed safely distant it was suddenly upon them, a rush of startling cold water that swept over their feet and ankles and halfway up their shins. Henry hopped back, but Alma clutched his arm again and held fast. "Stand still," she said. "For the next one, stand still. Let it bury you in the sand."

"What's that?"

"Just wait."

He felt her warm hand on his skin. He hoped it didn't look suspect from Effie's point of view, behind him—but what were they doing? Nothing. The sea receded again for a few moments, and then Alma pointed out another swell—he could see it darkly forming—which paled and crested and crashed, and once again they were submerged almost to the knees in the cold onrush of water. Henry stood still. The current pushed, stilled for a second, then tugged in the opposite direction, back out to sea, and when the water receded, sure enough, his feet were half buried in the sand. He looked at Alma and laughed.

"See?" she said, letting go of him. "Stand still a couple more times and you'll be buried to the ankles. You can't trust the ground around here."

While they waited for another wave she told him there were patches of quicksand all over the beach. "You can see them clearly, don't worry, they're little pools. But look out for them. They're old trenches or pipes under the sand, probably. I stepped in one a couple of days ago and fell to my waist. I had to claw my way out."

"Jesus."

"I know. But it just goes to show . . ."

Another wave crashed and swept over them, and this time, pointlessly, Henry took hold of Alma's arm—gripped it firmly, close to her wrist. She didn't pull her arm away, though she had to hold it at an awkward angle. As the wave withdrew, he let her go. Silently now they waited for another one. It came, and when it receded, it was just as Alma had said: Henry's feet were completely submerged in the sand, and hers were too, even farther, above the ankles.

"Just imagine," she said, pulling one foot and then the other free. "Just imagine all the things buried in here."

"A pirate's treasure."

"The bones of a sea monster."

They made their way back to the others. Alma sat on the bare sand beside her brother, and Henry took a corner of Effie's towel. She was curled up in a ball, her head resting on her knees, her arms hugging the back of the dress to her thighs. Her eyes were closed and her mouth hung open. Henry put his arm around her. "You look awful, baby," he said.

"Thank you," she said.

Clara gave Henry a theatrical frown. "She's really caught something, the poor thing. It's come on her so suddenly."

"I can't breathe out my nose," Effie said.

"Do you have a fever?" Henry asked.

"I don't know," Effie said miserably. "I feel cold."

In fact she was shivering. Henry held her close.

"You should get back in bed," Max said. "We'll layer you with quilts. I'll make soup—I saw lentils in the pantry. And Clara's got a pharmacy in her suitcase."

"I've got stuff that'll knock you out for a week," Clara agreed.

Effie made a pathetic groan. She thanked them, but she just wanted to go back to the cottage and disappear. She felt disgusting.

"Do you want to go back now?" Henry asked.

"I guess so," she said. "I'm sorry, Henry. You don't have to come with me."

"What are you talking about? Of course I'm coming with you."

Alma was looking in Henry's direction, behind her sunglasses, and she drew her bottom lip out in a pout.

"Get better before tomorrow night," Clara said as they got to their feet.

Tomorrow night was the night of the dance.

"I'll be there if Henry has to carry me," Effie said.

As soon as she peeled the dress off, with Henry's help, and got into her pajamas, Effie fell onto the bed in the attic room and gave up moving. Henry drew the covers over her shoulders. He kissed her cheek and asked if he could bring her anything to eat—some toast, at least? She shook her head.

"But you should eat something," he persisted.

"I just want to *sleep*," she said, not opening her eyes.

He smiled. "My little darling," he said, and kissed her again.

He picked Alma's dress up off the floor and without thinking brought it to his nose and breathed in. It didn't smell like Effie; it was a light, grassy scent. He draped it over the back of the vanity chair, ran his fingertips over the fabric, turned, and for a long moment looked at his wife. She seemed unbearably sweet to him there on the bed, her hair spread over the pillow, the gentle rise and fall of her back, and he thought that there was nothing in the world he wouldn't do for her. A tide of selfless, gallant feeling rose in him. He wanted to squeeze her and kiss her again—but she needed her rest. He would leave her alone.

Downstairs he made himself a sandwich and ate it on the back porch, watching the fallen leaves flutter in the backyard. In just a month, after he and Effie were gone, it would probably snow up here. He wished he could see it. He hadn't seen snow in years.

He wished he had a cigarette too. Next time he was out, he would buy himself a pack. It was time he took up smoking. He was a grown man.

He hated to be away from the others—from Alma—but the immediate future was bright, and in the meantime, with Effie dead to the world, he had the whole world to himself, and the thought tickled his stomach until, at last, something turned over inside of him, and he hurried inside, into the downstairs lavatory, where a week and a half of constipation came to an end.

The relief was exquisite. He felt light enough to fly. He bounded up to the second-floor bathroom like a gazelle and, in the twilight gloom of the stall, took a shower, whistling "Higher Ground" while he scrubbed himself. He tiptoed into the attic room for fresh clothes and found Effie exactly as she had been before.

"I'm going for a walk, baby," he said sweetly, but she didn't respond. He kissed her cheek again.

Fed, cleansed, healthy, young, and handsome, Henry strolled down New Hampshire Avenue, and at Philadelphia turned toward the beach. Small gray-bottom clouds raced across the sky, and the noon sunlight was always changing. He was a wanderer. Homeless—for the time being. Like Alma. He might run into her. Maybe Max and Clara had left, and she'd lingered at the beach—and then what? Nothing. Anything. He was at the top of a hill, where he could see his past, present, and all of his futures, and every future was real, because he had not chosen any one. He would have to choose at some point, he knew, but for now they were all arrayed before him, so present he almost felt he could touch them.

The beach was empty. He was wearing his trousers and loafers and didn't want to get them sandy or wet, so he sat for a while on a bench on the promenade, until he felt self-conscious sitting there by himself. He started for the grocer's, thinking of cigarettes, then decided it was too far for that purpose, thought of Effie in bed, worried that he'd abandoned her, and headed back to the cottage.

She had turned over on her back but there was still no waking her. Her mouth hung open, her breathing was wet and ugly. She would need to eat. At five, he told himself, he would force her to sit up and take something.

The afternoon began to drag. Every so often he tried the lights. Alma had been right: no one would notice until the spring.

He tried to read Boswell, but his thoughts wandered to the wedge in Alma's bathing suit, to her hand on his arm, to the way she'd pouted at him when he'd said goodbye. He went back into the downstairs lavatory, dropped his trousers, knelt at the toilet bowl, and finished what he'd started last night, before Alma had walked in on him—thinking first of Effie, out of loyalty, and then, giving in, of Alma, Alma pulling him aside somewhere lush and green, peeling her bathing suit off, and the orgasm seized him before he could quite picture her naked to his satisfaction, and a shot of semen struck the back of the bowl—and remained there after he flushed. He was impressed. With a wad of toilet paper he wiped it off, looked for any stray spots on the rim or toilet seat, and flushed again.

Afterward, lounging in the den and eating the last of the strawberries, he felt debauched and wasted. He lay back and tried to nap, but he was wide-awake.

Periodically he went up to the attic room to check on Effie. The room felt close and warm and smelled sweet, so he knelt and opened the windows, and Effie murmured her thanks. He got her to take some aspirin with water. Later, for supper, he warmed up a bowl of Campbell's chicken noodle soup and brought it up to her, along with the last of the bread. He got her to sit up, added a pillow behind her. The wind had calmed; evening was coming on. He'd found a kerosene lamp in a closet downstairs. She took a bite of the bread. She sipped spoonfuls of the broth. She was shivering, her face was mottled and swollen, her eyes were slits, and her voice was high and airy.

"I've been having these vivid dreams," she said. "Everything's amber. The sky's this dirty orange color."

"What are the dreams about?"

"I don't know. Nothing that makes any sense. There was one where me and Bernice DuPont were walking over this bridge, over this muddy river. And at the end of it these big men—like ten feet tall— were hanging around in rags, basically naked, and they were *dirty*, kind of copper, and the weird thing, they were missing some of their limbs, and they were looking at us like—I don't know. Like they wanted to eat us."

She handed the bowl of soup back to him. She was shivering more violently now—her pajamas were damp—and she lay back down and Henry pulled the covers back up to her chin. "I wonder if I should try to find a doctor," he said.

She shook her head. "It's just a fever."

"It's a bad fever."

"It'll burn itself out."

He ran his hands through her hair. She told him not to stop, and he said he would sit there for as long as she wanted him to.

After he'd made another bowl of soup for his own supper, and ate the bread Effie hadn't eaten, he alternated between the den and the front porch, reading, sipping Uncle George's whiskey, wishing the others would at least stop by to check in on them. Why hadn't they already? Wouldn't they wonder how Effie was faring? Wouldn't they figure Henry was feeling listless and bored, and invite him over for a game of charades? Not that he would accept, no—he would decline, magnanimously. But still, it seemed a waste of good health and youth to spend an entire evening alone. Out on the porch, he couldn't see any lights down at Clara's. Had they gone out? Where would they have gone?

He tried Boswell again, reading in the den by the light of the kerosene lamp. He had to hold the book just so to see the page. The whiskey was calming him, wrapping him in a bubble that was safe from all bad feelings. *Nor is it always in the most distinguished achievements that men's virtues or vices may be best discerned; but very often an action of small note, a short saying, or a jest, shall distinguish a person's real character more than the greatest sieges, or the most important battles.*

The words turned abstract. He drifted off. He was outside in the night and the stars and planets and galaxies, giant and bursting with color, were low enough in the sky that he could have touched them from the rooftops. And then a clatter startled him, and the book fell to the floor.

It was Alma. She was standing in the foyer, holding the screen door open.

"I woke you," she said. "I'm sorry."

He muttered a greeting, confused, and gathered the quilt around him.

"I hope you don't mind," she said. "I always seem to be walking in on you." She let the screen door slap shut behind her and stepped into the den, giving it a quick survey. "I saw the light in the window and thought"—she smiled sweetly—"I thought my fellow night owl must still be up."

"I was," he said. "I just nodded off." He looked at the clock over the mantel. It was after midnight.

Without asking if he wanted company, she sat down in the wicker chair by the sofa and smiled at him. She was barefoot, wearing her brown dress with the white polka dots, over it her old cardigan. But she'd put lipstick on, and he could smell her perfume, a stronger version of the grassy scent he'd made out earlier, in the fabric of her dress. "Your hair's sticking straight up," she said, and Henry felt for it and tried to press it down. She laughed. "Don't bother, it's no use."

It was dawning on him that she was there. That she had come to see him. "How's your day been?" he asked.

The question seemed to amuse her. "Dull," she said. She asked how Effie was feeling, and he told her, in too much detail, about the course of her fever, what she'd been able to eat—and then he cut himself short, and concluded that she would be fine. "That's good to hear," Alma said.

"Are you out wandering?"

"I was heading over to that house, actually," she said. "The big one we visited the other night?"

"The Bishops' house," he said. The image of her in her ruby-red flapper's wig came vividly to mind.

"I need to pick out a dress. For tomorrow. Plus, there's so much more to explore. Do you want to come?"

For a moment he didn't understand that she'd asked him a question. And when he did, it startled him. "With you? Right now?"

"No, next week," she said. "Yes, right now. You could help me find a dress."

He looked toward the front door, which she'd left open. "What are Max and Clara doing?"

"Who cares?"

He was alert now. He didn't know what to say.

"It's all right if you don't want to," she said. She drew the cardigan tightly around herself and looked at her long toes, which, when she stretched her legs out, could just grip the glass top of the coffee table.

"No—I want to," he said.

"Okay, good," she said.

"But," he said, and gestured toward the ceiling.

"She needs her sleep," she said. "The best thing you can do for her? Leave her alone. You might as well come out."

She smiled mischievously at him, and he returned it. He was shivering. The room, with the door and all the windows still open, was chilly. What would happen if he went with her? She would model dresses for him in one of the upstairs rooms of the big Victorian house, in the middle of a labyrinth, where no one could see them or hear them. She would ask him to zip her up, and his knuckles would brush the smooth skin between her shoulder blades. But he couldn't do it. If Effie awoke, and found him gone . . . "I can't," he said. "I'd feel guilty leaving her."

"You're a gentleman and a scholar," she said, and leaned back in the chair and patted the armrests. He wished she wouldn't give up. If she asked him one more time, he'd say yes—*Yes, to hell with it, let's go*—but now she was looking at the book splayed open at his feet. She reached her foot out, pinched the edge of the cover between her toes, and pulling it toward her, said, "What is this mighty tome?"

"It's *The Life of Samuel Johnson*," he said. It took on pretensions when he said it out loud. Why would he be reading such a book? "Uncle Carswall gave it to me. You know. It's hard going."

She picked it up and flipped through it, back to front, and imitating a man's voice, with a stuffy, aristocratic air, repeated, "Dear sir . . . Dear sir . . . Dear sir," and returning to her normal voice, "Oh, here's a poem." She scanned the page but must have found it uninteresting, because she flipped some more pages, and stopped on another. "Oh. Here's some advice for Sundays. Rise early, and—*and in order to it,* go to sleep early on Saturday." She laughed. "Examine the tenor of my life . . . Go to church twice . . . Instruct my family . . ."

"It was a wedding present," Henry said. "How to be a good man, or something."

She closed the book and hefted it in her hands. "You have so much to learn, obviously." She smiled at him, set it down on the coffee table, and stood up. Henry stood up too. He felt as if he'd failed her, as if he'd proven himself unworthy of her, or ridiculous.

"I wish I could go out with you," he said.

"Well," she said. "You can."

But he only smiled. He took up the kerosene lamp and followed her to the door, held the screen door open for her, and watched as she slipped on her deck shoes, which she'd left on the porch. Beyond her the darkness was absolute. It was hard to believe there'd be a dance in town the following night. She said, "Okay," and slapped her thighs. It meant: *last chance.* And when he only nodded, she said, "Well, good night," and he said, "Good night," and then, "Good luck finding a dress," and she laughed at that, and turned to leave.

Eight

The dress she'd chosen was silvery and long, with thin shoulder straps and straight lines, and the fabric was as light as a slip and had a sheen to it. She came slowly down the staircase, trailing her hand along the banister, and though she never looked at Henry, he was certain that she'd been waiting for him to arrive, that this entrance had been for his benefit. Her hair was pinned up, little tendrils falling from her temples, her makeup was light and glossy, and she wore sheer stockings and silver heels. He'd never seen anyone more beautiful.

"Aren't you a pretty thing?" Effie said, dabbing at her nose with a tissue. Her fever had broken, and though she was still weak, she'd been determined not to miss the dance. Henry had said little to dissuade her.

"You're a pretty thing too," Alma said.

They were all pretty, after so many days in swimsuits, wrinkled linens, bathrobes, and bare feet. Effie wore the forest-green dress she'd worn at their senior prom. Henry wore his wedding suit. Max wore a white tuxedo with black lapels—because why not, because it was the only formal thing he'd brought with him from New York, because it had been in his trunk, by happenstance, from some wedding or other—and Clara wore her white halter top from last week, spiced up with a silver choker and extra flourishes in her makeup and hair. In the foyer they'd said, "Look at you!" "And *you*!" "But *you* clean up well, don't you?"

They ate out at the patio table in the dusk, by the light of votive candles. The power was still out. Max had whipped up a simple pasta Bolognese with a canned ragout. Alma sat beside him. She seemed cheerful, in her way. Henry thought she might at least have smiled at him, gestured to her dress, let him smile back and nod his approval, but she barely acknowledged his existence. Maybe she'd lost interest in him when he'd refused to go out with her. Or maybe she was toying with him.

But the promise of the night, and of the days to come, cheered him, and set his nerves humming. He and Effie had decided to stay—maybe until the next weekend, though they'd play it by ear. He knew his family wouldn't like it, that Carswall would want him back at the farm, but he was a grown man, and he could do what he wanted. They'd call their families tomorrow, and move their things over to Clara's on Sunday.

After dinner they abandoned their plates and glasses on the table and piled into the Cadillac. Max kept the top up to preserve the ladies' hair. In the back, Effie sat in the middle and leaned her head on Henry's shoulder. "Are you going to make it?" he asked.

"I'm just saving my strength," she said.

The power outage didn't extend to the marina. As they crossed the bridge over the canal they could see lights blazing all along the length of the pier to the dance hall, which itself blazed against the dark of the sea and cast a river of light across the water in the cove. They turned into the marina parking lot and parked near the head of the pier. Outside, music drifted from the hall, big-band stuff, horns and heavy drums, and Henry wanted to run toward it—he wanted to leap up and smack the moon. He was eager for civilization. He imagined elegant jet-setters crowded inside the hall, people for whom physical distance was no obstacle, who might be in Cape May tonight and in Cabo tomorrow for another party, and he couldn't wait to join them.

But as they made their way down the empty pier he could see through the divided windows that the hall was mostly empty, and at the door they encountered a matronly, not-elegant woman behind a foldout table, who greeted them and informed them that the entrance fee would be five dollars. "Five dollars?" Effie said. "That's a little dear, isn't it?" The woman showed no offense, also no sympathy, and explained that it was to benefit the Cape May Historical Society. A hand-painted poster behind her said as much. "It's my treat, of course," Max said, but Effie insisted she pay for herself and Henry. Henry said he could pay for them, but Effie said that was silly, she had the money her daddy had given her. He didn't press the point. They paid, and went inside.

The music echoed in mostly empty space. The Cape May Historical Society had obviously gone to lengths for the band. There were twelve of them on a raised platform, all of them in white tuxedos, like Max, and the music was jumping. But aside from a few older couples trying to waltz in double-time, the dance floor was empty, and the rest of the crowd was scattered among the tables surrounding it. Most of the tables were empty. In the spaces between the windows hung nautical bric-a-brac: nets, harpoons, ships' wheels, anchors, flags, the jaws of a shark.

"Maybe we're early?" Clara said.

"I'm sure we are," Effie said. "It's not eight. I'm sure more people will pile in."

"From where, I wonder?" Max said.

A bar stood off to one side, under strings of lights, seemingly unattended, and as they made their way to it, a man in tweed stopped them. He was selling raffle tickets. Two dollars a pop, and the prize was that lovely painting of a sailboat and lighthouse displayed at the side of the stage. Max said he'd buy five, one for everybody. Clara laughed. "I don't want that thing," she said, and Max said, "Good, because I do. If anyone of you wins, you have to give it to me." He bought the tickets, and they went over to the bar, and the same man who'd sold them the tickets went behind it and asked what they wanted. Clara found this wildly funny. "Martinis all around," Max said grandly.

While they waited for their drinks, Henry's eyes adjusted to the scene. A group of Coast Guard cadets, easy to spot in their white uniforms, crowded around one table near the dance floor. The rest of the crowd looked old, except for a group of children who ran among the tables, playing a game of tag or something similar. Clara seemed amused. Alma seemed to be observing it with detached curiosity. But Effie, standing on tiptoe, her lips parted, seemed tense with expectation, with hope. His heart faintly broke for her. "The band's great," he said, and eagerly she agreed.

Their drinks appeared on the bar, Max paid for them, and they made their way to one of the tables beside the dance floor. For a couple of numbers they just sat and sipped their martinis—Alma was having one too—and watched the band, periodically looking back toward the door to see if more people were arriving. But no one was. It was a sad scene. People were dressed as if for church, and Henry felt eyes on their table—on Alma's shimmering dress, on Clara's exposed cleavage. After the first number the audience clapped respectfully, and the trumpet player said, "Thank you, thank you. It's great to be here," and without further comment, launched into the next number. They were earning a paycheck, Henry thought. Alma slumped back in her seat with her arms crossed. Effie drew her lips tight and gave Henry a look that seemed to say, *Well, we tried,* and he couldn't bear it. He clapped his hand on her thigh and said, "To hell with it. Let's dance."

"There's the spirit," Max said.

By this point the dance floor was completely empty. Effie seemed uncertain, but then Max stood up and offered his hand to Clara, and when Clara accepted, Effie said, "Well, I guess I went to the trouble of dressing up."

The band seemed relieved to see them. They were playing an easy swing number, and Henry turned and spun Effie around. They had always been able to move well together, to anticipate each other's steps. She seemed happy. Halfway through the song they swapped partners, and Henry danced with Clara, who was soft and vast in comparison. He stepped on her toe but she laughed, and soon they found their rhythm. He spun her out and brought her back to him, and she squeezed his arm and said he was very good. He said she was very good too. Alma sat by herself at the table, but on the next turn he saw one of the Coast Guard cadets bending to her, and by the next song the two of them had come onto the floor. An elderly couple joined them, and then a group of children came up as well, in a corner of the floor, kicking and flailing individually, as if to mock the beat—and suddenly the dance floor was hopping. The band launched into a fast jazz number, and the couples broke apart. Three more cadets stormed the floor. One of them engaged Effie. Henry tried to edge himself toward Alma, but another of the cadets, a tall one, had gotten her attention, taking her hand, turning her this way and that. Clara took Henry's hand and spun him around. Effie and Max, facing each other, did a kind of Charleston. One of the trombonists did a solo with a plunger, and it was funny the way he made it sound, the way he moved, and everyone laughed and whooped and clapped their hands. Then the band finished with a few measures of pandemonium and a crash of cymbals, and the little crowd on the dance floor cheered.

Clara and Max headed to the bar to order another round of drinks. Effie needed to rest a bit, and Henry followed her to the table. But before he could sit down Alma took his hand and said, "I need you to rescue me. Do you mind?" she said to Effie, and Effie laughed and said, "Of course not, honey."

The song was a slow one, an instrumental version of a tune he recognized, "I'll Be with You in Apple Blossom Time," and they were one of only three couples on the dance floor now. He took Alma's hand and slid his arm around her.

"Thank you," she said. Her eyes were locked on his, and she was grinning.

"Do I need to fight some cadets?" he asked.

"Not yet."

They moved lazily, out of step with the beat. She was slender and taut and warm, and the back of her dress was damp with sweat. She ran her hand up his arm and gripped his shoulder.

"The dress is nice," he said. "Good choice." He let his eyes linger on her bare shoulders, her collarbone, the little mounds of her breasts.

"I tried on a dozen of them. This one wasn't my favorite, but there were shoes that matched."

"Well, I love it."

"I'm glad. I guess I didn't need your help after all."

He turned her, touching his cheek to her hair, breathing her in, and through the dress he could feel the soft knobs of her spine, the clasp of her bra. He was going to get himself into trouble. Effie was watching them, smiling, but then Max and Clara returned with the drinks, and a couple of women Henry didn't recognize, and she turned her attention to them. The cadets had joined the table too.

"Ten to one Clara's going to invite all those people back to the house," Alma said.

"Another party?" Henry said, and she nodded.

"You'll need to stay by my side. I don't trust these boys."

He smiled like a fool. "I thought you wanted to meet people."

She made a face. "Not them. They're starved. They've been on the base too long. One of them said he fell in love with me the moment he saw me."

He laughed, and turned her again, pressing his hand to the small of her back. He thought he knew the cadet in question, the tall one, who was sitting at the table and watching them. "What did you say to him?"

"What could I say? I thanked him. I told him he was nice." She saw the cadet watching, smiled and twiddled her fingers at him, and Henry felt a flare of possessiveness.

"Well," he said, "I'll keep guard. I won't leave your side."

"You promise?"

"I promise."

They danced the rest of the song without speaking. She looked at their clasped hands. Her earlobes were tender and studded with silver beads. The hair at her temples was wet. He was under a spell. But then the song ended, and they parted, smiling, averting their eyes, and returned to the table.

The tall cadet's name was Carl, from Bloomington, Illinois, and his friends were Chance, Freddie, and David. They were trainees, fresh out of high school like Henry and Effie. That's what the base in Cape May was—a training center. They were on leave for the weekend, and were planning to head up to Atlantic City tomorrow. "Anyone interested?" Carl asked, looking at Alma, who pressed her lips together and shrugged—but one of the other women, Maggie, said that sounded like a grand idea. She and her friend Brenda were in town for the dance—Maggie's father was the president of the Cape May Historical Society—and they were looking for something to do. Maggie and Brenda looked older, in their late twenties, and seemed drunk already. The band had been Brenda's doing; she'd known the drummer in high school. Did they like it? Freddie, who was obviously angling for Brenda, said they were swell. David seemed to be sweet on Effie, until she introduced Henry as her husband, and Henry pulled a chair up between them. The band announced that they were taking a break, and they came over to the table. Henry stood up to shake the trumpet player's hand. Suddenly, their table was the center of the party. More drinks went around, from the bartender in the tweed jacket. The president himself, Maggie's father, a plump man who looked like a ship's captain, introduced himself and thanked everyone for their support. They would draw the raffle in half an hour. Max clapped his hands and rubbed them together. "That painting is mine," he said, and the president, oblivious to mockery, looked pleased. He'd commissioned it himself from a local artist. It sat on an easel beside the stage, a sailboat angling toward the lighthouse against a fiery sunset. Henry actually liked it. If he won it, he wouldn't mind taking it home.

Alma had been right: when the president left them, to mingle among the other tables, Clara said they should all abandon this joint and come back to the house. "You too," she said to the band. "We've got a full bar, and it's free."

"The lights are out, though," Max said.

"That only makes it more interesting."

The trumpet player said they were on the clock for another hour, but after that, they were up for anything. Maggie, looking aggrieved, said she'd have to stay and clean up, but Brenda said that was absurd, it was the booster club's job to clean up, and Maggie raised her glass and cried, "After-party!" Henry raised his glass too, and cheered.

The band went back on. Henry let David dance with Effie, and he danced with Maggie, who smelled of the mint gum she was chewing. "You have the most adorable accent," she said, and caressed his earlobe between her fingers, and he twitched his head so she would stop, laughing so as not to offend her. He wanted to be dancing with Alma again, but big Midwestern Carl was monopolizing her. A few minutes later they were gone, and when he rejoined Effie for a slow number he was distracted, looking around the room for them, looking through the windows to the pier outside.

"Lord, I'm fading," Effie said. She looked pallid.

"Are you okay?"

"I'm just a little woozy. I probably shouldn't go to this after-party thing."

"Oh?" Henry said. "Not even for a little bit?" If she didn't go, he couldn't go. And he couldn't bear the thought of missing out.

"Maybe for a little bit, sure," she said. "I can rally."

But then Henry remembered himself. "You shouldn't if you're feeling sick. Maybe we should just get you to bed."

"We'll see. I'd hate the night to end so early."

The band played a few more songs, and then the president and an older woman who might have been his wife took the stage and said it was time to draw the raffle. Max made a show of patting his jacket, as if he'd lost the tickets, then drew them out of his trousers' pocket. The president reached into the tin bucket the woman was holding, pulled out a ticket, called a number, and sure enough, Max raised his hand in the air and cried, "That's me!"

"Oh, for God's sake," Clara said.

The painting was his. The president congratulated him, invited him onto the stage to shake his hand, and after he and the woman had left, Max stayed up with the band. In his white tuxedo, he looked the part. One of the band members gave him a pair of maracas, and for the next two numbers he shook them and danced around the stage like an idiot. The band ate it up. Effie and Clara cheered and laughed, and gamely Henry applauded. Max was the center of attention, as ever.

Soon the band announced their last number, a slow one—"Moonlight Serenade"—and he and Effie danced to it. She rested her head on his chest, closed her eyes, and barely moved, and he rocked her side to side. Alma and her cadet had reappeared on the dance floor. He was looking intensely down at her, and she was looking away, as if lost in thought. When her eyes caught Henry's, she smiled at him.

The song ended, and the lights came up in the hall. They were unflattering fluorescents, and they made the crowd seem sparse and drab. Max took his painting down from the easel, and he and Clara hung back by the stage, waiting for the band to pack their instruments up. "The corner of New Hampshire and Madison," Clara called out, "New Hampshire and Madison."

Effie leaned heavily against Henry. He could feel her shivering. "I'm gonna collapse," she said.

"We'll just get you back to the cottage," he said, feeling chivalrous and terribly disappointed.

"I'm sorry," she said.

"What are you talking about? It's all right."

"You don't have to be with me. You can stay out."

"Don't be ridiculous."

They were standing near the dessert table by the door, where most of the crowd were lingering and gathering their things. Maggie, close by, was blathering to someone about the nightlife in Wilmington, Delaware, and when Henry turned, he saw that she was talking to the cadets, and that Alma was beside him. Carl stood on the other side of her, his arm around her waist. She was eating a caramel square, squinting at Maggie as if she were a puzzle to be deciphered, and Henry watched as she put the last bite into her mouth and licked her thumb and forefinger lavishly. And then, without taking her eyes off Maggie, she reached her arm out and wiped her fingers on the side of Henry's jacket.

That decided it. He would put Effie to bed, and then he would go to the after-party.

*H*e could hear the music all the way from Aunt Lizzie's front porch: horns, piano, maracas, and a chorus of voices, then cheers and applause. In front of Clara's, though he wasn't sure what he was seeing until he was almost upon it, stood a bus, a full-size school bus, with letters painted on it that he couldn't make out in the dark. It was the band's, naturally. Other cars were parked on either side of the street and in the driveway, and he felt his way among them toward the front door.

Inside, it was a more intimate gathering than it had sounded outside. The candles had been lit, the lamps were aglow. On the mantel over the fireplace stood Max's painting. Clara was at the piano, the band was lounging with their instruments all around the den, and everyone was singing a boozy rendition of "You Belong to Me." Max and two of the cadets were standing by the bar, Maggie and Brenda among them, and to Henry's surprise, a few of the older people from the dance were there too. Max raised his glass to Henry, and Henry held his hand up in greeting. He stepped uncertainly into the den, feeling strange without Effie, as though he were intruding, until he spotted Alma and Carl sitting on the rug by the coffee table, along with a rumpled-looking gray-haired gentleman and a few women he didn't recognize. They seemed to be playing cards. A bottle of whiskey stood on the table. When Alma saw him, she brightened and beckoned him over.

"Don't do it yet," she said to a Hispanic-looking woman, who was up on her knees across the table from her, holding a deck of cards. "I want Henry to see."

"Henry, darling!" Clara cried from the piano, then launched into another verse.

Carl eyed him warily. He'd unbuttoned his shirt, and underneath it he wore a white tank top, and he seemed to have spilled something on himself. "How's it going, Hank," he said. They were the first words he'd spoken to him all evening.

Alma told Carl to move over and make room.

"You're a tease, you know that?" he said, but Alma only smiled sweetly at him.

"I'm not teasing. I told you my boyfriend was coming back, and here he is. Now scoot."

Henry laughed, and felt a rush of heat. It was only a game, but he would play along. Reluctantly Carl scooted over, and Alma patted the space between them, and Henry sat down beside her, crossing his legs. She'd pulled her shoes and stockings off and was sitting with her legs tucked beside her, and when he asked what was going on, she shifted closer to him, so they touched.

"This is Zeynep," she said, nodding toward the woman holding the cards. "She's from Turkey."

"I'm from Cincinnati," the woman said.

"She's just shown us the most amazing card trick, and we're going to try and figure out how she does it. Here," she said, handing him a highball glass with two fingers of whiskey in it. "You need to help me with this. I'm getting tipsy."

"Gladly," he said, and took a swallow.

"Should I do it to him?" the woman asked.

Alma said yes, and laid her hand on Henry's leg. "Now, watch her very closely."

He would not be able to watch anything closely as long as she had her hand on his leg, as long as she was close enough that he could feel her warmth and smell her perfume, but he tried. The woman put the deck down on the table. She told him to cut it, and he took half the deck, set it down, and put the other half on top of it. She shuffled the cards again and held them up and made a fan, the faces in Henry's direction, and told him to take a card, any card, but not to show it to her. He picked the two of hearts. The woman told him to put the card on the table, facedown, and he did so, and she put the whole deck on top of it and then shuffled it again—once, twice, three times. He watched closely. She asked him to cut the deck again, and he did so, and she took one of the halves, put it between her knuckles, and held it out to him. "Now, slap it," she said.

"What?"

"Hit it—just slap the cards."

The others around the table laughed. Alma smiled at him. "Go on," she said.

It was some kind of joke, he thought, but what the hell: he got up on his knees, so he could reach the cards better, slapped them, and they all scattered and fluttered about the table—except for one, which was still wedged between the woman's knuckles. "Is this your card?" she said, holding it up.

And it was: it was the two of hearts.

Everyone around the table clapped, except for Henry, who was astonished—really and truly astonished. "That's incredible," he said. "Really, how is that possible?"

"I think I caught it that time," Alma said.

"I will not divulge my secrets," the woman said.

But how had she done it—really? She'd given him the card, and he held it in his hand like a sacred object.

Alma was enjoying his reaction. "It's impressive, isn't it?"

"That hardly says it. You know how she did it?"

She laughed and took the glass from him. "If I tell you, I'm afraid she'll kill me." She took a swallow and handed the glass back.

He put the card in his jacket pocket. It would bring him good luck, he thought.

They watched Clara and the band play. Clara was no joke on the piano. She was doing "The Entertainer," never looking at her hands, improvising little fills, turning half around to make eye contact with the trumpet player, who was playing a clarinet now. Soon the rest of the band had joined in—trombones, a kazoo, a chorus doing an a cappella bass line, and the drummer struck rhythmic accents on a ukulele. All the doors and windows were open, and breezes stole inside, disturbing the candles. Max and one of the cadets, Freddie, followed Maggie and Brenda outside, and the darkness swallowed them up. Henry finished the whiskey in his glass and poured some more. Now the trumpet player had wedged himself beside Clara at the piano, and together they played a rousing "It's a Long, Long Way to Tipperary," Clara laughing so hard she had trouble making the notes. The others followed along as best as they could. One of the old men, clearly very drunk, his shirt unbuttoned—a veteran of the Great War, maybe—stood and sang with feeling, swinging his fist in front of him.

The whiskey was going down easily. Henry thought of poor Effie across the street, in the dark, dead to the world and missing everything, and he felt for her. But he was happy to be on his own. He leaned back on his hands beside Alma, lightly swaying into her. Their fingers touched. She stole sips from his glass.

One of the other band members took over at the piano and played a ragtime tune. A small group by the staircase started dancing, including Clara and the trumpet player, who was running his hand up and down her side. *Scandalous!* Henry thought. Max was nowhere to be seen. Henry threw the rest of his drink back, got to his feet, and pulled Alma up with him, and they joined the group. Carl remained by the coffee table, looking darkly up at them.

The trumpet player was kissing the swells of Clara's breasts and caressing her behind, and Henry was shocked at the boldness of it, the shamelessness of it. Shocked, and excited too, because through the fog in his head he felt that nothing would be forbidden here. "Dear Henry!" she cried, tilting her head back. "Is Effie here?"

"She had to go to bed. She wasn't feeling well."

"My poor peach."

He was holding Alma's hand. "I would've stayed with her, but she made me come over." This was, in fact, true.

Clara reached out and put her hand on his chest. "I'm glad you did."

Alma pulled him away and turned him. The beat was jaunty, but they weren't following it. She put her arms around his neck, and he set his hands on her hips. He could feel her underwear through her dress. "This party's going to get ugly," she said, giving a glowering look over his shoulder, to Clara, presumably. "You can't leave me."

"I don't intend to," he said.

"Maybe we can escape," she said. "We've got our pick of houses. We don't have to stay here." She was smiling at him, full of meaning, and Henry felt dizzy. The lights seemed to dim, the music to come from far away.

"That's probably not a good idea," he said. Slowly he caressed her hips. "I could get myself into a lot of trouble."

She said nothing more. Something had turned. If the state of affairs between them wasn't plain before, it was plain now. They danced. There was another ragtime tune, and then Clara returned to the piano for a jazz number, and the party babbled along. Henry and Alma were separate from it.

Until Carl appeared, swaying in his unbuttoned uniform and tank top. "All right," he said to Alma, "why don't you quit this act?"

She pressed herself to Henry. "What act?"

"This"—he waved the back of his hand at them—"this boyfriend nonsense. You were with me tonight."

"I don't recall promising myself to anyone."

"Right," he said, and pressed his finger to her shoulder. "Like I said, you're a fucking tease."

Henry moved Alma behind him and with a bolt of adrenaline

said, "You ought to back off, son," and Carl laughed joylessly, and squared himself. He must have been half a foot taller than Henry.

"Or what, little hillbilly?"

Before Henry could answer, Alma put herself between them. "Or I'll gouge your eyes out," she said. Her voice was even and calm, just loud enough for him to hear over the music. She took Henry's hand and led him away. From the staircase she picked up a votive candle, and he followed her down the hall, past the bathroom, to a door near the end. They entered, and Henry closed the door behind him. "Is there a lock?" she asked, and he found the latch under the knob, and turned it.

The music came to them, muffled, from down the hallway. Henry expected Carl to bang on the door, but nothing happened.

"I think we're safe," Alma said. "God, what an asshole."

"What was his problem?"

"Who knows."

They were in a study. Bookcases lined one wall. A heavy desk and wingback chair stood on one side, and in the middle of the room stood a leather couch and armchair.

She sighed, and set the candle down on the desk. "Boys. They're so much more fragile than girls. Everyone thinks it's the other way around, but it almost never is. It's a burden."

He came over to her. He wanted to reach for her, but stopped short. "Sorry about that."

"I'm the one who should be sorry. I attract idiots." She took his hand. "Thanks for sticking up for me," she said.

"Any time." He looked around the room, which dimly shuddered in the candlelight. "I've never been in here before."

"It's nice." She moved her thumb in little circles over the back of his hand. "I hide away in here sometimes, when it's just the two of them and I don't want to hear them. There's quite a library."

She let his hand go and crossed over to the bookcases, and he followed her. They scanned the shelves, leaning against each other. He could just make out the titles. *Admiralty and Maritime Law. Black's Law Dictionary.* A lot of history too, ancient Greek and Roman, including Gibbon, in six volumes, leather bound. "Ah, your favorite book," she said, and from a shelf above them pulled down a copy of Boswell, the title in gilded letters. Henry laughed and told her to put it away, and as she did so, by instinct, as if to support her, he set his hand at the small of her back. She turned to him, his hand sliding around to her hip, and their faces were close. He could smell her breath—it was sweet, a faint note of whiskey. They were near a corner of the room, behind the desk. Her eyes shone.

"Can we hide here the rest of the night?" she asked softly.

"I mean, we can't go back out there, can we?" he said. "As long as what's-his-name is around."

"No."

Back in the den they were between songs. Someone shouted something, and there was a burst of laughter.

Alma moved her hand over his chest, over the contours of his muscles, up under his jacket to his shoulder. He could feel the warmth of it through his shirt. He was trembling. He was tipsy, maybe drunk, but he was intensely alert, every nerve ending alive. He pulled her by the hips against him, so she would know he was hard, and ran his hands over her behind, felt the soft flesh through the smooth fabric. She lifted her face so their noses touched, and breathed against him, waiting for him to go the last inch, which he did, and their lips met at last. The touch of her tongue against his. Her fingers running up the back of his head, the chills. He gripped her, and began gathering her dress up behind her.

Now she pressed her hand to the front of his trousers, gently squeezed him between her fingers, and the next moment she was pulling at his belt, tugging at it, finally drawing back to unbuckle it, using both hands, to unbutton and unzip his trousers, and as he drew her lips back to him, his trousers fell to his ankles and she slipped her hand into his boxers.

She smiled; he kissed her teeth. She stroked him slowly with her fist.

"Oh God," he said.

Their lips were still touching, but they weren't kissing, they were only breathing. "Do you want to fuck me?" she said.

"Yes," he said. His heart was pounding. "Yes, I want to fuck you."

"What are you waiting for?"

He kicked his shoes and trousers away, pulled his boxers off, turned her around, and brought them both to their knees—pushed her down and gathered her dress up over her waist, found the edge of her underwear and yanked them down her thighs, up under her knees, away from her ankles. The desk cast a dark shadow over them, and he could just see the pale mounds of her buttocks. He pressed his fingers between her legs, felt the wet of her cunt, the opening, and quickly, before it was all over for him, set his cock there, pierced and entered her—she let out a small cry—and for a few seconds fucked her savagely, holding his shirttails up with one hand, his groin slapping her buttocks and the backs of her thighs, until she reached her arm back and said, "Hey—easy, easy," and he slowed down, steadied himself, found a rhythm. She looked back at him from the floor, over her shoulder. "Don't come inside," she said. He didn't answer. All of him was focused on the dark cleft he was driving into. She closed her eyes. "That's it," she said. Her voice had turned airy. "That's it. That's it." And for an indeterminate time their bodies clapped together, until the orgasm choked him and, pulling out, pressing his forehead into her back, he ejaculated onto the rug between her knees.

For a long moment they held still like that. He felt the rise and fall of her back. "Did you come?" she whispered, finally, and he nodded.

He sat up and leaned back against the bookcase. She turned over, away from him, and pulled her dress down. She reached her hand out and felt the rug where they'd been. "Oh, my," she said, rubbing her fingers together. "Mr. Strauss will want this cleaned." Her head and shoulders were in the light. She smiled placidly at him. "I tried to escape one beast and ended up with another. Some luck."

All at once the magnitude of what he'd done came crashing down on him. "Oh God," he said, and turned away from her. "God, I'm sorry." He reached for his underwear. He didn't want her to see him, and angled away from her while he pulled them on. "I'm sorry."

"You're sorry," she said.

He pulled his trousers on, lifting his hips to pull them up to his waist, holding the buckle so it wouldn't make a sound. He felt too weak, too embarrassed to stand.

She was glaring at him, waiting for him to go on. "What are you sorry about?"

"I wasn't thinking," he said, buttoning himself up. "I'm sorry. This was a mistake."

She continued to glare at him for a long moment, until she looked away and seemed to come to some sort of conclusion. "Right," she said. She got to her feet.

"Alma," he said—but he didn't know what he wanted to say. He felt consumed by fire. "I wasn't thinking," he said again.

"I know." She turned her back to him and shimmied into her underwear.

"Alma, I'm sorry."

"If you say you're sorry again, I'm going to scream." She turned back around to face him, smoothing her dress. "I'm serious. Tell me you're sorry one more time. I'll scream. I'll say you forced me."

"No!" He stood up, his belt buckle ringing. "Please. You can't. You can't tell anyone."

She laughed. "Look at you. You're terrified."

"It was a mistake, that's all. I didn't mean to do it."

"Get the fuck away from me."

She strode past him. He grabbed her arm, and she swung around and slapped him in the face. The shock blinded him. His ear rang. She made it to the door and was unlocking it when he cried, "Alma—please. Please don't go. Please." She paused, her hand on the doorknob, and he held his palms up to her. "I don't know what I'm saying. Please. I feel crazy. I don't know what I'm doing."

She seemed to soften somewhat. Her eyes glistened in the light. He thought she might be on the verge of crying, but when she spoke, her voice was calm and clear. "Look, I'm not going to say anything. You can relax. It's nothing—nothing to report here. This was just . . ." She waved her hand at him. "It'll go down the memory hole." She opened the door, said, "See you later," without looking at him, and went out, closing the door behind her.

He was empty with shock. His face throbbed where she'd struck it. Finally he buckled his belt. He took his handkerchief—the nice blue silk one, which he'd bought especially for the suit—from his front pocket and knelt down where they'd been, to try to clean it up. It was hopeless. There'd be a spot. But there was nothing he could do. He stuffed the wet handkerchief in his trousers pocket, put his shoes on, blew the candle out, and stood in the dark, listening to the party down the hall. It had tamed down, but there was still a murmur of voices. The floorboards over his head creaked. He thought he heard a woman moaning. He had to get out—but not through the den. The study was at a corner of the house, facing the street, and through one of the windows he saw a space between the shrubs. He unlocked the window, lifted it open, stepped outside, closed it behind him, and escaped.

All was dark and quiet back at the cottage. He lit the kerosene lamp and brought it into the downstairs lavatory, where there was a shower stall they never used. But the water worked, and he made it hot. He pulled his suit off, left it crumpled on the floor, and stepped into the stall. Alma's scent was all over him. A desiccated cake lay in the soap tray, and he scrubbed himself with it. When he was finished he dried himself off, slowly, with the hand towel. He inspected his face in the mirror. It was bright red, and warm to the touch, but it didn't seem to be swelling. He slipped his boxers on, blew out the lamp, and carrying his suit in a bundle, felt his way upstairs to the attic room.

The windows were open, as usual. It smelled clean and fresh. He could see the mound of Effie's body under the covers. Quietly he deposited the ball of clothing in his suitcase and closed it, put on his pajamas, and slipped under the covers beside his wife. She whimpered, turned away from him, was still again. The wind whipped into the room and he stared up into the dark. He didn't have the heart to pray.

He couldn't believe he'd done what he'd done. And so he replayed it, moment by moment, as if in search of the proof, until in spite of himself he was erect again.

Nine

Never again. That was the refrain in his head all morning, while he straightened the den and mopped the kitchen floor: he would never be unfaithful to his wife again. It had been a horrible mistake, and that was all.

They were supposed to move over to Clara's tomorrow. It didn't seem possible now.

While he was mopping, Effie came down and stood at the edge of the linoleum. Her hair was wild. "Henry," she said, surveying the floor. "You sweet thing."

He stepped over to her, over the wet part he'd already done, and wrapped her in his arms. "How are you feeling?"

"Disgusting," she said. She turned again to the floor, and laughed. "You didn't sweep first, did you?"

He hadn't. And he could see, very clearly now, the wet balls of dust and stray hairs affixed to the linoleum. He took it as a sign of his uselessness. She looked up at him, and laughed again. It was all right, she said. It was helpful. They'd just let it dry, and then she'd sweep and do another quick pass with the mop—later.

She set herself up on the sofa, under the afghan, a box of tissues beside her, and he made her buttered toast and coffee. Her fever had come back in the night, she said, but she felt much better now. She was sweating like crazy, which was a good sign.

He caressed her cheek. "Are you sure you don't want to go back home? We can still make the train tomorrow. You might be more comfortable in your own bed."

"God," she said, "I don't want to think about that trip. Eighteen hours, three connections. Trying to sleep in that berth."

"Well—if you're *sure*."

She frowned. "Don't you want to stay?"

"Of course I do. If you do."

She asked how the party had been and what she'd missed, and he said not much. The band had been there. There'd been some sing-alongs, a little dancing. He'd left early.

She pouted. "I love sing-alongs."

*S*hortly after noon, to Henry's surprise and alarm, Clara knocked on the door. But she was her usual bright self. "Hello, hello," she said, and kissed both of his cheeks. He stepped aside to let her in. "How's my belle?"

"Don't look at me," Effie cried from the couch, covering her face with her hands. "I'm hideous."

"Nonsense," Clara said. "You're adorable." She was wearing her shimmering blue robe, and her presence seemed too big for the little den. She took it in and said, "God, I haven't been in here in years, since before Holly married. I barely recognize it."

"Uncle George redecorated," Henry said.

"Ah," she said, and he thought he could detect something faintly cold in her tone. She'd seen him dancing with Alma last night. He'd been fawning over her, right out in the open, like a fool. She asked again how Effie was feeling, and Effie said she'd be fit for public by evening, as long as they weren't doing anything too exciting. Clara rolled her eyes. "Don't worry. It's going to be a slow one tonight. Maxie overextended himself—typical. He's still asleep, if you can believe it. I wish we'd left all those people where we found them last night. A low-rent crowd if I ever saw one."

"I heard the band came," Effie said. "And there was singing."

"You were amazing at the piano," Henry put in. "You should have seen her, Eff. She was the leader of the band."

Clara seemed pleased at that, as he'd hoped, and smiled warmly at him. "The musicians were all right," she said, "but the girls, Jesus. The most boring pack of hangers-on I ever met. I shooed the one named Maggie out of the backyard this morning. She was asleep on the lawn."

"No!" Effie said, leaning forward, eager to hear more, and as Clara went on, about the girls, about "those awful Coast Guard boys," Henry's nerves calmed. She said nothing about him, or gave him any kind of suspicious look. Of course Alma wouldn't have said anything. And Clara had been absorbed in her own drama. He remembered how the trumpet player had been kissing her breasts.

"Anyway," she said, "assuming Maxie can rouse himself, we were planning to go to this little place in town that's open on the weekends. The Salty Dog? It's a bit of a joint, but the food's good, and our kitchen's depleted. Want to come? It'll just be us."

Effie said it sounded good to her, and looked at Henry.

"Sure," he said. "Of course."

*M*aybe she wouldn't come along. Maybe, knowing Henry would be there, she'd do what she usually did, and slip off somewhere by herself.

But at some point, if they were staying at Clara's, he would have to see her. And maybe, he thought, as he and Effie walked to the Western Union office to call their families, it wouldn't be so bad.

It was another fine day, sunny and warm, and since it was Saturday, the town wasn't completely empty. An old couple strolled ahead of them on the promenade. Down on the beach, a family was having a picnic. He and Effie held hands.

He thought of the days and nights ahead, and as always, the future cheered him. He and Alma would sit up again some night—maybe, probably, tonight—and they'd talk. The moon was already rising, a pale orb, barely visible. He'd tell her he understood, now that he'd had some time to think about it—that he'd reacted like a child, that he'd panicked, that she'd been right to be angry at him. But everything was all right with him now. It was no big deal. They would probably laugh about it. They would probably, in the days to come, exchange glances and smile at each other. Because they had this secret now.

They crossed Beach Avenue and headed into the town center.

There was a phone booth at the Western Union office, and Henry waited on the bench beside it while Effie called her folks. An old man sat behind the counter, reading a battered paperback.

Really, he *hadn't* been unfaithful to her, not in any important way. He loved her as much today as he had yesterday, possibly more. It had been a lapse in judgment, that was all. He'd been drunk. It had nothing to do with Effie, and she would never have to know about it. She *shouldn't* know about it, because knowing it would only hurt her pointlessly. That God knew was another matter, and when he thought of this, a shadow passed over him. But boys will be boys. Name an upstanding man who had never . . . Name a faithful husband who had never *once* . . . He could square it with his conscience. He could pray.

Effie was staring into space, holding the phone to her ear, and Henry could tell she was talking to her mother. "Uh-huh," she said.

"Okay. Right. Oh, neat." And then: "Hi, Daddy!" She told him they were having an amazing time. In an annoying, pouty voice she explained that she'd taken ill. But, brightening, she said they'd met the most interesting people, including a member of the *Hewitt* family. Didn't he know? Hewitt-Rowe, the shipping company? Henry stood up and paced to the other side of the room and examined a corkboard filled with out-of-date flyers. He disliked the importance she placed on money. It made their lives seem impoverished. Max and Clara never spoke of money—they never had to. It was the air they breathed.

When she wrapped up the call at last—"Bye, Daddy. Okay. Bye-bye!"—she seemed refreshed and happy.

"How'd they take it, about us staying?"

"Oh, Mama just fretted about Uncle George. Daddy asked if he should wire us some more money, but I told him we were fine." There was an ice-cream shop across the square, she said, and she thought she'd go there while Henry called his folks. She asked if he wanted anything, and he reminded her he couldn't take dairy. "Right!" she said.

In the booth, when the line connected, it was his mother who answered.

"I don't believe my ears," she said. "To tell you the truth, I'd pretty much forgotten about you."

He'd never gone two weeks without speaking to her, and the sound of her voice brought him immediately home and made him feel ashamed of himself. But when she asked how he'd been holding up, like Effie, he said they were having an amazing time. They'd gone to a dance last night. They'd gone sailing twice. They'd met lots of interesting people, people from New York, people from California, artists and actresses, writers and intellectuals. He didn't know why he was going on about it, she wasn't impressed by such things. He felt low and indulgent and disgusted with himself. If she'd really known what he'd been up to, she'd have been ashamed of him.

When he was finished, she waited for a respectful beat and said, "Well, we're about ready to have you back. I'll tell you the Old Wing won't be finished. You and Effie are going to have to make do with your old bedroom for the next couple of weeks. Carswall had to fire one of the Fletcher boys. He showed up drunk the other day and couldn't hit the damn nails with his hammer. But Bo's going to finish it off, and you could help him when you get here."

"Actually, Mama," he said, "we're probably going to stay here a few more days."

"You're going to stay there a few more days? You've *been* there for two weeks."

He and Effie had worked out earlier what they'd tell their families, but just now it occurred to him that what they'd agreed upon—that an old friend of Effie's was coming into town to see her, and they wanted to spend a few days together—would seem frivolous to his mother, who already considered Effie a frivolous woman, not because she was, but because she was Daisy Tarleton's daughter. So he explained that Effie had come down with a bad flu, that she'd been bedridden for two days, that she was feeling a little better now but was in no condition to travel, and his mother agreed. She took illnesses seriously.

"You take her to a doctor yet?"

"No, Mama. It seems like it's running its course at this point."

"Take her to a doctor anyway. If it's strep or something it could lie low and come back as scarlet fever—believe me. I nearly died of it when I was a girl."

"I know, Mama," he said. "Okay, we'll see a doctor."

She said Carswall wouldn't be happy with their extended vacation, and that piqued him.

"He can be as unhappy as he pleases," he said. "We can stay as long as we want to—we're adults now. And I'm not his employee. We talked about this."

His mother chuckled. "It's all right. I'll talk to him." And then: "You're a fine boy, you know that? A fine married man now. I can't believe it."

After he hung up he felt like crying, and he sat in the booth and stared at the floor, until the man behind the counter asked if he needed anything. He shook his head and stood up to go.

He was a poor excuse for a man.

He remembered a story his mother had told him, a few weeks before the wedding, about a great-uncle of hers who had tried to desert from Hood's army after the Battle of Chickamauga. He'd made it all the way home, she said, but at the door his wife had pulled a shotgun on him and told him to go back until they'd won the war, or else she would kill him. He'd rejoined the army and, "obediently," as his mother put it, died of dysentery soon after the surrender.

Effie was waiting for him on a bench in the square, holding an ice-cream cone. Sunlight dappled her face. She was immeasurably precious to him.

"How's the Angel of Darkness?" she asked, meaning his mother. It always made him laugh.

That evening, Alma stood on the sidewalk in front of Clara's, in her brown dress with the white polka dots, and the sight of her there in the gloaming burned away every line of reason he'd articulated to himself that day, along with any trace of shame. Clara had come to fetch them, and she and Max were waiting. She glanced in his direction, then away.

They started toward the town center, down the residential streets on the other side of Madison. The streetlights were out, and the evening was soft and warm. Alma trailed behind. He wished he could fall back and ask how she was, but she would only look at him like he was an idiot. So he listened to Effie telling Max and Clara about her mother, how anxious she could be, how she wished she'd take up drinking, if only to calm herself. The streetlights worked past Ocean Street, and as they neared the town center they saw lighted windows here and there, and people on the sidewalks, as if they'd crossed an enchanted barrier into the living world.

The Salty Dog, on Decatur Street, was a dilapidated black house with a dim light by the door. It looked forlorn, but inside was a lively murmur, and a fair crowd of weekenders in their linen shirts and V-neck sweaters. There was a bar along one wall, and in a corner a trio of musicians—a guitarist, a violinist, and a man with a ukulele—was playing what sounded like a sea chanty, or an Irish ballad. The air was smoky and smelled of fried fish.

"This must be everyone in town," Effie said.

They were seated at a small bench table near the bar. Henry and Effie took one side, Max and Clara the other. Alma sat beside Max—as far from Henry as possible. The room was warm, so she took the cardigan off. She crossed her arms over her chest, and focused her attention on the trio. Her smooth, bare shoulders, her long neck, the soft line of her jaw, her chin, her lips that he'd kissed only last night. Her features were familiar to him now but she was new enough to him that every time he saw her they took him by surprise, the particular arrangement of forms, suddenly remembered, that made her herself and no one else. Her beauty was startling. He even loved the careless, messy way she tied up her hair. He studied the menu, which was printed on loose, weathered paper, so as not to stare. The choices alarmed him. Squid. Octopus. Swordfish. But also fish and chips, thankfully.

The conversation was subdued. They mostly watched the musicians. Max seemed distracted. Effie asked if he was all right, and he said he'd been too cavalier with the whiskey. "Also with Maggie," Clara added pertly, and Max waved her away and said, "Nothing happened. I'd have told you if it did." Effie made a face to Henry—*Okay!*—but said nothing. Max held up the mug of beer he'd ordered and said it would restore him to health. Henry had ordered a mug of beer too, and clinked glasses with him. That was a Viking tradition, Max said: you clinked mugs so your drinks would slosh together, and that way you could be sure your host wasn't trying to poison you.

Their food came. Alma had ordered the swordfish. It looked like steak. She dug into it, eating steadily and methodically: first a cut of the fish, then half a baby potato, then a piece of asparagus, and then back to the fish again. She always cleaned her plate. That, too, he found charming. Like Effie, who ate as well as any good Southern girl. Clara picked at hers. Max was thorough but slow.

The fish and chips were delicious. Fresh cod. Henry devoured it.

Clara asked if they were moving over that night, and Effie said no, they still had the cleaning to do. Though Henry, she said, smiling at him, had gotten a start on it this morning.

"You're a better man than some I know," Clara said.

"We'll need to restock," Max said. "I hope the stores are open tomorrow."

"The grocer's is, I know," Effie said.

"But the liquor store," Clara said.

"How much longer are we staying here?" Alma said, and everyone stopped to look at her. She held her fork aloft, a chunk of swordfish on it.

"I don't know," Max said. "For as long as we want, I suppose."

She nodded, turning back to her plate, and stuffed the swordfish into her mouth.

"Why?" Max said. "Is something the matter?"

"No," she said, cutting into a potato. "I was only asking."

"Because if you're unhappy, or bored . . ."

"I'm not," she said. "I'm perfect."

"It's nice here," he went on. "I can feel myself think for the first time in ages. I think I might start writing tomorrow."

"You know, dear," Clara said, leaning forward so she could see past Max, "you don't have to stay if you don't want to. There's a train straight from here to Penn Station."

"Clare," Max said.

"I'm only saying, darling," she said, putting her hand on his forearm. "In case she wants to go home. She can take care of herself."

"I appreciate it," Alma said. "It's good to know. Maybe I'll do that."

Henry fought the urge to beg her not to go. As it turned out, Effie did it for him: "You *can't* leave. It'd be too sad."

"No one's leaving," Clara said, chuckling, waving her hand, and took a sip of her martini. "You're all trapped here with me."

They finished their dinner, ordered another round—Alma was drinking Coca-Cola—and listened to the music. Max, Clara, and Effie clapped along to a jaunty number. Finally the check came. Max paid, and to Henry's relief, Effie didn't protest.

When they got outside, Alma said she wanted to walk out to the point, and Max said nothing to dissuade her. She put her cardigan on and started away from them, down Decatur Street toward the promenade. Henry wished he could go with her.

"Poor girl," Clara said. "My mother taught me that if you can just pretend to be cheerful for a little while, you'll actually turn cheerful. It's been a great skill for me. I could teach it to her."

"You'd better not." Max laughed wearily. "Maybe she should go. I have to remind myself she's not my problem."

They got back to Clara's a little after eight. There was enough brandy for each of them, but the gin and the whiskey were all gone. It was all for the best, Max said, tipping his head back in the armchair and closing his eyes: he would be dead to the world soon. Effie said she would too. They'd need to call it an early night.

"No sleep is better than when you're sick," Clara said.

"The dreams are weird," Effie said.

"God yes, the dreams."

As soon as Effie settled herself under the covers, she was gone—off into her strange dreams. Henry took the lamp and went back downstairs. It wasn't yet ten o'clock.

Tomorrow night they'd be settled at Clara's, and after everyone had gone to sleep, he'd stay up and wait for her, for as long as it took, and they would talk. But that seemed impossibly distant now. He couldn't bear another day in which she ignored him, in which she hated him. He lay on the sofa and stared at the ceiling. He was done with Boswell. He didn't feel like reading anything. Restless, he blew the lamp out and stepped out onto the front porch. The moon was out somewhere, low and weak. He could make out the houses across the street. Clara's place lay hidden in shadow. He was barefoot, but he'd not changed out of his shirt and trousers, and he had a fleeting impulse to go back over there now, crouch in the bushes, and lie in wait for her. Instead, he sat down. If he saw a light over there, maybe he would go. Or he might see her slipping by on the sidewalk, like a black cat in the night.

That was when it occurred to him. He stood up and stepped down to the sidewalk and looked down the street, toward the big Victorian house. He could make out its sharp tower, the second-floor balcony. And in one of the windows, a dim glow.

He started toward it without thinking. It was three houses down. When he reached it he saw that the light was coming from the balcony door they'd entered the other night, and he climbed the metal staircase, the grating digging into his feet. He crossed the porch and tried the door, and it opened with a chirp, the hinges creaking. Down the narrow hall, the big game room was aglow. He stepped inside, pushed the door closed behind him—the panes rattled loudly—and as he turned and made his way down the hall, he considered for the first time that Alma might not be here, that it might be the owners of the house come to stay for the weekend. But as he entered the big room, there she was, in the hallway across from him, holding her hand to her heart.

"Jesus," she said. "You gave me a heart attack."

"I'm sorry," he said, holding up his hands. "I saw the light. I thought it was you."

They both looked at it, a small lamp of frosted glass, which she'd left on an end table by the sofa. She crossed over to it and blew it out, and for a moment all was dark. And then he saw, at the end of the hall she'd emerged from, soft light spilling from an open door.

"What are you doing here?" she asked.

He could just make her out, the line of her shoulder, the side of her head. "I couldn't sleep," he said. He took a step toward her. "I saw the light, and I figured . . . I just wanted to talk to you."

"You should go," she said.

"But Alma—"

"What do we have to talk about?"

He wished he could see her face, because her voice wasn't cold. There was something gentle in it, willing—he wasn't sure. It was enough to encourage him. "Last night," he said. "What happened . . ."

"Nothing happened," she said. "It was a mistake, I get it. It didn't happen. We don't have to discuss it, for Christ's sake."

"Alma, please." He came closer to her. She didn't move away. "I'm . . ." Not sorry. Or she would scream. "I acted like an idiot last night," he said. "I mean after. I shouldn't have acted like that. I was—I wasn't in my right mind. I was stupid."

He waited, but she said nothing to this.

"I thought about you all day," he said. "I couldn't think of anything else. And tonight, at dinner—I wanted so badly, so badly to . . ." To do what, he didn't know, all words failed him. Still she said nothing. "Alma . . ."

"Henry," she said gently, "you should really go."

"I don't want to go," he said.

She made a halfhearted sound of annoyance, but there was nothing more to say. He knew with every nerve what he wanted, and there was no need to put it into words. He stepped closer and took her hips and pulled her toward him, felt her crossed arms against his chest, but after the slightest resistance she uncrossed them and put them around him. She rested her head on his shoulder, and they held each other. He was shaking. "You should think very carefully about what you're doing," she said. He lifted her chin and found her lips, and she sighed and seemed to collapse inward, giving in. He gripped her behind, held the back of her head. She bit his lip. He kissed her nose, her chin, tasted the salt on her neck, took her earlobe into his mouth, smelled the sun in her hair. And then she pulled away and took his hand and led him down the hall, toward the lighted doorway.

It was a bedroom. He remembered it from the other night. An old tin hurricane lamp stood on the nightstand, beside a heavy four-poster bed with a thick blue duvet almost completely buried in dresses, which Alma must have been taking from the open closet and inspecting. The wallpaper was blue, and by the wall opposite the bed stood a heavy oak dresser and mirror. She pulled him toward her by the front of his trousers. Suddenly their movements were rushed and urgent. She unbuttoned and unzipped him, he began gathering her dress up her hips—but it was faster to do it themselves, so he stepped away and hurriedly unbuttoned and removed his shirt, dropped his trousers and underwear in one go, hopping on one foot to free the other, and when he looked up, free at last, Alma was naked—fallen back onto the bed, up on her elbows, legs dangling over the side, so beautiful he felt light-headed. She had a neat V of straw-colored pubic hair. Small, upturned breasts, bright pale where her bathing suit had covered them. A constellation of moles on her stomach, one prominent one, raised like a third nipple, just under her left breast. Her secrets. He could have turned back. He could have apologized again and gathered up his clothes. She would have screamed at him, thrown the kerosene lamp at him and burned the place down, but he could have run, and convinced himself that he was still a faithful man. But he was standing there naked himself, his cock sticking out from him like a bowsprit, and there was no turning back. He must have been standing there at the precipice for a long time, because at last she raised her knees and spread her legs and said, "Do you just want to stare at it all night?"

*I*t was dawn before he knew it. She lay against him, trailing her finger over the soft skin at his hips. They'd kept the lamp burning and no time seemed to have passed, but suddenly the windowpanes stood out blue behind the blinds. He got up on an elbow. She rolled over to see. "It's late," she said dreamily. "Or early, depending."

"Shit," Henry said, and sat up. It must have been five thirty at least, maybe six. The Art Deco clock on the wall read eleven fifteen. "Shit," he said again. "Effie's going to be up soon. If she isn't already."

It was the first time he'd said her name, and now Alma looked up at him sharply, and her foot, which had been caressing his calf, halted. He bent down to kiss her and smoothed a lock of hair behind her ear. "I have to go."

"Don't," she said.

"Alma—I have to."

She smiled and pressed her fingertip to his lips. "I know. It's okay."

He pulled himself out of the bed, and while he picked up his scattered clothes and put them on he wondered, in a detached way, whether he had already ruined his life. Effie might very well be awake. It was

Sunday morning, and she'd probably want to go to church. He wouldn't have the opportunity for a shower before she saw him, and Alma's scent, hers and his, was all over him—the room was dense with it: the smell of semen, of Alma's vagina, of something feral they'd made in common, which hung close to his skin like musk. They'd made a mess of the bed. The dresses, which they hadn't bothered to push aside, were probably ruined.

Alma rolled over onto her stomach, resting her head in the crook of her arm, and smiled back at him as he zipped and buttoned his trousers. She was posing for him: displaying her behind, giving him one last peek through the star-shaped gap between her thighs and buttocks. How could he leave her, even for a moment? He sat on the edge of the bed and ran his hand over the smooth skin, the hairs at the small of her back, the raised mole between her shoulder blades. Incredibly, he felt himself getting hard again. He had to go.

"I'll wait a while after you're gone," she said. "Before I leave. In case anyone's passing in the street."

He smiled. "You can't be too careful."

"I'll see you soon?"

"In just a few hours. Hopefully." He caressed her hair. "We're going to be roommates now," he said.

"That'll be interesting."

He kissed her long on the lips and kissed her head, breathing her in. If the worst happened, he might never see her this way again. But he got to his feet and crossed to the door, and after one last look at her from the doorway, he made his way out.

New Hampshire Avenue lay clearly visible in the dawn. The detachment he'd felt about his future was beginning to wear off, now that he was walking back to the cottage. His carelessness astonished him. It was as if he were courting ruin, as if he wanted to be caught. But he didn't, he knew he didn't. He went inside the house and up the stairs like a condemned man. It was just after six.

She was still asleep. He stood at the doorway and looked in on her. She was sprawled diagonally under the covers, like she'd tried to reach for him and found nothing. Maybe she'd gotten up sometime in the night to look for him. The thought of her padding downstairs, checking the den, the front and back porches, calling his name— *Henry? Henry, boo, where are you?*—made him sick with love. Or pity. He had a strong urge to hold her, to tell her it would be all right, as if not he but somebody else were breaking her heart.

He went down to the second-floor lavatory and ran the shower. The sound of the water calmed him. He was safe. She could wake up now, and he could tell her he hadn't been able to sleep, that he'd gone for a walk in the early morning and then, since he was up, had decided to take a shower. He leaned his head against the tiles and relished the hot water on his skin. He emptied his bladder where he stood. It burned. He'd been up for twenty-four hours, and most likely he wouldn't have time to sleep now.

Back in the attic room he put his clothes into his suitcase, over his bundled-up wedding suit, and stepped into his last pair of clean underwear. When he turned around, Effie was rolling onto her side and squinting up at him.

"How long you been up?" she asked, pulling her hair away from her face.

"A little while," he said. "I had trouble sleeping. How are you feeling?" He sat on the edge of the bed and rubbed her shoulder.

"Okay, I guess." With effort she sat up, coughed and winced, and held her hand to her chest. Then she smiled at him and laid her head on his shoulder.

To his profound relief, she wanted to skip church that day. Jesus would understand. That preacher was abysmal. And they had enough to do.

"We'll just be sure to thank Him throughout the day," she said. "For whatever. Not aloud, but in our minds, like. 'Thank you, Jesus, for this cup of coffee. Thank you, Jesus, for toast and butter.'"

And Jesus was pleased, obviously: a little later the radio in the den came to life—rousing orchestral music—and the end-table lamp shone. It was a miracle. Henry cried, "Thank you, Jesus!"

They spent the rest of the morning cleaning to music, following King George's instructions—sweeping and mopping, wiping the counters and dusting, stripping the sheets off the bed and leaving them in the hamper, throwing out the perishables—and then Effie bathed and dressed and they packed their suitcases and brought them down to the den. In order to avoid a full-blown diplomatic crisis, Effie said they'd better try and restock the bottles they'd used. And so after a sandwich for lunch they headed out, to see if the liquor store was open.

Another beautiful day. He thanked Jesus for this too. As usual, they took the long way to the town center, down along the promenade, and unaccountably, Henry wanted to whoop for joy. It was the music, it was the eternal sea beside him, it was how alive and invincible he felt, now that he'd escaped ruin, the night still white-hot in his nerves, on his skin, the day and the night to come already trembling with promise. He wasn't tired at all—only time felt strange: it was incomprehensible to him that only six hours ago he'd been with Alma in the blue bedroom, and that that time was continuous with dinner at the Salty Dog and also with this bright, clear, perfect afternoon, while the waves struck the shore again and again like a metronome. The secret to life was hidden from us, Henry thought, because we couldn't be awake to see every moment of it. If you could forego sleep a little while and see it uninterrupted, something essential would be revealed to you. But you could only just grasp it, because eventually the veil had to be lowered, you had to sleep. He wished he never had to sleep.

The liquor store was open. They bought a bottle of Cutty Sark, a bottle of Remington's, and two bottles of Beefeater's gin—one for Uncle George, another for Clara's. Maybe Effie would have her daddy wire them the extra money after all. The clerk provided them with a box to haul it. "Must be some party," he said.

Back at the cottage they latched all the windows, locked the front door behind them, and left the key in the hanging pot with the dead fern.

"Bye, little place," Effie said from the sidewalk. "I guess I'll never visit you again."

"We'll be back," Henry said. "One of these summers."

"Maybe," she said.

They let themselves in at Clara's and dropped their suitcases in the foyer. No one was in the den, but all the windows and doors were open, drafts played through the house, and here too classical music was coming from the record player. "We're here," Effie called, and from above Clara cried, "My loves!" and then Henry saw her—Alma—out by the pool, lying in a deck chair in her white bathing suit and sunglasses, reading a magazine. When he came to the patio door she glanced at him, drew her lips taut—the faintest trace of a smile—and returned to her reading.

Ten

Sunday, Monday, Tuesday, Wednesday: the days passed in a haze. The hours were strange. Henry only slept in short, deep bursts, when he laid his head back, wherever he was, and closed his eyes, and time jumped and someone, usually Effie, shook him awake, laughing at him, and he leapt up to follow whatever they were doing—another excursion into town or out on the boat, another drink, another meal, another game. If he was acting strange, no one seemed to notice. They'd all given themselves over to some kind of enchantment. They drank all day. In the morning Max and Clara worked, and these were the quiet hours. Effie lay out by the pool. Alma slept upstairs. Henry napped fitfully in the shade. In the afternoon they took the boat out. At night they danced in the den. They played hide-and-seek in the house and out in the yard. They sat around the fire and played games. In the first couple of days Effie never made it to midnight: she would fall asleep on the sofa, and Henry would wake her and take her up to their room, where he'd lie beside her for a while, listening to her steady breathing, waiting for the house to still, until he could get up and slip away, downstairs and outside, a shadow in the night, down the street to the Bishops' house, where Alma would be waiting for him.

At every moment his intention was fixed on that one object: to be alone with Alma. Sometimes she seemed so much herself, so natural and indifferent to him, that he was sure something had changed, that she was no longer accessible to him, and he'd feel panicked, he'd try to meet her eyes, he'd want to clutch her and beg her, out loud, for a sign, and then he'd feel rotten and ashamed of himself. But then she'd do some little thing—a passing touch, a smile, the way she said *hi* to him—that would carry him for hours, and the secret was almost as sweet as the thing itself. He loved to see her around the others, ignoring him. He loved to see her in her clothes and know that, in a few hours, he would take them off.

They took *The Mistral* out most days, even when it threatened rain. Clara pointed them into the wind, and they pitched and dove through the waves. Alma stood on the deck, holding on to the mast, facing the elements. Slate-gray sea, low, racing clouds. Her tan calves flexed as she kept her balance, her hair whipped behind her.

Now the sails were down, the sun had returned, the boat rocked drowsily. Picnic basket, gin, ice from the marina. Strawberries and grapes and soft cheeses. Henry sat with his back against the bulkhead, and Effie rested her head in his lap. Alma sat on the deck above him, her legs dangling by his side. Softly, when no one was looking, she caressed his arm with her toes.

At the fish market by the marina she joined him at the lobster tank and said, as if commenting on the lobsters, that she was soaking wet.

The others stood safely by the scales. Nearby, an attendant was scrubbing the inside of an empty tank.

"I only thought you should know," she said. She was up on her tiptoes—her flexed calves—looking down into the churning water. "Every time I look at you, I get wet."

"You're giving me a hard-on."

"Let me see," she said.

He laughed, looking around. No one was paying attention to them.

"Just a peek," she said. "Come on."

And so he pulled the elastic of his trunks out and down, exposing it for an instant, and she smiled at it and left him there, by the tank, to stare at the lobsters and cool off.

Max fried scallops for dinner and they ate outside in the dusk. Alma had showered and changed into her green dress, the one Effie had borrowed. She sat away from him, out of his reach. He felt a hand on his leg—Effie's—but she was looking at Max and laughing at something he was saying. She was feeling much better. It was all the gin, she'd said. A grape fell to the flagstones and Clara picked it up with her toes and, lifting her foot to Max's mouth, fed it to him.

They played hide-and-seek. It was Max's idea. Clara thought it was stupid, but now she was It, and the rest of them scattered throughout the house and outside while she went into a closet and counted to fifty. Henry went outside, and Alma followed at a distance. He called to her from behind a cluster of chinaberry trees. He only wanted to steal a kiss, maybe a quick feel up her dress, but she got to her knees and pulled his trunks down to his ankles, and while her head bobbed at his groin, and he ran his hands through her damp hair, he could see Clara through the windows, searching the den, now stepping out onto the patio to search the dark brush on the other side of the yard—"Christ, where is everyone?"—and Henry bit his lip so he wouldn't make a sound.

Later, Alma sat in her chair by the fire, absorbed in a book of maritime ghost stories. Shades of dirt on her knees. Max was giving Effie and Clara a tarot reading. He'd found the deck in a junk drawer and was making everything up, but Effie was riveted. "Don't worry," Max said, "it doesn't mean death. Not necessarily. It means . . . it *could* mean a new beginning . . ." After a while Alma got up and drifted out to the patio. She wouldn't be back. Effie gathered the afghan around her. It was just after eleven o'clock. Soon, she would be asleep.

But not soon enough—never soon enough. Monday night he didn't get away until almost one in the morning, and outside, he jogged down the street—to Alma, his Alma.

The Bishops' house was all theirs. She'd leave the front door open, and he'd walk in and feel his way through the dark rooms until he caught a sliver of light and found her. She was always inspecting some curiosity—a nested doll, a collection of lacquered fans, a jack-in-the-box that wouldn't open—and she'd pretend at first that she wasn't interested in him. "Maybe it's a joke," she said, shaking the jack-in-the-box. "I don't hear anything inside."

Never mind the jack-in-the-box. He kissed the back of her neck and ran his hands down her sides, began lifting the green dress up over her waist. She turned to him.

"I thought you would never come."

"I thought they would never go to bed."

They dropped to the rug, pulling at each other's clothes. They didn't bother with the dress, only her underwear, his trunks. She hooked her legs around him and drew him in. That first blissful entering. He came quickly, just to get it over with. Hours lay ahead of them.

They'd christened the game room, the kitchen counter, all of the bedrooms. That first night, in the blue bedroom, she'd introduced him to the term *coitus interruptus,* which was Latin, she said, for "pull out." And so he'd pulled out and jerked off, flinging a little shower onto her buttocks and onto the backs of her thighs. They made a mess of the sofa, of the throw pillows, of the sheets, until he was spent. But his need for her was insatiable. He kissed every mole. He breathed her pits in, the faint onion and baby powder. He sucked her toes. (She wasn't ticklish, like he was.) He spread her thighs and devoured her. She was finer, less profuse than Effie. He pressed his tongue in as far as it would go, the taste of her tart like a plum, until she spread herself with her fingers and tapped a tender bulb, the size of a bb, nestled in a hood of delicate skin, and told him that was where the gold was. And when he toyed with it she whimpered and arched her back, told him harder, softer, until she cried and shuddered and squeezed his head between her thighs.

They wandered the house, exploring things. She did. He couldn't keep his hands off of her. While she looked through the kitchen drawers he nestled his penis between her buttocks and cupped her breasts. He told her again and again how much he wanted her, how beautiful she was, how he never wanted these nights to end. They were the best nights of his life, he said. She told him she loved his hands, how he touched her, that she loved the sharp tan lines around his neck and arms, that she loved his chest and stomach and the line of hair under his belly button, that she loved his voice, his accent, the way he said her name—*Awlma*—a name she had always hated until now. "Awlma," she tried, but it wasn't right. "Say it," she said, and he said, "Alma," pulling her hair aside, kissing the back of her neck, "Alma, Alma, Alma." He was up again, pressing it against her.

They made use of the fresh baby carrots they found in the refrigerator, of the jar of strawberry jam, of the canned sliced peaches. They made themselves slick with olive oil. Their knees slipped on the linoleum, they fell, laughing. In the dining room he bent her over the sideboard and, lubricated already, gave it to her in the French manner, as she'd called it the first time, when he'd asked if she wanted it that way. ("I'll let you, if that's what you mean.") A shaft of light fell over them from the kitchen, and he spread her buttocks and watched the livid rim she made around his cock. Her muscles fluttered. She brought his hand around to her front and made him rub her where she liked. He pulled out, almost, stopping at the edge of the rim, slowly started again. She let out a groan. He felt like a god. She worked herself, pressing his fingers with hers. And when he came he pushed in deep, rattling the decanters on the sideboard, the orgasm like a long wave that rose slowly, slowly, to an unbearable height, and then slowly, slowly faded.

Out in the living room she put on an Andrews Sisters record and danced around the room to "Rum and Coca-Cola," pulling her oiled hair up, a shiny nymph, while he watched from the sofa, trying to stroke himself back up. He was aching and depleted. She sang off-key, her voice too low for the melody—but the next number suited her better: "Bei Mir Bist Du Schön." A dim, red-light melody, a minor key, a strutting tempo. She flung herself back against the grizzly bear by the bookcase. He beckoned to her and she came to him and pulled him to the rug. Straddled his head and bent down to swallow him whole. She could always bring him back from the dead. He buried his face up into her, the dusky scent of her that he loved.

Then the windows stood out from the gloom, and suddenly—it always seemed to come so suddenly—it was time to go.

They lay on the rug, on pillows, a quilt spread out beneath them, tracing each other. Nothing was barred. He could know her completely. He knew places on her body that she would never know herself. He hid nothing from her either—mostly. He was shy of the calluses on his feet and kept them away from her. He clenched tight when her fingers went between his buttocks.

"Say my name," she whispered, tugging at his armpit hairs, and he said it, and she smiled and kissed him. "Now tell me you love me," she said.

It startled him. But it was easy to oblige, because he did love her, he thought: it had been on his lips all night, his all-encompassing need for her. "I love you," he said, running his hand over her stomach and over her breasts, caressed her chin and her lips, and kissed her. "Alma, Alma, I love you. I love you. I love you."

They showered together in the upstairs bathroom, rubbing the lavender soap onto each other's skin. It wasn't like the soap at Clara's, but the scent was light, and he hoped, if Effie smelled it on him, it wouldn't arouse suspicion. She leaned her forehead on his shoulder as the hot water beat down on them. He loved her long toes, her slender ankles, the healthy veins that crossed them. He loved her shins and knees and thighs, he loved the soft swell of her hips, he loved her belly button, he loved her ribs, he loved each of her moles and freckles individually, he loved her small breasts, the nipples, fairer than Effie's, that stood up half an inch when they were stimulated, as they were now, he loved her little attached earlobes, he loved the wet hair at her temples, he loved the smell of her head under his nose, he loved the warmth of her body, which seeped into his. He didn't think what it meant, only that he loved every part of her.

*T*uesday morning, seven o'clock. Blue sky, brisk fall breeze. He was pushing it this time. But he was only out for a walk, and to show he had nothing to hide, he strode in through the front door at Clara's and let the screen door slap shut behind him.

Effie appeared at the archway to the kitchen, holding a spatula. "There you are," she said, frowning. She was dressed already, bright and clean. Before now she hadn't risen until nine, but she was feeling better, clearly. "Lord, Henry, how early do you get up for these walks of yours?"

It was this damned insomnia, he explained. He came over to her and kissed her head, felt suddenly wretched. "I was up and down all night."

She didn't seem satisfied. "What's wrong?"

"Nothing," he said. "I don't know. I get this way sometimes."

If she suspected he was up to something, she said nothing about it. And it amazed him, because he felt like he was saturated with guilt, that it gave off a feral smell. But if you aren't looking for signs, he supposed, you are blind to them. She was making eggs, she said, if he wanted any. He did—and coffee, he was dying for coffee. He joined her in the kitchen, and while she finished the eggs and he made the coffee, he worried about Alma coming in, whether Effie would hear her, whether it would be enough for her to suspect. But then, from the stereo in the den, the sunny opening of Beethoven's "Pastoral" began, and a moment later Max strode in, singing, "Good morning, friends!"

There was music all morning. Beethoven, Strauss, Bedřich Smetana, the heavenly "Vltava." Henry dozed to it out on the patio. "Poor baby," Effie said, running her fingers through his hair. Max and Clara had decided, apparently, to take a break from work today. Max set himself to cleaning the pool, and as soon as he'd cleared the leaves from the surface he dove in, and Clara and Effie dove in after him, though the water was still green and full of who-knew-what. As if from a great distance, half asleep, Henry watched them splashing around, taking turns at the diving board, playing a game of Marco Polo. At some point he drifted off, behind a wall of light, their voices reaching him, the sighing of the trees overhead.

Now Alma appeared, finally—he didn't know what time it was—pirouetting out onto the patio to "Dance of the Sugar Plum Fairy," wearing white shorts and a striped T-shirt. The shorts made her legs look extra-long, like the little ice nymphs in *Fantasia*. She smiled at him. He smiled dreamily back.

"You're perky today," Clara said to her.

Max suggested they sail all the way to Atlantic City—it would take, what, two or three hours?—but the water was choppy, and they turned back to Cape May after an hour.

That evening, after grilled hamburgers and baked potatoes, while they played Max's dice game out on the patio, Effie pressed her hand between Henry's legs, where no one could see, and leaned into him and kissed him on the neck. Alma, across the table, met his eyes.

What could he do? He pulled Effie's hand away and muttered into her ear, "Hey, now."

"What?" she said.

He kissed her temple. "Save that for later."

"You promise?"

"I promise."

A little later, after ten, Alma went away.

And then it was eleven, and midnight, and one in the morning. Henry watched the clock over the bar. He nursed his drink, trying to stay alert. The rest of them got drunk.

They were playing Kings Cup, a drinking game with a deck of cards. It was Effie's idea, a game they'd played in high school, when they could get their hands on beer. Every card drawn had a rule to it—"two is you," "three is me," "five up high," "queens are girls." They made up most of the rules. If you drew an ace, you had to remove a piece of clothing. Max had come up with this one—and then drew the first ace. But he was only wearing trunks. Effie found this unbearably funny. Clara handed him the afghan, and he draped it over his lap and pulled his trunks off and tossed them to the rug. Effie drew the next one, and removed her engagement ring. ("Sorry, boo," she said.) There was some debate about whether it counted, but then, later, she drew the next one too, cried, "No!" and, laughing, facing away from them, removed her panties, held them up so Max and Clara could see—Henry laughed uncomfortably, unsure how he felt about this—and tossed them onto the sofa. When Clara drew the last one, she took her sundress off entirely and played the rest of the game in her underwear. She sat to Henry's right, her legs tucked under her, vast and white and soft as dough, and it was all he could do not to gape at her. He was distracted, he was hot and bothered, getting tipsy in spite of his best efforts, feeling more panicked with every minute that Alma waited for him, wishing at the same time that there was another ace and that Clara would draw it. Desire engendered desire. He wanted to fuck everyone. He was going mad.

Finally it was over, and he led Effie, stumbling drunk, her panties in her fist, up to their bed, where she fell on him in the dark, smothering him, clawing at him, pulling at his shorts. She'd never been this way before. They hadn't made love in almost a week. She felt soft and round and tender, and he sank into her, and the orgasm was like the sun breaking through clouds.

She groaned into his neck. "That was nice," she said. And then she was asleep.

The house was dark and quiet. He should have been half dead, but he was wide-awake. It was almost three in the morning. Alma was waiting.

Outside at last, in the black of a cloudy night, he ran down New Hampshire Avenue.

She was up on a footstool in the living room, looking at a row of ivory figures on a high shelf: a devil, a big-breasted woman, a tiger. She didn't acknowledge him when he entered. "Alma—God, Alma, finally. I couldn't get away. It was torture." He ran his hands up her legs and pressed his face to the back of her shorts. "I got here as soon as I could." He reached around to unbutton and unzip them but she stopped him, stepped down from the footstool, and turned to him.

"You were with her tonight, weren't you?" she said.

He'd been too late this time—he knew it. "I was with all of them," he said. "We were playing a stupid card game."

"I mean her—Effie. You were with her before you came here."

It was the first time she'd spoken her name. She didn't wait for him to answer. She crossed over to the bar, where, unlike her, she had poured herself a glass of scotch. "Alma," he said, going to her. "Alma, what's wrong?"

"Do you do it every night?"

"No," he said, reaching for her, but she backed away. "No, I swear. Tonight was the first. I couldn't—"

"I knew it." She laughed and turned away from him, set her glass down and went toward the sofa. "No wonder you're so late. You fucked her. And now you expect to fuck me. Two girls in one night. You're drowning in pussy, aren't you?"

"What am I supposed to do? She's my wife, for Christ's sake. I can't turn her away."

"Yes, you can." She laughed again. "Did you even wash yourself before you came over here?"

He didn't know what to say. Why was she being this way? He went to her and grabbed her arms. "I came here as fast as I could. I only want you. You're all I can think about. I love you."

"What do you want?" she asked.

"What? I want *you*. Only you."

"I mean," she said, "what are you going to do? What is this? Are you going to leave her?"

The question floored him. He let her go, stepped back. Of course he wasn't going to leave her. The thought had never entered his mind. But no other thought had entered his mind either, except to be alone with Alma, to touch her, to have her. The future had not been a consideration. That she was thinking about it astounded him. "I don't know," he said.

She stood looking at him with her arms crossed, waiting for him to say more.

"I don't know anything," he said. "I only know I want you."

"You can't have everything. You can't have this for free. You have to give me something."

"What can I give you? What do you want? I'll give you anything." He knew this wasn't true. He was being reckless.

"Just don't be with her," she said. "If you're with me, don't be with her too."

"How can I do that?"

"I don't know. Say you're sick. Say you're not in the mood. Just don't be with her."

"Alma, you have to be reasonable . . ."

"Don't be with her, Henry, or else don't touch me again. You were fawning over each other today—right in front of me, mocking me."

"That's not true."

"You were. Do you have any idea how that makes me feel? It drove me crazy, Henry. And then I have to sit here for four hours and imagine you fucking her, and I can't stand it. You're mine. Right now, you're mine, Henry. You're not hers."

To his amazement, there were tears in her eyes. He was gob-smacked. It took him a moment to collect himself. "Are you asking me to leave her?"

She wiped her eyes with a finger. "No," she said, and sighed. "I don't know. I'm crazy—I know I am."

A wave of tenderness spread through him. He took hold of her arms. "Alma, I'm sorry, I didn't mean to hurt you. I love you." He ran his hand over her hair. "I won't be with her," he said, not thinking of what he was saying, nevertheless sincere, "I won't be with her. It's just you, it's only you. Alma, I love you." He pulled her to him and kissed her, until eventually she uncrossed her arms and held him. "I love you," he said again, "I love you," and then: "Alma, do you hear? Do you love me too?"

"Yes," she said softly.

"Tell me."

"I love you."

"Tell me again."

"I love you, Henry."

At dawn they lay up in the tower, on the floor beside a small bed, on a quilted rug made of random colorful scraps of fabric in no discernible pattern. A floor lamp shone down on them. They'd spent most of the night talking, lying against each other, caressing each other. She told him she'd wanted him since the first day out on the boat, when she'd seen him with his shirt off, his muscles that had come, she knew, from good hard work. And when he spoke, that accent—it made her melt inside. She could imagine a home with him somewhere, his voice always reassuring her. He'd wanted her that day too, he said, when she stripped to her bathing suit and lay on the deck, and all that evening he hadn't been able to take his eyes off of her. She knew he was looking at her, she said, she'd always angle herself so he could easily see her legs, her ass—he knew it, he said—and after the night they'd stayed up together talking, she said, she knew she would have him. "You're very sure of yourself, aren't you?" he said. "I'm on my honeymoon, you know. I'd have to be a horrible man . . ." "I'm not usually so sure," she said. "But with you, I knew. Like it was fate." They talked about what it would be like if they ran away together, and where they would go. Everywhere. To Hawaii, to South Africa, to India, to Papua New Guinea. She needed the sea. He loved the sea too. Max would give her money—she could get it out of him. They wouldn't have to work. They would just eat and drink, fuck and sleep. And then they'd settle down somewhere, somewhere pretty and safe. They weren't talking seriously—he didn't think they were—it was just idle, but still the subject thrilled him. "I wish," he said. "I wish I could." She said nothing.

She was curled between his legs, resting her head on his thigh, running her finger up and down his penis, bringing it back to life, until it was taut and smooth. She touched a sore spot—he winced—and she apologized. He showed her where: a little raw patch. She inspected it closely, and kissed it. She caressed his testicles. He told her about the root of the word: *testify*. She laughed, lifted them gently to her nose, and breathed in. They smelled like pancake batter, she said.

After a bit of silence she asked, "What kinds of things does she do to you?"

"What?"

"Effie." She tugged at his hairs. "What's the wildest thing you've done together?"

"Why would you want to know that?"

She shrugged. "I just do."

She got up and straddled him, guided him into her, began rocking her hips. The light was growing brighter outside. He didn't care. He held her hips and told her about the night they'd walked naked together down the street. How he thought they'd seen her, Alma, from afar, walking along the promenade, and how seeing her had excited him. She smiled at him and moved his hand down her stomach and pressed his thumb to her little bulb. He told her they'd had sex on the neighbor's lawn, in the bright moonlight, and that part of what had made it so exciting was that she might see them—that she *would* have seen them, if she'd been walking down the street. That was the wildest thing they'd done, he said.

"We'll be wilder," she said.

"We already are," he said.

*I*t was almost eight in the morning when he returned to Clara's, but the house was still, and upstairs, Effie was fast asleep. He slipped into the bed beside her. He'd meant everything he'd said to Alma, every promise, but now, away from her, beside his wife, he felt lost and afraid. He saw the sanctuary of Signal Creek Methodist, the white crepe ribbons running down either side of the aisle, the pews filled with people in their finest clothes. Hoke and Maynard looking awkward in their suits. His mother in the front row on his side, beside Uncle Carswall. Reverend Miller smiling at him. He would never be able to face these people again. He could never go home. He couldn't imagine Alma there. Maybe years and years from now.

He fell asleep.

When he woke, Effie was gone, and it was the middle of the afternoon.

Alma was downstairs on the sofa in her green dress, reading. She beamed at him. "Look who's alive."

He was in a fog. A film lay over his eyes. He came down from the landing. "Where is everyone?"

"They took the boat out, per usual."

He didn't understand. They'd gone—Effie had gone—without him? "Why didn't anyone wake me up?"

"They tried. And then Effie said you'd been having a terrible case of insomnia or something." She laughed. "She said maybe it was a good idea to let you sleep."

"But . . ." He was still confused. Effie—with Max and Clara—had gone without him. He would never have gone anywhere without her.

"You look adorable right now, do you know that?" Alma stood up and came to him, put her arms around his neck and kissed him.

"Why aren't you with them?"

"I didn't feel like going out. I mean, enough with the boat."

"You love the boat."

"I love you more."

He smiled at her, slipped his arms around her waist. They were alone—he understood now—these were stolen hours.

"I told them I'd stay here until you woke up. Better than a note."

"That's nice of you."

"They'll be another couple of hours at least. Want to fuck?"

"You're going to kill me."

"You'll die happy."

They showered upstairs, and she brought him into her room. It must have been Scott's old room. Model airplanes hung from the ceiling. He recognized a Hellcat and a Corsair. On the floor was a small valise, which was empty, and Alma's clothes and underthings were scattered all over. He recognized all of it. She hadn't packed much.

She wanted to draw him. She took up her pad and pencil from the little desk by the window and made him pose back against the pillows, one arm behind his head, one knee bent, the foot of the other leg hanging off the side of the bed. She sat Indian-style at the end of the bed and began to work. Sunlight streamed through the open windows. Her breasts glowed. For the first time in days, he felt clean and well rested. For a long time they said nothing. He loved the look of concentration on her face, as she scratched the pencil on the paper, how intensely she looked at him. His penis wouldn't stay still. She laughed. She told him to hold it in place, where it naturally fell when he was on his back: angled slightly toward the right of his belly button. He held it, and then it was hard, and stayed there on its own. Perfect, she said. When she was finished she showed him, and he was shocked: there he was, exactly, lying back on the bed, legs spread, everything exposed. He'd never been drawn before. It made him shy to look. It reminded him of the view he'd had of himself when he was younger, with the hand mirror. She'd even got his tan lines, the shading, his mussed hair, even the furls in the sheets where his weight pressed into them. "That's amazing," he said. "Really. You're incredible."

She was pleased. "Thank you."

"I hope you won't leave that lying around," he said.

She gave the drawing an appraising look, closed the pad, and tossed it back onto the desk. "Don't worry. It's for my eyes only. I'll keep it forever."

He pulled her to him.

By the time the others returned, Alma had left the house, and Henry was lying on the sofa under the afghan, reading the book of H. P. Lovecraft stories.

"Baby, how are you?" Effie cried. "You're not angry we went with-out you, are you? I hated to leave you."

He wasn't angry at all. He'd needed the sleep. "I don't know, but I might be coming down with what you had."

"No!" She sat beside him on the sofa and pressed her cheek to his forehead. "You don't feel hot."

He told them Alma had gone out, he didn't know where. They'd stopped by the fish market and would have fried cod tonight. They were all exhausted. They'd overdone it last night. Tonight would be an early one. That sounded good to him.

Effie was tired but radiant. "Let's never leave," she said. "Let's just stay here forever."

"This is Circe's island," Clara intoned, "and I am Circe."

They didn't stay at the Bishops' house that night. It was still early— just after one in the morning—and the night was warm and clear. Henry wanted to go outside, under the stars, and Alma had an idea: they should go down to the beach and skinny-dip in the ocean. Henry still hadn't been in the ocean.

They left their clothes where they'd dropped them in the living room and went out the front door, and as they made their way down New Hampshire Avenue, toward Philadelphia, the same way he and Effie had gone—ages ago, it seemed—he felt the twinge of his be-trayal. This had been their secret, and now he was reenacting it with someone else. But the air on his skin was wonderful. The night was darker this time, the sky was teeming with stars. They came to the streetlights at Philadelphia and turned toward the sea, walking through the shadows of trees, over lit patches of exposed sidewalk— walking easily, without a care.

Beach Avenue was bright with streetlights and traffic lights, the lights along the promenade. They kept to the shadow of a motel on the corner and peered up and down the street, to make sure no one was coming. Then they dashed across the street, up the steps to the promenade, and down the long, sloping ramp into the darkness of the beach.

On this side of the promenade the sound of the waves surrounded them, though the tide was out, and they walked over a vast moonscape of soft, dry sand, cool under their feet. The darkness wasn't impenetrable. By the lights of Beach Avenue, and by the brighter lights of the hotels farther down, their pale bodies were illuminated and exposed, and yet it wasn't until they were almost upon it that they saw a large rowboat half-buried in the sand, the words "Cape May" painted on its side in blue letters. The light was deceptive out here. Henry could see its sources, brightly, and by it he could see Alma vividly beside him, but if she walked a few paces ahead she was almost entirely lost in the dark. They were hidden here, and safe. The faint glow of the Milky Way arced down toward the horizon. Finally they reached the smooth, damp, cold sand that was easier to walk over, and they made their way quickly to the edge of the surf.

It struck their feet, icy cold, and Alma shrieked and took hold of him, pressing her body against his. The surf was high but not frighteningly so. It crashed and made a glowing field all around them. They waded farther in, the depth varying with the waves: now it was at his shins, now it was halfway up his thighs. The water stunned him. The first time it struck his balls he cried out, and Alma laughed and dragged him farther ahead, but by then the water was going out and it was only to his knees.

"You just have to dive in," she said.

"It's freezing," he said. "I can't do it."

"Of course you can. Be a man."

She bounded in up to her waist—one last flash of her behind—and dove headlong into the next wave. The same wave struck Henry's middle, shocking his skin with cold, and a moment later he saw Alma's head and shoulders several yards ahead of him. He forged on, all of his muscles seizing. The water here was an element entirely different from the creek where he'd skinny-dipped back home, where the water caressed his skin in the summer. There the water was domesticated, here it was wild. The next breaker hit him square in the face, tumbled him over in darkness, and for the first time he tasted the heavy salt of the ocean in his mouth and nose. The saltiness, the intensity of it, surprised him. He got his footing back and stood up, and still he was only waist-deep, and Alma was an indistinct shape beyond the breakers.

"Come on," she cried, "swim for your life."

"I'm trying," he shouted back.

"Get past where it breaks. You have to dive into it. It's calm out here."

He let the next wave hit his chest, waded farther in as the sea drew back again, and when he saw the next wave coming he dove beneath it, pushed forward with his feet, and swam as hard as he could against the current.

When he surfaced, the ground had disappeared beneath him. The sea swelled, lifting and dropping him, and he treaded furiously to keep up with it, until he willed himself to relax and rode the pushing, jarring waves—stroking up the slopes, gliding back down. For a moment he couldn't see Alma, he faced the open sea, thousands of miles of it ahead of him, above him nothing but the stars—but there she was, farther out now, up on a swell: he could just see her waving at him. He swam toward her, working against the current. Already he was out of breath. His skin was numb. He rolled onto his back and kicked and pushed—he could swim more powerfully on his back— and a few minutes later, finally, he was level with her.

"I thought you'd never make it," she said.

"It's"—he felt like he'd been in a sprint—"it's exhausting."

They were twenty, thirty yards out past the breakers. The lights along Beach Avenue glowered at them.

"It's amazing, isn't it?" she said.

"It's amazing. Yes."

His voice trembled, his teeth were chattering, the salt water stung his sinuses. She told him to lie on his back and catch his breath, and he did.

The sea was gentler here. He moved his arms and legs easily and his body rode the swells. The stars seemed not so far away now: an arbor of luminous, low-hanging grapes. When he'd caught his breath he pitched upright again and dove under.

They floated, dove, treaded water close enough to see each other's faces. On one dive she found him and took hold of him, their limbs intertwining, her skin as slick as an eel, and he panicked and kicked free. When they surfaced, she was laughing. He laughed too, but kept his distance. Out here, he thought, the elements meant business. He thought of undertows and riptides, he thought of sharks and giant squid, he thought of the immense spaces hidden in the dark. In an instant any one of these things could erase him.

Alma treaded close to him again. "I'm peeing at this very moment," she said. "Can you feel it?"

He laughed wildly. Everything felt exaggerated. "You're disgusting," he cried.

"This is what disgusts you?" she said. "We're in the sea. We're nothing but animals."

He relaxed, and let himself go too, and felt the warmth of it spread up his abdomen. Alma leapt on him and pulled him under again.

They were drifting, fast—they were even now with one of the big hotels. It was a strong current, Alma said. It would play itself out. Or they could swim in, walk back up the beach, and go in for another ride. They treaded in the current until they were almost to the town center, before one of the large piers, and started in. Heavy swells again, and then the pounding surf. It was impossible to see the waves coming out of the dark, from behind—one struck him and toppled him head over heels. But he made the beach, and found Alma waiting for him. She took his hand, and they made their way back up to where they'd started.

They rode the current again and again. A half-moon rose—giant at first over the sea, the color of a paper lantern, then smaller and brighter as it rose higher, casting a broad silver river over the ocean. The stars dimmed, the sky brightened with moonlight. He could see Alma's face in the water now, her nipples when she floated on her back or leapt from the waves like a mermaid. He'd become acclimated to the cold, but gradually the heat left his body, until he was shivering constantly. But he didn't want this to end—he'd let himself die of hypothermia.

Back on the beach she hugged him, rubbed his arms and back as the surf ran over their ankles, cupped him until his scrotum relaxed in her palm. They sat on the smooth, wet sand, just out of reach of the surf, huddling close. He had never been so in love with anyone. His voice trembled, from the cold, from his nerves. Their bodies were silver. They were nymphs of the sea. "We can just run away together," he said. "There doesn't have to be a scene. We can just go."

"We can go tonight," she said.

"Not tonight," he said. "We need to prepare. Pack a bag. Meet at the house tomorrow night, maybe, like usual."

"There's tons of clothes and things there."

"Yes. Meet there and get whatever we need, then go to the train station."

"We'll need to go to New York first. I have things I want at Max's."

"I've never been to New York."

"From there we could go anywhere. We could take a ship to Europe if we wanted."

"I don't have much money with me."

"I have some. Max would give me more—as much as I wanted."

"Do you think he would? Do you think he'd approve of this, I mean?"

"He'd think it was all funny, probably. He'd be glad to get me out of his hair."

"I can't believe I'm doing this."

"I can't believe my luck. That we found each other."

"I love you so much, Alma."

"Say it again."

"I love you, I love you."

She smothered him in kisses and he ran his hands all over her, trembling, and pulled her on top of him. When he came, he didn't pull out but pushed into her deeper, squeezing her to him, feeling their hearts thumping together.

They watched the moon rise, hypnotized by the sound of the waves. The wind picked up and the surf crept toward them, reaching their feet. Alma said, "Oh," and sat up, and he sat up, too, to see what she saw: a haze of light stretched over the horizon, and everything around them—the sheen of the sand below the tide line, a lifeguard's station close by, the big pier to their right, the hotels behind them—was clearly visible.

They ran to the surf to wash the sand off of them and started back up the beach. They were at least a quarter mile from where they'd entered, and as they jogged back along the smooth part of the sand, the sky grew brighter until, by the time they reached the ramp up to the promenade at Philadelphia Avenue, the sun had pierced the horizon and they were two naked people in the clear morning. Alma covered her breasts and crotch as they streaked across Beach Avenue. Henry saw headlights approaching from afar, down near the town center, and they ran down Philadelphia until they reached New Hampshire, rounded the corner, stopped to catch their breaths. No more cars. They had nothing to fear. It was a beautiful morning. They strolled easily the rest of the way down the street to the Victorian house. He took her hand. She smiled at him.

It was after seven. It seemed impossible that so much time had passed. Effie was likely up already, but it didn't matter. They ran a hot shower and lingered in it for a long time.

"Tonight, then, my love," she said down in the foyer, seeing him out.

"Yes. Tonight." He kissed her.

"It'll be torture until then."

"It'll only be a short time now."

"Are we really going to do this?"

"Yes."

"If you don't come, Henry . . ."

"I'll come. I'll be here. Just wait for me."

Eleven

He could hear them laughing in the kitchen when he arrived. It was after nine. He went up the stairs. The guest room smelled like Effie now, the light cedar that hung around her and suffused the Tarleton household and that still reminded him, when he noticed it, of their first days together as a couple, only last year, when he'd visit her at her house. He sat on the bed and stared at his open suitcase. She'd done their laundry yesterday and hung it out on the clothesline in the backyard, and now his clothes, even his underwear, were folded and placed neatly back in the suitcase. As if she'd packed for his departure. The care she'd taken broke his heart. He felt, suddenly, sick to his stomach. He couldn't think about this right now. When the time came, he wouldn't think at all. He'd just go. He'd leave the suitcase behind.

"There he is," Clara said, smiling brightly, when he came into the kitchen. The three of them were sitting at the table, the remnants of breakfast in front of them.

"I guess you aren't sick," Effie said, "if you were out walking."

"No," he said, "I think I'm fine." He bent down to kiss the top of her head. She didn't move her hands from her coffee cup. He sat at the table.

"Still can't sleep?" Max said.

"Not well."

"I can make you an egg if you want," Effie said. "There's some bacon over there."

"I'm fine for now."

She seemed slightly cold. He scrambled to think what might be the matter—what she might know. But then she brightened, looking past him, and said, "Hey, honey."

Alma had come into the kitchen, looking refreshed, wearing her brown dress with the white polka dots. She laughed. "I love when you call me honey." She took a piece of bacon and leaned on her elbows at the island counter, obviously in a good mood. "What are you all up to today? Let me guess: sitting around, drinking, going sailing."

"And what are you going to do?" Max said.

"I think I'll take my leave today," she said.

"What's that, dear?" Clara said.

"I'm going back to New York."

Henry went cold. They hadn't discussed this. She didn't look at him.

"Oh, no," Effie said, and made a pouting face. "That's too sad."

"You're just going—by yourself?" Max said.

"Why not? I don't want to break up all the fun. You all keep on frolicking."

"Alma . . ."

"Max," she said, standing up straight, holding her hands out, "everything is fine here. I just want to go home, that's all. I'm okay. You don't have to worry about me."

"But what about the city being miserable, everyone's mean and ugly, you'll never have a home and all that jazz?"

Her face hardened for a moment. "I feel differently now. Honest, Max, this trip, I think it's been good for me. I've had a lot of time to think. I want to go back and maybe apply for some jobs. Magazines. Fashion houses. You were right."

"That sounds wonderful, dear," Clara said.

"What's going on?" Max said. "When did all this happen?"

"This week," Alma said, and pointed to her temple. "Up here."

He still seemed confused. He made to say something, then stopped. "Well, if you're set on it," he said.

"I am. I'll just go up and pack my things. I can stay for lunch."

"I'm not sure when the last train leaves," Clara said. "You might want to get to the station before then."

Alma gave her an even look.

"I'll drive you," Max said.

"It's not a long walk," Alma said.

"Alma. I'm not going to let you drag your suitcase across town. I'll drive you."

"I hate to see you go," Henry said.

So she was doing it. She was setting it in motion already. Max would take her to the station, and she'd make the walk back to the Victorian house, where she would wait for him, her valise all packed. It was happening too fast, and he felt disoriented and outside of himself. He was already trembling with nerves. But it would take nothing to set off this cataclysm—the simplest of actions. All he'd have to do is go outside and walk, meet her, and keep on walking. Under cover of night. They'd go back to the station and wait. She'd know the timetable. The train would arrive, they'd get onto it, and then they'd be on their way to New York.

She came downstairs with her little valise. Under her arm she held her drawing pad with his picture in it. She set them both down at the bottom of the stairs. For travel she'd put on heels and stockings, she'd put her makeup on, and from her neck hung a small pendant

with a blue gem in it. She looked pretty and respectable. Like someone he could bring home to his mother.

They said their farewells. A cursory hug from Clara, a warm em-
brace from Effie. She hugged Henry last, a quick, friendly goodbye.

"I hope we'll meet again sometime," she said to them both.

"We'll look you up—you and your brother—if we're ever in New
York," Effie said.

"Yes, please."

She took up her valise and drawing pad and followed Max out
the door.

"Sweet relief!" Clara cried when they were gone. "I feel like the
clouds have parted."

"You're terrible," Effie said. "I like her. She's . . . *cool.*"

"Right." Clara started for the bar. "We're out of Champagne, but
you're a good Christian, maybe you can tell me: where in the Bible
does it say you can't have a gin and tonic before lunch?"

Henry said he'd love one too. Effie said to make it three, she didn't
want to feel left out.

They made ham sandwiches with pimento cheese and ate them
out by the pool. The sun was bright but the temperature had dropped
over the course of the morning, and by noon, for the first time in
days, it felt like fall. Like it was supposed to feel in the middle of
October. They finished their sandwiches and went back inside. Clara
closed the patio doors. Max had been gone for over an hour, and
Henry began to worry what was taking him so long. Maybe she'd
decided to tell him everything, to ask him for money before she left,
and they were fighting now, and soon he'd come to beat Henry to a
bloody pulp. Or maybe he'd caught a peek at the drawing somehow,
and the same scene was playing out. The gin helped calm his nerves.
He made himself another drink, and Clara joined him. Effie put on
a Johnny Mercer record. He was a good Georgia boy, she said. Was
he, really? Clara said. Effie said Henry should build a fire—yes, a fire

would be nice, Clara said—and as he began stacking the wood, Max returned at last. Alone. Henry watched him closely. But there seemed to be no change in his manner.

"Ah, good, a fire. It's getting nippy out there."

"You were gone an eternity," Clara said.

"I wanted to see her off."

"Really, Maxie, you didn't have to sit with her. She's a grown woman."

"I think it's precious how you worry over her," Effie said.

Before he could stop himself, Henry said, "She got on the train?"

It was stupid of him. But he was confused. Max smiled at him, a smile he couldn't read. "Does that surprise you?"

Effie was looking at him too, sweetly blank, registering only that he'd spoken.

"I mean," he said, "you waited with her until she got on the train."

"Because," Clara cut in, "he thinks she'll run off with the circus or something if he isn't watching her. Honestly, Maxie."

The moment passed. Max rubbed his hands together and said how about that fire. Like a dummy he'd driven with the top down. Clara said he should have a drink too, and join the party.

Gradually the day turned dusky and windy outside, but inside they were warm. The fire was strong. There was no question of sailing. They made more drinks, and the gin made Henry feel nicely cocooned. Effie manned the record player. She was on a kick of elegant crooners—Frank Sinatra, Johnny Mathis, more Johnny Mercer. Max teased her for her taste, but she didn't care, she was a romantic, she said. They settled into their usual places, listening to music, talking, drinking, passing the time until dinner.

The more hours separated him from Alma, the more the whole thing seemed unreal. Like a fever dream. Effie put her feet up on

Henry's lap and he massaged them, and she smiled and closed her eyes. He lifted her foot and kissed it, and she squirmed and said it tickled.

Alma had gotten on the train. Which meant she was either on her way to New York without him, or she was trying to make her way back. Maybe she'd gotten out at the first stop—Egg Harbor? Atlantic City?—and was now waiting on a platform for the next train back, intent, whatever it took, on making it to the Victorian house tonight. Max had insisted on seeing her off, so she'd had to get on the train or else tell him everything, which might have led to disaster. But would it really have been so hard to make him leave? She could have said, *Max, Jesus, I just want to be alone*—and he'd have shaken his head, eventually, and left her. *Fine, whatever you want.* But she'd gotten on the train. And maybe, he thought now, maybe it was because she'd had the same misgivings he was having—that had been roiling in him all along, that in fact had made the idea of running away with her so exciting—and as soon as they'd parted, she'd come to her senses and understood they were being foolish, that they'd been drunk on each other, and determined that the only way to put an end to it was to go away, as soon as possible. That was why she'd seemed so determined when she told them she was leaving. It had not been a ruse: she was going home.

By six they were hungry but fairly tipsy already, and no one felt like cooking. As a group they went back into the kitchen and scoured the refrigerator for leftovers. A bowl of rice and beans. The baked chicken from Sunday, a couple of hamburger patties from Tuesday. Bread and butter and garlic. Smoked gouda and soda crackers. Clara put the chicken and hamburgers onto a baking sheet to warm in the oven, and they carried everything back out to the coffee table. Max opened a new bottle of gin. Effie put on a Bing Crosby record. They settled around the table and ate.

She was on her way to New York—away from him, out of his life forever. It was clear to him now. Of course they were never going to run away with each other. He had known it all along, and so had she. It had been a wild game, intensely lifelike. He wished they could have said a proper goodbye. But what would a proper goodbye have looked like? He respected the way she'd gone. Simple and clean, no words. She was gone, but he would have the vivid memory of her for the rest of his life. He felt as if he'd escaped with a precious gem, something he'd hold close and take with him to his grave, and no one would ever know, only the two of them. He'd be loyal to her in his dreams. He would always love her.

But now, he had to admit, he felt safe. As if he'd arrived home out of a frightening storm.

Clara lay down on the rug by the coffee table, having finished her plate, and stretched her arms and legs out long like a cat. She was wearing a white-and-green flowered dress, and when she stretched, her bosom swelled and the top edge of her bra peeked out. She sat up and leaned back on her hands. "I'm so, so very glad it's just the four of us," she said. "I felt like we couldn't be ourselves," she added, to Max. "No offense to her."

"I know," Max said from the armchair. "Let's not talk about it anymore."

"I hope we aren't inhibiting you too," Effie said. She was down on the rug too, with Henry, leaning back against the sofa, her warm hand on his leg. They were full. It felt good. He hadn't had much of an appetite all week.

"Are you kidding?" Clara said. "You make everything more interesting. I wish it weren't so chilly out. We could go skinny-dipping in the pool."

Henry's senses quickened, but she was looking at Effie, who shrugged and answered coolly: "I told you, I'd do it if it was warmer."

"Really?" Henry said, and she smiled at him.

"If you approved," she said. "If you did it too."

Clara held up her glass. "Henry would approve. He's no stick in the mud."

He laughed uncertainly. "I hope not."

"There's always Kings Cup," Max said.

"That was fun," Clara put in. "I'd play that again."

"We could make it a dare. Pull the ace of spades and you have to strip and jump into the pool."

"Not in this world," Effie said. "I would refuse."

"There would be a penalty."

"I don't care." She shook the ice in her glass. "Could you replenish me, boo?" she asked, and he said of course and struggled to his feet—he'd better slow down, he told himself—and took their glasses over to the bar.

Clara got up too, and joined him, and as she waited for him to pour the gin she stood close to him, close enough that he could smell her Chanel perfume and feel the warmth of her skin. "I hope it rains the rest of the week," she said. "I just want to nest in here and forget the rest of the world."

"That sounds nice."

"Do you know the world could be ending right now, there could be war with Russia, and none of us would know it?" She took the gin from him. "I suppose we'll have to go home someday," she said. "Assuming it's still there. But not just yet."

It occurred to him, as he handed Clara the tonic, that he wasn't quite sure what day it was—Wednesday, Thursday, or Friday—nor how long it had been since he and Effie had called their parents. "Is there a phone here?" he asked.

"Do you need to make a call?"

"I just realized we never gave our folks a number or address. Nobody's got a way to reach us."

Clara laughed, and put her hand on his arm. "Oh, baby, you're lost in the woods, aren't you? Don't worry, you're safe here."

"I just mean they might be worried."

"We'll call them tomorrow."

They settled back around the coffee table to play Kings Cup again. Skinny-dipping was out—the wind outside was rattling the window-panes. Clara suggested an alternative, to keep things exciting: if you drew an ace, you had to play the rest of the game in your underwear, like she had done the other night. What if you drew a second ace? Effie asked. Then you got to choose someone else to do it, Max suggested. Effie laughed. "We might as well get down to our undies right now."

"No," Clara said. "It has to happen naturally."

"I think this game's rigged," Effie said to Henry.

"It's good, clean fun," Clara said. "We're all adults here."

"I'm game," Henry said. He was feeling expansive and excited. Thrilled and relieved from his escape, the wild memory of Alma locked safely away, the comfort of his wife beside him, the unspeakable possibilities that were upon them now, which they could share. And anyway, it wasn't a big deal, it was like being in trunks and bikinis.

Max set the deck of cards at the center of the table and they started. Henry's reflexes were terrible. If someone drew a four, they all had to put their thumbs to the edge of the table, and the last one had to drink. Henry took tiny sips, but the gin went down so easily. Fives were high—everyone raised their hands—and this time it was Clara who was distracted. "Fuck," she said, and drank. Max drew a joker, which meant he could make up a rule on the spot. Until the next joker was drawn, he said, they all had to speak with a British accent, and anyone who slipped had to drink. For Henry this was easy, he'd always been good with voices, but Effie's entire understanding of the English way of speaking seemed to rest on beginning every sentence with the words "I say"—"I say, dear Max, could you spare a girl a cigarette?"—and the rest of them, Henry included, could barely contain themselves. Max ordered Effie to drink, and drink again. "I'm just going to shut my mouth, dammit," she said, which forced another drink.

Henry drew the first ace—"Bingo!" Clara cried (in a British accent, impressively)—and groaning, as though he dreaded it, he removed his oxford shirt and trousers, tossed the bundle behind him, and sat Indian-style in his thin, baby-blue boxers. Effie laughed, leaned into him, and kissed him. He was in no danger of an erection, his nerves kept it down, but no matter what he did with it, the slit at the front of his boxers gaped open in Clara's direction. She wasn't looking, she was concentrating on the rounds. He missed the five-up-high and had to drink.

He drew the second ace as well, and was forced to choose. They all looked at him. "Who's it gonna be?" Clara said. Effie to his left, Clara to his right, but both were fraught, and so he chose Max across from him.

"Hank," he said. "I had no idea." He pulled his T-shirt and khaki shorts off, complained jokingly of a draft, and got up to put another log on the fire. He wore tight white briefs, and his bulge was indecent. Henry saw anew his thick athlete's build, which didn't square with all the loafing and gorging they'd been doing the past two weeks, and supposed he lived a different life in New York. While he stoked the fire Effie stared openly at him and laughed, her cheeks bright pink, but Henry didn't care. The gin made everything fluid. He leaned back on his hands and stretched his legs out in front of him, let anyone who cared see the open gap in his boxers.

Effie drew the third one. She was wearing one of the modest dresses he knew from church, and he helped her with the zipper in the back. She shimmied it up over her waist and with effort pulled it up over her head and off. "Huzzah," Clara said. She wore a pointy tan bra and matching panties, open lace at the hips. She hugged her knees to her chest and said, "Don't look at me, I'm a whale"—"Drink," Max said—and Clara said, "You're an angel, my little belle"—"You drink too."

For the rest of the game, Clara was the only one dressed. Henry drew the other joker, and said they all had to speak like Southerners now. "Not fair," Max said, and Henry ordered him to drink. But there were only a few cards left. Max picked up the last one—the final ace—and without having to be told, Clara reached back to unzip her dress, pushed the shoulder straps off, and worked it down past her hips, down her legs, and kicked it away. She wore mismatched underwear—white bra, blue panties. "Free at last," she said, and Henry admired her without restraint, the soft, broad expanse of her. She smiled at him. "Should we play again?"

"No!" Effie cried. "I won't be able to stand up anymore."

Nevertheless, she asked Henry to refresh her drink, and he went back to the bar with both of their glasses. Max put on another log. He'd been right, there was a draft in the room—Henry could feel it by the bar—but instead of putting their clothes back on they huddled closer to the fire, which Max had stoked up high. Clara took a few pillows down from the couch. The music had stopped long ago, and Effie got up to put another record on. She read the back of a record, holding her left leg out *en tendu,* and put on Vic Damone, "On the Street Where You Live." She sang *la-di-da* to the melody, swept back to them, and by the couch spread her arms out and spun around a few times, until she stumbled, laughed at herself, and plopped down on the floor beside Henry. She lay back and stretched her legs over his lap, and he ran his hands over her bare skin. A few strands of hair peeked out from the edge of her underwear, and he tucked them back in. He wasn't bothered. It excited him that they might see. She smiled at him. "I'm sure I'll be embarrassed about this in the morning," she said.

"No, my belle," Clara said. She lay close to them on her side, her back to the fire, head propped on her hand. "There's nothing to be embarrassed about. We're all in it together." She reached out and ran the back of her fingers over Effie's arm. "It's nice, isn't it?"

"Very nice."

On his way back from the bar Max turned out the end-table light. The big den was dark all around them, but the fire was warm and bright. When Vic Damone finished singing, there was only the wind outside and the crackling of the fire. Things seemed to have become serious. Max was telling them about certain problems with his novel (the U.S. airman on leave in Italy, the torrid affair with the woman in Tuscany), a problem of diction, specifically: there were no words in the English language to capture the immediacy of their actions and emotions. He thought it was because Anglo-Saxons had so thoroughly cut themselves off from sexuality. Max's points had a tendency to become complicated when he was drunk, and Henry only partly followed them. He was drunk too, and at the same time alert, his heart beating strongly, his armpits sweating. Effie sat up to sip her drink. She looked down at her breasts and adjusted them, leaned back, and seemed to admire the firelight shining on her bosom. "I told you," she said over her shoulder, "you're writing a love story."

"No," Max said. "It's just a game for them. It's not love. They're both traumatized, you see. By the war. They're trying to forget themselves. What I'm trying to get at is the act, the intensity of it, which I think is profound, but it's almost impossible to express."

"What I've read is beautiful," Clara said. Max was leaning back with his ankles crossed and she was rubbing her toes lightly over his bulge, and with a primal longing Henry saw that he was hard under his briefs. It was angled to the side, threatening to pop out of the top.

"Whatever you say," Effie said. "It's a love story."

Max laughed. "Okay. How so?"

"I just mean it'll be advertised that way, whatever you have to say about it. I mean I haven't read it, so don't listen to me. But I bet you'd be best to focus on the love stuff instead of all that other mess."

"All that other mess is the point."

"Well," Effie said, and let it go at that, leaning back, shaking her hair out behind her, rubbing her legs together over Henry's lap.

"Women like to feel," Clara said dreamily. "Men like to see." She dropped her head back to look at Henry. "What do you think?"

"I don't know," he said. He felt flummoxed. "I don't really follow, honestly. I think I like both."

They had another round, and settled into the subject of love and sex. Max said love was multifaceted—part involuntary desire, part empathy, and part something willed, like a code of ethics. Effie laughed at him and said he was very smart, wasn't he. Clara said love and sex had nothing to do with each other, and that she'd had sex, maybe her best sex, with men she despised. Max said that wasn't true, she adored him. They were both shocked, and then delighted—Clara was delighted—to learn that Henry had been a virgin until about two and a half weeks ago. No, Henry said, he would not describe it. Effie said there were certain things that were none of their business— but then she smiled, as if to invite them to ask again. She said there was no prohibition in the Bible against enjoying sex, none that she knew of. God had given them these bodies, and they were meant to feel.

They didn't finish the next round. They were destroyed. But Henry had the feeling they were all, like himself, acutely alert, focused on the same obscure object. They had come to this point deliberately. Max moved behind Clara and held her—she was cold, she said— and eventually he was kissing her shoulder and running his hand over her stomach, and after a while, he slipped it into her underwear.

Effie found this funny. Henry couldn't take his eyes away. He saw the feathered edges of her pubic hair, which was light as wool. Clara hoped they weren't embarrassing them—they were just fooling around. Effie said it was a free country, they could do what they wanted. Henry didn't mind, either. They spoke softly. It was just a little fooling around. It was exciting. They could watch. They could watch each other. They were flickering shades, bare skin in the fire-light, half illuminated. The dark made it all right. Max leaned back on his elbows and Clara pulled his briefs off. He had a large, thick penis, bronze in the light, an upward curve to it that struck Henry as diabolical. The balls of a horse. Clara stroked it. Henry and Effie watched. Effie opened her legs, and Henry pushed her underwear aside at the groin. He hadn't felt her in so long. Her prodigious hair, her plump labia. She was soaked. He rubbed her where Alma had liked it, and she sighed, closed her eyes, clutched the cup of her bra, opened her eyes again to see. Clara's head was down in Max's lap, and he was kneading her back, concentrating, silent. They were all silent now. She'd freed her breasts, and they hung heavily from her. She was on her knees, her hips and thighs within Henry's reach, and Henry longed to touch her but held back. He wouldn't cross that line by himself. Effie was closer to Clara's head, and while Henry rubbed her she looked down on it as if in pain—until she reached her hand out and pulled Clara's hair away from her face, so she could see, and a tormented look came into her face, and she sighed deeply. That was the line. There was no turning back. It was the look on her face, so transfixed and free of self-consciousness. Henry took his hand away from Effie and reached for Clara, her great expanse of skin, to touch her soft thighs and hips, to feel if her underwear was damp like Effie's, and in the next instant, it seemed, she was facing him, up on her knees and surrounding him. She reached down and drew his cock out from his boxers and stroked him. Effie, beside him, was oblivi-ous, her head thrown back. Max was behind her, kissing her neck, pulling the straps off her shoulders, moving his hands down to cup her breasts. *Henry,* Clara said. Her breath was hot in his ear. *Henry. Do you mind this?* He didn't mind it. He wanted it. Her breasts filled all the space in the room. He gripped them. He sucked her nipples. He reached between her legs, into her underwear, and felt a vast, dense carpet there, felt her open, wet, on his fingers. He breathed in the scent of Chanel—and suddenly came, and looked down to see a glaze over her fingers. She whispered, *Oh, baby,* stroking him still, *oh, you came, I made you come,* and she smiled, and kissed his lips. *Just don't stop. I'm not through with you yet.* He wasn't going to stop, he said. She drew away from him and pulled his boxers down, he freed himself from them, and she bent down and enveloped him with her mouth. He was stunned, and in ecstasy. Effie's underwear was stretched tight between her knees and Max's hand was down below, lost in shadow. One of her feet was pressed against Henry's hip, and he felt her toes grip his skin. Henry saw them as if from afar, as if they had nothing to do with him. He felt a dull ache, like longing, when he saw her reach back and put her little hand around Max's cock. And then Clara nudged him onto his back and got on top of him, sat up and straddled him, her breasts looming, and covered his stomach. She was warm and slick. She brought her groin to him and he filled his mouth with it. She was tart from the long day. He turned her over and sank in, buried from nose to chin. She was bottomless. She couldn't hold still. She rolled him over again, lay on him, wanted to feel his skin all over her. Straddled him again, and reached behind her to feel him. His erection was indestructible. She slid back onto it. *Oh. Oh, Henry. There you are, finally.* She moved her hips back and forth and in circles. He pushed up into her. *Oh,* she tilted her head back, *oh, oh.* And he closed his eyes, lost in her, imagining he could float forever up into her generous body, until after a time he heard Effie softly crying, and brought himself up to his elbows to see. She lay under Max a few feet away, her neck arched back so her face was almost upside down—eyes closed, lips parted—and she drew her knees up as Max's hips slowly undulated between her legs. His face was buried in the crook of her neck, his hand ran up her side and over her breast, and he seemed to smother and overwhelm her. They were half-moons and lighted curves. They were a riddle Henry couldn't work out. He was mesmerized. Effie dug her fingers into Max's back. He wished she would look at him, but she was nowhere near him. Clara pulled his attention back to herself—*Oh, Henry, you feel so good, baby*—and he gripped her savagely. She fell forward and put her weight on her hands, and between her breasts he watched his silhouetted cock pump up into her groin. She got down to her elbows and breathed into him, *Oh—oh, you're going to make me come,* and he sank his teeth into her shoulder, trying to concentrate on the feel of her all around him. But all he could hear was Effie's breath, her whimpering and panting, noises he'd never heard her make before. And he couldn't keep himself from looking. Max held the backs of her knees. She clawed the rug. If only she would look at him—to say, I'm here, I'm with you. But all the world, including Henry, seemed to have fallen away from her, and there was only her body, and Max's. Clara, breathing heavily into his ear, asked if he was okay, and he said he was fine, he only needed a minute, and she sighed and slumped beside him. And he watched as Max turned Effie over and brought her up to her knees. Saw the thick, bronze cock slide into her from behind. Heard her bellowing into the crook of her arm. Watched until, at last, he groaned and pushed forward, bent her spine and then flattened her onto her stomach, lay heavy on her back, groaning still, moving his hips as if to burrow himself entirely inside of her, and when he rolled off, finally—withdrew his curved, evil-looking cock—she was splayed out on her stomach, and the insides of her thighs shone wet in the firelight.

He felt sick, suddenly. He drew away from Clara and got unsteadily to his feet.

"Where are you going, baby?" Clara said.

"I need to go to bed," he said. He started for the stairs, not bothering to search for his clothes, stumbled into an end table, found the banister, and made his way carefully up. He was going to be sick. He felt his way into the upstairs bathroom, closed the door, didn't bother finding the light. Avoided his ghoulish reflection in the mirror. Fell onto his knees and vomited into the toilet.

He lay on the floor for a while in the dark, waiting for the nausea to pass. The tiles were cold. He expected someone—Effie—to knock and ask him what was wrong, but no one did. His little Effie, his wife: he didn't know her anymore. What she'd done, what she'd let him do to her. It was one thing for Henry, but for her, his wife, his girl. A lady. He should have stopped it before it started, he should never have let it go so far. But he didn't know himself either. A degenerate with no fixed center. Less than a man. Only yesterday he'd been professing his love to Alma, promising that he'd run away with her, and no sooner had she left than . . . He wished she hadn't gone, that they had run away together. But that was only because he wanted to erase himself.

Out in the upstairs hall the fire faintly revealed the balcony rail, and he turned away from it and felt his way into the guest room. Fell onto the bed. She wasn't there. Her absence turned his stomach. He slipped under the covers, and he was still awake when, sometime later—he didn't know how long, but he was relieved—she came into the room. She sat on the bed in the dark and was still for a moment. She must have been dying of shame. He listened for her crying, for her to call his name—he wasn't sure he would have answered—but she only sighed, finally, and lay down. He turned his back to her and lay as far away from her as he could.

Twelve

When he woke, she was gone, and the room was bright. He had no idea what time it was.

The night swiftly asserted itself. It settled like ice in his stomach.

The wardrobe stood open and empty. On the ledge of the bay window lay Effie's suitcase, and on the floor below it, his own. So they were leaving. At the foot of the bed, on the corner farthest from him, clean clothes had been set out for him.

He heard voices down on the patio. Clara's laughter. He got up from the bed and went to the window, covering his groin, pointlessly, with his hands. They were all sitting together at the round table by the pool. Max and Clara. And Effie. It was sunny out, but they were dressed for the fall. Effie wore her cashmere sweater. She was nodding at something Max was saying, her expression mild. The scene confounded him. How comfortable they all seemed together.

He dressed and went quickly downstairs and out to the patio, thinking vaguely that he would catch them out. It was a brilliant day, cool under the sun. Clara was standing in one of her bright sundresses, a shawl over her shoulders, gathering plates from the table, and when she saw him she greeted him warmly. "Henry, dear. There he is."

"Hey, boo," Effie said.

He stopped before the table. "What's going on here?"

"You're leaving us, apparently," Clara said, let out a mirthless laugh, and headed toward the patio door, carrying the plates inside.

"How are you faring, Hank?" Max asked. The sight of him was loathsome. He was slouched in his chair, smoking a cigarette. He wore khaki shorts in spite of the chill, and Henry saw—would never be able to unsee—the bulge at his crotch.

"What's this about?"

"I packed our things while you were sleeping," Effie said. "I hope you don't mind."

"No," he said. "Are we going home?"

"There's the ten o'clock to Philadelphia tomorrow morning. We could stay in a hotel, but I thought we might as well go back to the cottage, if it's just for a night, and save us the money. Uncle George would never know."

He was confused. "Were we going to talk about this?"

"Do you want to stay here?" she asked.

"No," he said. "Not if you don't want to."

Max pushed his chair back and stood up. "I'd better go in and help Clare," he said, and Henry watched him cross the patio and go inside.

"How are you feeling?" Effie asked.

He didn't know. He was in a fog from sleep. There was a sharp ache in his temples, and he was dying of thirst. But he said he was fine, and pulled a chair out to sit down. There was no way to talk about what they'd done. "So we're going home," he said.

She rubbed her forehead and closed her eyes. "We can call our folks from the station tomorrow. I can't face it today."

He didn't need to ask why they were leaving. What disturbed him was how calm she seemed. She sat with her legs crossed, elbows up on her armrests. She was wearing her knee-length skirt, her sheer white stockings, and black pumps—her travel attire.

"What day is it?" he asked, and she laughed wearily.

"It's Friday," she said.

The air had a sharp edge to it when it stirred, and he noticed, with surprise, that the trees in the backyard, the birches, and even the chinaberries and shrubs, had lost most of their leaves already. It had happened overnight, or it had happened gradually and he hadn't been paying attention. Henry's insides were churning. He looked down at Effie's stockings, the kind young women and girls wore back home at church, and the image of her from last night seemed impossible, like a nightmare.

"How are you feeling?" he asked softly.

She tipped her head back and sighed. "I feel like I could sleep for six days."

It wasn't the answer he wanted. But then he had no idea what answer he wanted.

*H*enry brought their suitcases down. He'd been surprised to learn it was almost three in the afternoon.

Max was working—or hiding, Henry thought—back in the study. Archly, Clara had put on a Johnny Mercer record, and to Henry's shock she was fixing herself a gin and tonic. You had to muscle through it, she said. You had to face the enemy head-on.

The big living room seemed open and clean, and no sign remained from last night. Effie must have gathered up his clothes at some point and put them into his suitcase.

Clara called down the hall for Max—"Maxie, they're leaving us now"—and Max appeared, smiling, in his shorts and T-shirt and wool cardigan. So easy and carefree. Henry couldn't get away from him quickly enough. They gathered at the edge of the foyer, and for an uncomfortable moment, no one said anything.

"I think you're being ridiculous," Clara said, finally, to Effie, and Effie smiled.

"You can think whatever you like."

"You're still a child," Clara said. "I should have understood that."

Effie turned toward the door. "Let's go, Henry," she said, and Henry, bewildered, took up their suitcases and, because he couldn't bear to be impolite, said, "Thank you for having us."

Clara laughed. "Darling. The pleasure was mine."

"Katie Scarlett," Max said, as if Henry weren't standing there beside her, "I hate for you to go this way." And when Effie looked back at him, holding the screen door for Henry, something fluttered across her face—a little tremble of feeling, which Henry couldn't read.

"I know," she said. "I'm sorry." And they went out.

They walked down the street to the cottage without saying a word. Effie's expression was dark. She never looked at him. They stepped up to the porch, retrieved the key from the hanging pot, and let themselves inside. The musty smell of the place was like a whiff from another time. Henry set their suitcases down at the foot of the stairs. Effie dropped her pocketbook, sat heavily down on the couch, and rested her head in her hands.

"Could you bring me the aspirin, Henry?" she said. "And a glass of water?"

He stood by the coffee table and watched her. He would never be able to erase it from his mind. How she'd *been* with him. How she'd bellowed like an animal. She looked up, pulling her hands down her face, making basset-hound eyes.

"Henry, please. Aspirin."

"Don't you think we need to talk?" he said.

She hid her face again and sighed. "Oh God," she said. "I can't, Henry. I don't have the strength for this right now."

"You don't have the strength?" He was trembling. Everything about her—her tone of voice, her posture, her whole physical being—it stabbed into him and wrenched his insides. "I don't care if you don't have the strength."

She gave him a dark look.

"Effie," he said. "How . . . *how* are you not—dying of shame right now?"

"How am *I*?" she cried, slapping her hand to her chest. And then she bolted up from the couch and strode past him. "I'll get the fucking aspirin myself."

He followed her through the dining room, calling her name, and stood at the bar counter while she went into the kitchen and opened a cupboard. "Effie, you don't talk to me like that. Do you hear me? Look at me, goddammit." But she didn't look at him. She took down a glass and began filling it at the tap. "Effie, do you hear me? I'm trying to talk to you. We have to talk about this."

She turned the tap off and spun to face him, water sloshing out of the glass, and cried, "What do you want me to say?" And for a second he couldn't speak. Did she really think there was nothing to say?

"Do you even remember?" he said. "Or are you going to tell me you were too drunk?"

"I remember," she said, turning away from him again. "Jesus, Henry, of course I remember."

"Because I remember," he said. "I can remember every fucking detail."

She opened another cupboard and took down the bottle of aspirin, and he watched as she poured a small pile of the pills into her palm, threw them all at once into her mouth, and guzzled the water down.

"I keep seeing you with him," he said. "I see you and it makes me sick to my stomach, Effie. How you acted with him. I'll never get it out of my mind."

She set the glass down and bowed her head, and when she spoke, her voice was weak. "You were doing it too, Henry."

"How would you know?"

She glared incredulously at him, her eyes welling with tears. "What is that supposed to mean?"

"You never looked at me," he said. "You never once looked at me."

"Would that have made it better?" she cried. "If we were staring at each other the whole time? Jesus Christ, Henry, I *saw* you. You were all over her, and you were doing it—you were doing it with her right in front of me."

"No," he shouted. "Not like you. We were fooling around—"

"So were *we,* Henry."

"No—no, you weren't. Don't tell me that's all it was." He'd found his voice, and it felt good to shout. The words poured out of him. "What I did, it didn't mean anything, but you—that was something else. I was looking at you the whole time, Effie. You wanted him, you were begging for him, I could see it. You made yourself his little whore. I've never seen you that way before. You've never been that way with me—never—that, I can tell you. You wanted him, you liked it, don't tell me you didn't."

Tears streamed down her face. "God, Henry," she wailed, "how can you talk to me like that? You're rotten. Do you know that? You're a rotten son of a bitch." She started out of the kitchen, and when he went to grab her she jerked with surprising strength away from him. "Don't touch me, you bastard."

He followed her back into the living room. "Tell me you didn't want him, Effie. Tell me you didn't like it."

"Get away from me."

She started up the stairs, and he followed. "You wanted him all along, didn't you? This whole time. You laughed at all his fucking jokes. You were dying for him."

At the second-floor landing she turned and shouted, "Get away from me, Henry!" and ran the last flight up to the attic room. He ran after her and caught the heavy glass door just as she was sliding it shut and shoved it open, so hard he thought the panes would shatter. She backed away from him, sobbing. "Get away, Henry, get away from me."

Behind her the attic room lay bathed in midafternoon light, and there was the bare mattress where they'd shared their first two weeks of marriage. She stood before it now, arms slack at her sides, and the way she cried made his heart ache for her. He wished he could go to her and hold her. "Do you love him?" he asked.

"What?"

"Do you love him, Effie?"

"No," she cried. "God, Henry."

"But last night, when you were with him . . ."

"I don't love him," she cried, "for Christ's sake." She held her hands out as if in supplication. "What do you want me to say? I wanted him—okay? I'm a human being. I thought about him. I wondered—I wondered what it would be like if . . ." She held her hands up, and then dropped them, as if words had failed her.

"If what?" he said, his voice faltering. He was dying inside.

"I'm ashamed," she said. "Do you really need me to tell you that? I've never been so humiliated in my life."

He said nothing.

"You should have stopped it," she said. "You should have done something."

"This is my fault?"

"You're my husband, Henry, and you should have been there to protect me. But you let it happen—you son of a bitch—you just let it happen." She put her face in her hands, and sobbed.

He left her there, and made his way downstairs. In the kitchen he poured himself a glass of water and drank it down. He paced the den. He imagined grabbing his suitcase, right then, without another word to Effie, and going to the train station. He could take the train to New York and find Alma, somehow. But his thoughts were wild. He wasn't thinking of Alma, he was thinking of Effie's bewilderment, her desolation and ruin.

He needed to bathe. Last night lay like a film all over him. In the second-floor bathroom he ran the shower hot and scrubbed himself twice over with the washcloth and soap. Then he stood, letting the water beat down on him, and wept.

He had never felt his heart break like this. The pain seared his insides. He remembered Ida June and how miserable she'd made him. But it was nothing like this.

He'd never be able to look at Effie the same way again, he thought.

He remembered how she'd been there, after Ida June, to offer him solace. It was she who had asked him to the homecoming dance, not the other way around, as she always told it. And he'd been grateful for her. He'd liked how assertive she was. How clear the world was to her. *She is white trash and that is all,* she'd said, and it had flattered him—more than that, it had touched him deeply—that she liked him, because her judgments could be so severe. He'd always thought she was pretty. A little more short and plump than he liked. (*Sturdy,* his mother had said, a word he could never quite erase from his mind.) But when she'd brought his attention to her, he'd wanted her. And as they'd grown closer, and he'd begun to imagine her as his wife, part of what had comforted him was knowing that she'd never be capable of making him miserable, the way Ida June had, because she'd never have that kind of hold on him. If he lost her, he'd thought, he'd be sad, but he'd get over it.

And now here he was, and the pain seemed unendurable. He would not get over it—he didn't see how he could.

He loved her. He hadn't realized, until now, how much he loved her.

Women, Uncle Carswall might say, if Henry could somehow tell him what had happened in a way that removed the sordidness from it, and his own culpability. *Damn them, son, they'll bring you nothing but misery. But you have to bear it.*

And he would. He knew this already. He wasn't going to walk out on her. She was his wife, and she belonged to him.

He'd brought his suitcase up to one of the second-floor bedrooms—a bright-yellow room with white curtains—and he dressed there and, taking a moment to collect himself, went up to the attic room. But Effie wasn't there. He went down to the living room and she wasn't there, either, and he panicked, calling her name—until he found her, to his relief, sitting out on the back porch steps. She glanced back at him miserably.

He sat down beside her. Streaks of sunlight lay across the fallen leaves in the backyard. Fall had arrived.

"I can't stop crying," she said. "I knew if I started . . ."

She wept, hugging herself, and after hesitating a moment, he put his arm around her. She leaned into him, and rested her head on his shoulder.

For supper they ate at the diner they'd gone to their first day—almost three weeks ago now—and sat at the same booth by the window. It was a Friday evening, and a few other people were there. A man in a plaid shirt and suspenders, eating alone. A trio of women in nurses' uniforms. Their waitress was an old woman with horn-rimmed glasses. Henry ordered the chicken-fried steak, Effie ordered a Cobb salad, but when their food came, she only picked at it. Her stomach didn't feel right, she said. Neither did his, he said. But he hadn't eaten in over a day, and so he forced himself. They said little. On the radio behind the bar a news program was playing. The Soviets had sent a machine of some kind up into outer space, and all the world was in a clamor. It was enough to draw their attention away from themselves.

"Huh," Effie said. "That's interesting."

They walked back to the cottage in the last light of dusk. Halfway there he took her hand, and she smiled up at him, her eyes watering, whether from emotion or because of the wind, he didn't know. They passed Clara's, on the opposite side of the street, and made no comment. The downstairs windows were alight. He could smell chimney smoke in the air.

Effie didn't feel like making up the bed in the attic room. They could sleep in the yellow room—or wherever he wanted, it didn't matter. The room was fine. While she was in the bathroom washing up, Henry changed into his pajama bottoms and T-shirt and got under the covers. The bed was comfortable, and the thick duvet enclosed him safely. They would put this all behind them. They would forget it had ever happened. He could feel it receding already. For the first time since they had arrived, he was looking forward to going home.

Effie returned in her slip, her face shiny with cold cream, and knelt at the side of the bed to pray. She didn't do this regularly, as it had turned out—the last time she'd done it had been their first night at Clara's—and what made her do it, or not do it, was still a mystery to him. When she was finished she got in under the covers, and before turning out the light she lay there looking at him. Her expression, it seemed to him, was full of remorse, her eyes big and dark.

"I love you, Henry," she said softly, and he felt the sting of tears. She'd never said those words to him without irony. He told her he loved her too, and kissed her, and she turned out the light, and they settled down to sleep.

He drifted off soon after, feeling depleted but warm.

And was startled awake, only seconds later, it seemed, by a hand pushing at his shoulder, and out of the dark came a familiar voice, clear and smooth: "Henry, my love? Did you forget about me?"

Thirteen

He'd swept her out of the bedroom and down the stairs before he was fully conscious what he was doing. Effie hadn't stirred. He didn't think she had.

"I waited for you," Alma said as she followed him, and he tried to shush her. "At the house, like we planned. I watched the sun rise. I slept on the couch all afternoon—you would have seen me there. You never came."

When they reached the den he turned and whispered, "What are you doing here? Are you out of your fucking mind?" He couldn't see her in the dark.

"Why didn't you come?"

"But"—he could barely speak, he was so bewildered—"what are you *doing* here?"

"You were supposed to meet me," she said, making no effort to conceal her voice. "Did you forget? I've been waiting for you."

He took her arm—she was wearing her cardigan—and pulled her through the dining room and kitchen and out onto the back porch.

"Why didn't you come?" she asked again. She was a shadow in the dark. It was cold out, and the stars were dazzling.

"I thought you went to New York," he said.

"What?" She laughed. "I didn't go to New York, Henry. Are you an idiot?"

"Max said you got on the train. He said he saw you."

"I didn't get on the train," she cried, and he took her shoulders and begged her to be quiet. She wouldn't. "I got on, I got off. How could you not know what I was doing?"

"Alma, please, please be quiet."

She dropped her voice, finally. "How could you not know? Honestly, Henry, how dumb are you?"

"I thought you'd gone."

"Well, I didn't go. I'm here."

"Alma"—he squeezed her shoulders—"Alma, I'm sorry," and he felt her shoulders relax.

"It's all right," she whispered, and brought her hands to his stomach. "You're dumb, but it's all right. I'm here. I didn't leave."

"Alma."

"You can't go like this." She felt the waist of his pajama bottoms. "Can you change? Or we can find you something at the house. A clown suit, maybe."

"Alma," he said, "I can't go with you."

She stiffened. He braced for her to strike him, or worse, to scream, but she did nothing.

"Alma—I'm sorry."

She stepped back away from him. "I knew it. I knew it before the sun came up."

"Please understand. I wanted to, I really—"

"Did you change your mind?"

"No," he said, "it's not like that. Alma, please. I thought you'd gone, and then Effie and me . . ." But it would be impossible to explain last night to her, and where he and Effie stood now. He couldn't explain it to himself. At some point, he supposed, she would hear from Max some version of what had happened, and she'd draw her own conclusions about him. He was glad he couldn't see her face. "I can't go with you," he said. "You know I can't. We weren't thinking straight. We let ourselves get carried away."

"Was this all just a joke to you?" she said.

"No—Alma—of course not. It meant everything to me."

"Have you been toying with me?"

"How can you ask me that?" He stepped forward and took her shoulders again, and she let him. She felt weak in his hands, as if she'd fall over if he let her go.

"You told me you loved me," she said.

"I do love you."

"You told me you loved me and you wanted to be with me."

"I do, Alma."

"No, you don't. You've had your way with me, and now you're done with me."

"That's not true," he said, shaking her. How could he make her understand? He wished she'd gone to New York—then their nights together would have been sealed off in the past, perfect and complete. And it could still be that way, he thought, if only she would understand, and kiss him, and go away. He loved her, he said again, but he couldn't run off with her. He had a wife. He'd made a commitment to her. He couldn't just leave her. Didn't she see? But as he tried to explain these things she began to laugh, slumping forward against him, pressing her forehead to his chest. She was delirious, he thought. He glanced back at the house. He'd left the sliding door open, but everything was dark and still.

"Oh God, Henry," she said. "That's rich, really. A commitment. You amaze me."

"I don't see what's funny about anything."

"You're such a devoted husband, aren't you?"

He drew away from her. "You don't have to be cruel."

"Who's being cruel?" she cried. She wasn't laughing anymore. "You led me on and said you wanted me, and now you're tossing me aside. Like I'm nothing. And now I don't have anywhere to go."

"That's not true," he said—quietly, hoping she would be quiet too. "You have Max. You have a home in New York."

"I'm just a burden to Max," she said. "You don't understand. He doesn't want me. Nobody wants me."

"I want you, Alma."

"No, you don't. You're casting me off."

"I want you," he said, and drew her to him again. "If I could lead two lives, I would. Don't you understand? I've never wanted anyone so much in my life. But I can't do it—I can't just run away with you. I have a responsibility here."

She leaned against him. "You only have the one life," she said after a moment. "You shouldn't waste it." She was speaking softly now, into his ear, which he was thankful for. She slid her hands under his shirt, like ice on his back, but her body was warm. He loved the smell of her unwashed hair. "It could just be the two of us," she said. "We could go anywhere."

"We can't. You know we can't."

"I *don't* know that. You told me we could. It's as easy as coming with me to the train station."

"I wasn't in my right mind. You know that. You know you make me crazy."

"You make me crazy too."

They spoke like this for some time—she beckoning, he refusing—until he felt her tongue on his neck, and after glancing again at the house, and seeing nothing there, he closed his eyes. She kissed him, and he sank into it. He couldn't resist her. They would have this moment, he thought, and then he would make her understand. He couldn't bear to hurt her. He wanted to leave her warm and intact. He squeezed her and ran his hands over her, as if to memorize every curve. She reached her hand, warmed now by his skin, into his pajama bottoms, and stroked and kneaded him until he was stiff. She whispered, Come with me, come with me, and he whispered, I can't, you know I can't, and dug his fingers into her back.

"Alma—God. I wish I could. But I can't. Can't we just have this? Then you'll be with me, always."

To his relief, she gave in. He knew it by the way her muscles slackened in his arms, how she withdrew her hand and laid her head on his shoulder. They held each other a long time. He kissed her head, breathing her in. He felt expansive and generous. He asked what she was going to do. She didn't know. She'd go back to New York. Maybe go to the station tonight, catch the first train up to Penn Station in the morning. He mentioned, by the way, that he and Effie were leaving in the morning too, on the ten o'clock to Philadelphia. She would hide, she said, if she wasn't gone by then—he didn't have to worry. He wasn't worried, he said, and ran his fingers through her hair.

"I'll never forget you," he said.

"I know you won't."

Later he would try to imagine the scene as Effie saw it. He would never know for certain what she saw, or for how long. From the sliding-glass door they would have been barely discernible, their bodies blurred together but unmistakably there. The moon hadn't risen yet, there were only the stars, which were out in the millions. The cold air swished through the trees. They never heard her—Henry didn't hear her—step out onto the deck and come close enough to touch them. Until she cried, in a high, choked voice, "Oh my God."

He tore away from Alma. "Effie," he said. "You're up."

She covered her mouth, and through her fingers said again, "Oh my God. Oh my *God*."

He held his palms up as if to ward off a blow. "Effie, this isn't . . ." He changed tack. "It's Alma," he said. "She's still here."

Alma had backed away from them. "Hey, honey," she said.

Very calmly, it seemed, lowering her hand from her mouth, Effie turned and walked back across the porch and into the house. Henry was too stunned at first to move.

"I guess this is goodbye," Alma said, and he glared at her. "It doesn't have to be," she said. "I can wait for you."

He left her there without a word, and went to follow his wife. He felt his way into the den, calling Effie's name, but she wasn't there. "Effie, baby?" He ascended the stairs, and at the first landing saw the closed door of the yellow bedroom, the sliver of light beneath. He ran up to it. Of course she'd bolted it.

"Effie," he said. "Please, baby, please let me in. Let me talk to you. Effie, baby, please, I love you so much. Let me in."

She didn't answer, not even to tell him to go away. He could hear her moving things around. He gripped the doorknob and rattled it. "Effie!" he shouted, and struck the door several times with his palm until, giving up, he slumped his shoulder against it and slid to the floor.

He cried. All the pent-up guilt and shame and longing, all of his exhaustion, the nights without sleep, his frayed and exposed nerves— all of it broke inside him, and he lay against the door and cried. He wasn't thinking—not grasping for a defense, not imagining what was to come, not even considering what he'd done. All of that would come later, when the shock faded and he was left, horribly, alone in his head. For now he was only a creature of feeling. He cried, and the only word in his head was *please—please, please, please.*

Finally Effie slid the bolt back and opened the door and he sat up straight. She wore her tan overcoat and her stockings and heels. From her shoulder hung a large paisley bag he didn't recognize. She looked down at him. She hadn't been crying. She'd put her makeup on and pinned her hair up. Her calmness was unnerving.

"Effie," he said. "Can we talk, baby, please?"

"I don't want to talk to you," she said. "I don't want any explanation from you. I don't want to be in the same house with you."

"Where are you going?"

"I'm going out," she said. "It's none of your business where. If you come after me, if you touch me, Henry, I'll kill you."

She stepped over him and started down the stairs into the dark.

*H*e got to his feet and went into the bedroom. Whatever he was going to do, it seemed important that he get dressed. He was pulling his trousers on when he saw, lying on Effie's side of the bed, the drawing—his drawing, in all its vulgar detail, an exact image of himself, like a reflection of his deepest shame.

Thanks for the memories, it was signed. *Love, Alma.*

Fourteen

He had ruined his life. As he dressed and went downstairs, turned on all the lights in the den and the dining room and the kitchen, poured himself a scotch and then put it aside, disgusted by the taste of it now, he felt as if he'd betrayed every object in the house and everything he owned, even his own clothes. They were reminders of what he'd destroyed. His argyle socks made him want to cry. He'd imagined happier times for them.

So much had happened, and it wasn't yet eleven o'clock. He wished he had cigarettes. He stood out on the front porch, antsy to roam the town in search of Effie, in spite of her warning, but worried too that he'd miss her if he went out. The lights were on down at Clara's. The thought that she was there—that she'd gone to Max, if only for revenge—made him panic for a moment, made him want to run down there and stop it—but then he couldn't believe she'd actually do such a thing, he was sure he knew her that much: she'd be sickened by all of them. And she'd assume Alma was there, anyway, and would want to avoid her. Unless she wanted to tear her to pieces. (Against Effie, he thought, Alma wouldn't stand a chance.) But in fact Alma wasn't there, as Henry knew, because there were lights down at the Bishops' house too.

An hour passed. He imagined Effie wandering Cape May, letting herself cry, now that she was out of his sight, or going down to the boardwalk. Yes: that must have been where she was, not crying at all, but sitting on a bench and watching the waves roll out of the dark, one after another, trying to decide whether or not to leave him.

He thought he knew the verdict already. A long line of tribulations had queued up in his near future. The trip back to Signal Creek by himself, the cavernous stations full of strangers. His solitary homecoming, and his explanation, to his mother and Uncle Carswall, of what had happened, or some version of it. How they would look at him. The inevitable confrontation with Effie's father. *There is a special place in hell for you, son.* Word would get around—it would probably get around before he made it home. He'd be shunned by the town, even by his friends, because what he'd done was unforgivable. *There's that Henry Faircloth, who was married to Mayor Tarleton's pretty little daughter. You know he cheated on her—on their honeymoon?* He'd have to move away. To Macon, where, with Uncle Red's recommendation, the railroad would probably take him. But he would do better to go farther. Maybe he wouldn't go home at all. Maybe he'd go up to New England—Maine—Prince Edward Island, like Anne of Green Gables—and become a fisherman. Let everyone back home think he was dead, like he deserved.

He was shivering. After a while the lights at Clara's went out. At the Bishops' house they shone on—through the side door at the second-story balcony, and through the windows downstairs.

He'd torn the picture into little pieces and flushed them down the toilet. Alma had intended to hurt him, even before she'd seen him tonight. Maybe she'd only intended to leave the picture in the bedroom, for Effie to discover, but when she'd seen him there she'd been unable to resist waking him—to confront him, or to see, if only

for the sport of it, if she could tempt him away. In fact he had no
idea what her intentions had been, what had been in her heart. He
could only speak for himself, and he was a fool.

Love. He didn't know her at all.

He couldn't sit still any longer. He left the porch and made his
way toward the Bishops' house. He would tell Alma she had ruined
his life. He would strike her with the back of his hand. Then, maybe,
they would run away together after all. What else was left for him?
They could be exiles together. His thoughts were muddled. He ran
up the porch steps and threw open the front door and shouted her
name.

A lamp was on in the living room, but she wasn't there. "Alma!"
he shouted again, so strenuously it hurt his throat and strained the
tendons in his neck. It felt satisfying. He stormed across the living
room and back into the kitchen, where the lights were on, shouting
her name again and again. She wasn't in the kitchen, and she wasn't
in the dining room, and when he entered the living room again he
stopped short, halted by the sight of a small old man at the foot of
the stairs, in his bedclothes and slippers, pointing a gun at him.

"You stop there," the old man said. "You stay right there and don't
you move."

Henry held his hands up. "Sir," he said. "There's been a mistake."

"I'll say."

The gun seemed too big for the old man, and it trembled in his
hands. Henry had never had a gun aimed at him before. Even at ten
yards away, the little black hole of the barrel dominated the room.

The stairs popped and he looked up to see an old woman standing in her nightgown, looking down at him in terror, her hand to
her chest. "Oh, Francis, do be careful."

"Call the police," the man said, not taking his eyes off Henry.
"And don't come down here until I tell you."

The woman hurried back up the stairs.

"Sir," Henry said, "there's no need to do that. I'll just go. I came in here by mistake. I'm sorry."

"You're the one's been in here," the man said. "You and this— Alma?"

"I'll never come back here again, I swear. I'm not a bad person."

"You stay right there," the man said. "I have shot a man before, and I am not afraid to do it again."

*T*he police arrived in minutes. Two officers, who left their blue-and-red lights flashing outside, and who had to tell the old man to set his gun down. The old woman watched from the stairs. Henry was made to sit down. The officers, one of whom was much younger than the other, almost a boy, were polite, even jovial. They called Henry sir. Questions were asked, answers were given. The old man and his wife had arrived from Philadelphia that evening and found the place a mess. No, nothing had been stolen, as far as they could tell. Yes, Henry confirmed, he'd broken into the house multiple times. No, he said, he hadn't stolen anything. Yes, he'd had an accomplice, a friend, whose name was Alma. He didn't know where she was. They'd only been looking at things. No, that wasn't all, they'd been having sex too. The old man was appalled. The officers' faces turned beet red, they cleared their throats. He was from Georgia. He was on his honeymoon. No, not with Alma. His wife's name was Effie—he spelled it. No, he didn't know where she was either. He could have lied and made things easier for himself, but he felt too miserable and penitent to say anything but the truth.

"Heck yes, we want to press charges," the old man said.

The officers placed Henry in handcuffs and led him outside and into the backseat of the squad car, and as soon as they were on their way, they laughed.

"So let me get this straight," the young one said, turning in his seat to look back at Henry. "You're on your honeymoon, but you and this sweetheart—not your wife—you just break into that house every night—to screw? Oh, Mack, we can't arrest this fellow," he said to the other one, who was driving. "We should give him a medal. He's my hero."

Cape May swept darkly by outside. He rested his head against the window. It was a short trip: the police station, along with the City Hall and courthouse, occupied a building on Washington Street, near the town center, a stretch he and Effie had passed many times. They led him into the station, where the lights were bright and the air smelled like burnt coffee. Only one other officer was on duty, manning the front desk, and he seemed to enjoy the story even more than the other officers had. "I bet you're glad you're in here, aren't you, pal? We can tell your wife we never heard of you. You'll be safe here." It was probably the most excitement they'd seen in months. They uncuffed him, took his information—reluctantly, he gave them his address and phone number back home—and took his prints and his picture. They told him the judge would be in first thing Monday morning, to set bail.

"Monday?" he cried. It was only Friday night—or rather, early Saturday morning. The clock on the wall read half past one.

"Sorry, Romeo. Next time, get nabbed on a weekday."

They said he could make a phone call, and dully he searched his mind. There was no phone at Aunt Lizzie's, and anyway, Effie probably wasn't there. It would do no good to call home. Clara was his only choice. He asked for a phone directory, and the officer at the front desk slapped it down in front of him, a slim volume. He flipped through it, expecting nothing, but—a bit of luck, finally—found "Strauss, A.," with a New Hampshire Avenue address. He connected to the number and waited, and waited, until Clara's voice came through. He could tell she'd been sleeping.

"Clara," he said. "It's Henry."

She paused for a long time. "Henry," she said, drawing his name out. "Henry, Henry, Henry. Have I heard a story about you."

"Is Effie there?"

"No, dear, I haven't seen her. I suppose she's left you?"

"Oh," he started, but his voice broke, and he began to cry. The officers looked at him with real pity. "Clara," he said, "I've been arrested. I'm at the jail."

"My God, what did you do?"

He explained what had happened, turning his back to the officers. He said nothing about Alma, but he guessed he didn't need to.

She laughed. "Oh, Henry. You are in a pickle, aren't you?"

"I don't know what to do," he said, and when she didn't respond to this, he tried again: "What am I supposed to do?"

"How should I know, dear?"

She wasn't going to help him. And why should she? But he had to try. "I mean, can you . . . is there any way you could bail me out?"

"Oh, Henry." She sighed loudly into the receiver. "Dear, sweet Henry. I'm afraid money is a sensitive issue at the moment."

"You mean you can't . . . ?"

"Listen," she said, "I'm going home tomorrow. But if I see Effie, I'll tell her what's happened. If I don't, I'll leave a note for her. That's all I can do." She sighed again, and clucked her tongue. "Poor Henry. I feel terrible for you, I do. You and I are a lot alike, you know. We want everything."

*T*he block of cells was tiny, only four of them in a square, separated by bars, with a passageway down the middle. One of the cells was occupied, by an old man in a pea coat sleeping on a cot. They put Henry in the cell diagonal from him, against the back wall. He had a cot, a sink, and a toilet bowl. No privacy, of course. No windows. Another wall clock hung at his end of the passageway, and when the officers left the block, he could hear the second hand ticking.

He held his head in his hands and cried, quietly, until the man in the pea coat said, "Quit your blubbering," and he looked up to see him glaring at him over his shoulder. "Fucking prep-school pansy," the man said, lowering his head again.

Henry looked down at his trousers and loafers and supposed an old drunk could see him that way. But his life had veered in another direction. He'd be an old drunk himself soon enough. He curled up on his cot, facing the cinder-block wall, and closed his eyes tight. The light in the block remained on, which seemed unnecessarily cruel. He'd always felt generously about himself, but now he knew what he was. A liar, an adulterer, and a criminal. He could never go home again. He could never face his family.

The hours passed slowly, one second at a time. He fell in and out of consciousness. He dreamt that he was wedged in a coal chute and was suffocating, and he woke with a loud breath. The cell was silent, aside from the old man's snores, and the second hand of the clock, and the faint buzz of the light. He couldn't hear the sea. He could have been anywhere.

Seven o'clock looked no different from one thirty, except that now a new officer entered the block, bringing oatmeal and water for breakfast. Henry drank the water but had no appetite, and set the oatmeal aside. He felt bloated, but he couldn't have relieved himself here if his life had depended on it. He curled up again and tried to sleep.

Just after noon an officer woke him, kicking his cot, saying, "Up and at 'em, kid. Time to leave."

Behind him the cell door stood open. Henry sat up, baffled, and put his loafers on.

He followed the officer out of the block and down a short corridor into the lobby, where Clara was standing at the front desk in her sunglasses, a white scarf tied about her head. Right then, she was the most beautiful thing he'd ever seen.

"My poor dear, there you are." She kissed his cheeks and hugged him, and he breathed in the scent of her Chanel. He didn't understand what she was doing there. "I'm a sorceress," she said. She'd paid the Bishops a little visit that morning, she explained, and convinced them to drop the charges. They'd called the station before she came over. Didn't he remember? They'd been old friends of her mother's. They'd been enchanted with Clara when she was a little girl. "Actually, I groveled," she said. "I'll probably hear it from Mother."

"I don't know what to say."

"Say nothing," she said. "I feel like I owe you one."

He didn't ask what for. He collected his wallet from the officer at the front desk, and just like that, he was free to go.

It was a bright fall day. Leaves skittered along the sidewalk. Clara took his elbow and they started down Washington Street. He was free, he thought. All hope wasn't lost. She asked if he was hungry, but he only wanted to get back to the cottage. He asked if she'd seen Effie, and she gave him a sympathetic look, and shook her head. "Maybe she's at the house," she said. "I thought of looking in, but I have a feeling she doesn't want to see me." She took his hand, entwined her fingers with his. "Don't worry, dear. I bet she just went to a hotel to sleep it off. She's a devoted girl. You're both so young, you know."

He nodded. They walked on, and turned right onto Madison Avenue.

Max and Alma were gone, she said. They'd left first thing that morning. "There was quite a scene last night, when Alma came back. Max wanted to kill you."

He stopped, and let go of her hand. "He did?"

"You're surprised? Alma was in pieces, you know. I don't know what you did to her, darling, but she was inconsolable."

"That's hard to believe."

"Believe what you want. I'm only telling you what happened."

They walked on. He didn't know what to think about anything.

"Anyway, he wanted to beat you to death, but Alma begged him to leave it alone, for what it's worth. She said you were in the dog-house already."

"She made sure of that," he said.

"She said she just wanted to leave, and Max said yes, it was about time they went away—and so they're gone. Just like that: gone, gone. Like always, everything comes to exactly nothing."

They came out of a bend in the street and the sea loomed ahead, sparkling, electric blue. The sight of it pained him. He wished he and Effie had gone, like Effie had wanted to in the beginning, before they'd ever met any of these people.

"I suppose we've both been abandoned," Clara said.

"I'm sorry if I ruined things for you too."

"Nonsense," she said. "I was getting bored."

She amazed him. "Do you care about anything?" he asked, and she laughed and asked what that was supposed to mean. "I just mean, nothing seems to bother you."

"Oh, Henry, sweetheart," she said. "That's all a ruse."

They turned onto New Hampshire Avenue and stopped in front of her house. From her pocketbook she withdrew a card with her address on it—Manhattan, East Seventy-fourth Street—and handed it to him.

"Please write," she said. "I love long letters. I like to read them on Sundays in the bath. And if you're ever in New York, you'll come visit?"

He said he would. They said their goodbyes, and she kissed him on the lips, and licked the tip of his nose.

———

*E*ffie wasn't at the house. The door stood open, just as he'd left it last night, and the lamp on the end table was still shining.

He showered. He packed his suitcase and made up the bed in the yellow bedroom. Effie had taken everything but a few dresses and some of her underclothes, but they were enough, he thought, to bring her back. She wasn't careless. She'd never leave things behind. He put her things in her suitcase and carried it down to the den and set it beside his. And waited. The shadows grew long. A car horn beeped outside and he looked out the window to see a taxicab waiting at Clara's. A few minutes later, it passed by on the street.

Then it was dusk. The windows were open, and the den was cold. He lay back on the sofa and pulled the quilt over him. He waited, and night fell. The lamp lit the room. The wind billowed the curtains in and sucked them back against the screens. He could hear the waves. Which meant they must be big. He knew their power now. He thought of Alma in the sea under the moon. She'd been inconsolable, Clara had said.

*H*e fell asleep at last, and when he woke, Effie was sitting on the coffee table beside him, smoking a cigarette and observing him. At first he couldn't be sure she was real. She didn't move when he opened his eyes, and she didn't say a word.

He sat up and pulled the quilt aside. "Effie. Baby."

"You look so peaceful when you're sleeping," she said. "Did you know that? You look like a little angel." He went to put his arms around her, but she held up her hand and said, "Don't touch me." She got to her feet and moved to the other side of the coffee table.

"Baby," he said. "You came back."

She said nothing.

"I've been a wreck," he said. "You wouldn't believe the night I've had. Baby—I missed you so much. I've been dying. Where have you been?"

She had not changed her clothes. Her eye shadow had faded and there was a haunted look on her face. He wondered if she'd slept at all. "I've been sitting here looking at you," she said. "I've been trying to decide if I can stomach you."

He got unsteadily to his feet, but she told him to sit down. She took a last drag from her cigarette, dropped it into a glass of water, and picked up a pack of Winstons and a silver lighter he didn't recognize.

"How long has it been going on?" she said, drawing another cigarette out.

"Baby, please . . ."

"How long, Henry?"

He put his head in his hands. "A few days," he said. He looked up to see the effect this had on her, but her face betrayed nothing. She lit the cigarette and blew out a thick stream of smoke. "It meant *nothing*, baby. I swear to Christ. Absolutely nothing."

"She's pretty," she said. "Anyone can see that. She's a good artist too. Is that what you want? A pretty little artist?"

"Baby, please—please listen to me."

"Do you want someone like her? Am I not enough for you, Henry?"

He stood up again. "You're everything to me. The only thing I want is you. I love you, baby—I love you so much."

She laughed, a hollow laugh, and pressed her palm to her forehead. "Great," she said. "Thank you. You love me. You sound like a love song."

"I don't know how else to say it."

She took a drag from her cigarette and stared at him for a moment. "I feel so stupid, Henry. That's the thing: how fucking stupid

I feel. It was right under my nose all the time, wasn't it? All those times I reached for you and you weren't there. Your fucking insomnia." All this she delivered in a calm voice, with a smile. It left him speechless. "You're a monster, Henry. You're a hypocrite. You made me feel ashamed of myself, but all the time . . ."

"Effie, baby, I don't know what I was thinking. I wasn't in my right mind."

"I don't want an explanation. I know what you are now. What I need to know is can I live with it. Are you worth the trouble?" She glared at him, and seemed really to want an answer. "What do I gain with you, Henry?"

He held his hands out to her. "Baby, I'm worth it. I'll prove it to you. I'll be devoted to you, only to you, for the rest of my life."

"What good is that?" she said. "Any man could be devoted to me. I have everything to offer. I don't need you to tell me that. The question is—what do I get with you?"

His mouth hung open. It seemed impossible to answer. "Baby. You have my love. My loyalty—from this day forward, baby, I swear. You have . . ."

"One thousand acres," she said. "That's the only sure thing I can think of. One thousand acres of land—that'll be ours someday. With that, and Daddy's business, we'll have a fortune. We'll be secure, for our children. Everything else is bullshit."

For a moment he was speechless again. He only wanted to hold her. "Does this mean you'll stay?"

Fifteen

They would stay a few more days in Cape May. Until Effie made up her mind. Before they went home, she said, she wanted things to be settled, one way or another. If Uncle George came, so be it: they'd move to a hotel, or they'd go home. She put the sheets back on the bed in the attic room, but she didn't want him to share it with her. It wasn't a punishment, she said, it was only that the thought of him touching her made her sick to her stomach. He took the room with the rose-patterned wallpaper, where they'd made love the first time.

He woke late on Sunday and she was gone, but soon she returned, in a nice blue dress and overcoat and white stockings, carrying a bag of groceries. She'd gone to church. She'd bought a few things for supper. She'd called her parents, and suggested he do the same. As soon as she'd unpacked the groceries, she changed into a sundress and sweater and went out again.

That evening, after a quiet supper of chicken and rice, she went to bed early, and Henry stayed up drinking gin, from the new bottle they'd bought before moving over to Clara's. He got drunk and talked out loud to himself. A grand confession, a vow for the future. There would forever be a shadow over their marriage, he admitted to himself, but maybe all of this would enrich it somehow. It was a trial, which over time would deepen their love. He repeated this point over and over again, as if Effie were sitting in the empty wicker chair beside him.

She went on long walks by herself. She'd go out with barely a word—"I'll be back in a little bit, Henry"—and he'd sit around the house, feeling anxious, until he decided to go for a walk himself. He'd wander the town, hoping to run into her. He'd sit on the cold beach and watch the waves. At dusk he'd make his way back to the cottage, hoping Effie would be there—that he would see, with satisfaction, an edge of anxiety on her face as she asked him where he'd been. But she'd either still be out, or she'd be in the kitchen making supper already. When he said hello, she gave him a feeble smile, and that was all.

All this time he felt an acid chill in his stomach, and as he wandered the town, he recited arguments to himself. He was a *man*, wasn't he? What did Effie expect? If she thought he was the first husband to cheat on his wife, she was a fool. In fact it was likely that *every* husband cheated on his wife at some time or another—it might be argued that such a devotion to one person was not, in fact, what nature had intended, for either men or women, but especially for men, who, from the dawn of time, had been used to wandering. In every man's heart, from the town drunk's to the mayor's, even in the reverend's heart, there was the memory of an affair—he would bet on it. The abandonment of reason to desire. Vividly, intensely carnal: the thoughts would rise up and take over. There was no stopping them.

She'd been spoiled, that was the problem. She was a little princess, doted on by her father, made to believe in fairy tales.

But that wasn't fair, he thought the next moment. She wasn't at fault. He was the monster. He'd broken her heart, and he deserved whatever she gave him.

Or neither of them had been at fault—that was more true, maybe. It was Clara, Max, and Alma, who had swept them up into their drama and confused them. It had nothing to do with their love for each other. They had temporarily lost their minds, but soon they would go back to normal again.

Tuesday afternoon the sky was dark, the clouds a featureless steel gray, and the wind was so strong and cold that Effie, relenting at last, closed the windows. To Henry's surprise, she asked if he wanted to go with her to see the waves.

The tide was high and the ocean, as far as they could see, was roiling violently. It was the kind of sea that foundered ships. They sat on a bench, their hands buried into the pockets of their coats. Only a few days ago he and Alma had leapt into the same sea. The elements were ever changing, time rolled on, it would be winter soon and then, later, it would be warm again.

"I think I'm pregnant already," Effie said.

He wasn't sure he'd heard her correctly.

"I'm pregnant," she said. "I mean, I think so. I should've had my period last week."

"Your period," he repeated stupidly. He understood next to nothing about this. It involved blood, and was governed, like tides and werewolves, by the moon.

"I could be wrong," she said. "It could be the change in climate, or my schedule. Or all the drinking. I don't know. But I'm usually so regular."

She looked at him, tentative, pulling a lock of hair behind her ear, and it began to dawn on him what she was saying. "Effie," he said, sitting up straighter. He put his arm around her shoulder, and placed his hand on her stomach. "Do you really think so?"

"I wasn't going to tell you," she said. "I wanted to see the doctor first. But it's been on my mind. It might be nothing."

"It's not nothing," he said. "I can feel it." He kissed her head and drew her to him, and she let him. They were going to have a baby. She belonged to him. Nothing else mattered. Her shoulders began to tremble, and she put her hand over her mouth and cried.

After supper that evening, he asked if he could come to bed with her. Just to sleep beside her, nothing more. Her tone, when she replied, was not angry or resentful, only tired. "I just want to be alone tonight," she said.

But sometime in the night, he woke to her weight on the bed. She got in under the rose-patterned duvet, and he opened his arms to her. She was in her slip. She laid her head on his chest, her bare leg over his thighs. He said nothing. Questioned nothing. He held her. Lifted her slip to feel her skin. Felt the expectation in her muscles. He tugged her underwear off her hips, and she helped him, and quietly, they made love.

"Tomorrow," she whispered afterward. "Let's go home."

Yes, he said. And then: "I love you, Effie."

"I know you do," she said.

In the morning the frost was so thick on the small lawn out front and on the rooftops of the houses that he mistook it at first for snow. He could see his breath on the air. Cheerfully, humming "Chances Are," he made coffee, but he reined the cheer in when Effie came down from her bath. If they wanted to catch the ten o'clock to Philadelphia, she said, they had to be out the door in two hours. They could walk to the station, but she would appreciate it if he'd run down to the Western Union office and call them a taxicab, and then they wouldn't have to carry their suitcases. He would do it, he said.

An hour and a half later the taxicab arrived outside, and on the short drive to the station Effie crossed her arms over her chest and stared out the window. She seemed veiled in darkness. He didn't yet know that this had nothing to do with him, that traveling, which for him was always hopeful, was for her always sad. She could never say why. She'd feel better when they arrived.

Sixteen

By noon the following day they were home, and on Monday
Dr. Reeves confirmed what Effie had suspected, that she was pregnant, and in July of the next year their daughter Kate was born.
Henry was relieved by how much she favored him. Joyce came in
August of the following year, and in the next year came Anne, and
several years later, they had a son, finally, Brian, who died with a fever
when he was ten days old.

Until then they had been happy. After Joyce they'd moved into
the main part of the house, and Henry's mother and Uncle Carswall
had moved into the Old Wing. (Henry's sister had moved out and
gone to secretarial school in Atlanta.) The doors and windows stood
open, and in Henry's memory, their two dogs, Rex and Colonel, were
always making laps from the back door to the front, around the yard
and back again, and their three girls were screaming and chasing after
them, and often on a Saturday morning he and Effie lingered in bed
together, the door latched, until some crisis involving the girls drew
them out. By then Henry's mother would have finished making
breakfast, which Effie, though she never said anything, always took

as a reproach. From the beginning they disliked each other but, being good Southern women, they kept this to themselves, and anyway Effie was often out of the house on errands. In those days Henry was protective of her, and jealous of the attentions of other men.

After Brian, she fell into a depression that lasted the better part of three years. She spent a month at her parents' house, in her old room, and refused to see Henry. Without consulting him first, she had her tubes tied, so she could never have children again. When she came home she began to clean constantly, and the house always smelled of bleach and Lysol. And cigarette smoke, because she'd taken up smoking for good. She drank every night until she was drunk, and sometimes she never came to bed. She fought with Henry's mother, who called her a mean-spirited and neglectful woman, and after one particularly nasty fight, Effie, on her own, moved a heavy sideboard against the door connecting the Old Wing to the main part of the house, and for good measure, she nailed the door shut. It remained shut for twelve years, until Henry's mother died.

Henry worked a signal freight to Brunswick, Georgia, three runs a week, where he'd stay the night in a boardinghouse, and he had an affair with the young widow who ran it. He would believe, later, that the change in Effie had made him stray, but in fact the affair had started while she was pregnant with Brian and things were bright. Her name was Rose. She had red hair and freckles, like Ida June, and she was ten years older than he was. One of her legs was slightly shorter than the other, and she had to wear a special shoe on that foot, with an elevated sole. He'd come into Brunswick after midnight and she'd run a bath for him, and in the morning she'd fix breakfast for him and the three other boarders, including J. P., another brakeman on the signal freight, who had become Henry's best friend, and who kept the secret. But after a year, Henry was bumped up onto a better run, up to Atlanta, and he never saw Rose again.

Effie, he told friends, had left him for Signal Creek United

Methodist Church. He meant it fondly, because it coincided with
happier times. She joined and eventually led the church's finance
committee. When part of the church caught fire, she formed the
booster club to raise money for repairs. She had a reputation for
toughness. She got along better with men than with women. One
woman, Vivian, another member of the finance committee—whom
Henry would kiss, years later, at the end of a party, when they were
both drunk—said to him, "I love her, Henry, I really do, but you are
an angel to put up with that broad every day of your life."

In the summer of 1971 a revival minister came to town, a young
man named Charlie Morrell, and for a week every girl in Signal
Creek—especially Kate, who had just turned thirteen—lost their
minds over him. He was in his twenties still, handsome and gently
passionate, charismatic under the hot, bright tent set up on the
town green. Reverend Lyle (Reverend Miller had retired) had invited Mr. Morrell to town, but it was Effie who stepped in as the
church's main emissary, and helped the young minister organize the
revival.

She was thirty-two that year, and still pretty—she would be pretty
all her life—but four children and a Southern diet had made her fat,
and Henry no longer feared that she would attract another man's attention. In this, as with so much else, he was naïve. Charlie Morrell
left town after the revival, but a few months later he was back, staying with Reverend Lyle's family for a few weeks—on what business,
Henry didn't know—and when Henry went off on his overnight runs
up to Atlanta, Effie would see him. Henry never knew what they did
together, but she was rarely at home, Kate said, and would often come
back late, after the children had gone to bed, and Vivian had seen
the two of them walking together around the Indian Mounds. When
Henry said to Effie, as casually as he could, that he'd heard she was
spending a lot of time with that revival boy, Effie said yes, he was a
dear young man. And when Henry asked outright, "Is there some-

thing going on between you two?" she glared at him and said, "You of all people don't get to ask me that."

But she'd been drinking, and the next morning she apologized for snapping at him, and said no, nothing had been going on, she promised—he could ask Reverend Lyle if he didn't believe her. But he told her he believed her, and put the matter to rest in his mind, and as far as he knew, Charlie Morrell never returned.

They still made love, occasionally, when he was home. He'd bumped up to engineer by then, and was seeing a girl in Atlanta, Genie Taylor, a waitress at the Shoney's where he had breakfast before heading to the switchyard. She was twenty-four, and lived in an apartment by herself. But after a few months she said she loved him, and asked him to leave his wife, and he said he couldn't do that, and broke it off.

It was a happy time, all things considered. Effie drank. She'd pour a full pint glass, half gin, half seltzer water, with a squeeze of lime, what she called her "fizzy drinks," and she'd have four or five of these a night, and sometimes Henry would wake alone in the wee hours and find her sitting by herself in the den, muttering to herself. He couldn't go near the subject with her, not even on the mornings when she woke chagrined and self-loathing. So he let it go, because he liked to drink too, and Effie was in her best moods when she'd had a couple. "I believe it's fizzy-drink-o'clock," she'd say gaily at six or seven in the evening, and at that hour the house often took on a celebratory atmosphere. They were frequent hosts. Dinner parties, barbecues. Friends would stop by to shoot the breeze and stay for supper and cocktails. J. P. and his wife, Nell; Maynard Givens and his wife, Helen, and their children; Bernice DuPont, who was now Bernice Clarke, and her husband, Jaime, whom everyone tolerated. (Hoke had enlisted in the navy and was stationed on an aircraft carrier in the South China Sea.) Sometimes, late on a Friday or Saturday night, Effie's voice would begin to slur and something sharp and dangerous would enter her mood, and politely their friends would comment on the hour and take their leave. If the children were up, Henry put them to bed. (Kate was getting wise, and would linger, asking if everything was okay.) In those moods, Effie could start talking about anything—gardening, say—and the subject would veer into dark terrain. "Mrs. Jackson," she once said, meaning their seventh-grade science teacher, who had once given her a C on a project involving bean sprouts, "that bitch—I never felt good about myself after that. She ruined my fucking life."

Carswall had a stroke and died in 1975. By then Signal Creek had become a suburb of Macon, and a state highway ran through the town center. For years developers had tried to get Carswall to sell the land, but he'd refused, and as soon as he was dead, Effie hired a real estate agent and started taking offers. Within a few months she'd sold or rented out all the land, and within a few years the thousand acres of fields and woods had been transformed into subdivisions and strip malls, and Henry and Effie had become, by any measure of the word, rich.

In the year before Effie died, when she was in and out of the hospital, Kate told Henry that she and Joyce and Anne had always been certain that, as soon as the last of them had grown up and moved away, he and Effie would separate. It was a surprise, she said—a happy surprise—that they were still together.

Henry was shocked. "I never dreamed of leaving your mother."

Of himself and Effie he'd sometimes said, with a grin, rolling his eyes, "We love each other, we just don't like each other that much."

Their friends, and the people at church, said, "They're a good team. They lean on each other."

They were old. Loving and leaving were no longer questions they asked of themselves. After Genie Taylor, and the unfortunate kiss with Vivian, Henry was never again unfaithful to her. He might have been, if the right woman had ever approached him, but none had. He was still handsome, he thought, though he'd lost his hair and developed a generous paunch. He and Effie barely spoke; they could read each other's minds. He always made a big to-do for her birthday, which she pretended to hate. Whatever they said, whatever anyone said, they belonged together.

A few months after Effie died—she'd been just shy of seventy-three—Henry went through the things in her room. (They'd slept in separate rooms for more than twenty years. It was the secret to a happy marriage, he liked to say.) Under her bed he found a shoe box packed with letters—dozens of them, all from Charlie Morrell, addressed to no name, only to a P.O. box in Signal Creek. He flipped through a few of the envelopes, looking at the postmarks. 1971. 1976. 1985. A faint spicy scent rose up from them. He pulled one of the letters out, from 1974, and opened it, and read:

> *Darling,*
> *It should be easy to tell Millie I have business that*
> *weekend, if you really think he'll be away, but I'm not*
> *sure my heart can take it again if . . .*

He folded the letter and slid it back into its envelope, put the envelope back with the others, and closed the shoe box, then slid the shoe box back under the bed.

His heart ached. He spent the rest of the day in front of the television, paying no attention to it. But they had been through so much together. Joy and misery. Everyday comforts and complaints. They'd had a life together, and they'd loved each other. What did Charlie Morrell matter? Kate came by after work that evening with the groceries and sat with him for a while, and they chatted amiably.

He thought of the shoe box often, but never read the letters inside.

That fall he raked a pile of leaves in the backyard to burn them, and on an impulse, after he'd started the fire, he retrieved the shoe box from under the bed and threw it into the flames. The box smoked and caught and split open, the envelopes caught, the letters inside, but then the burning pages took flight in the draft and swirled up high over his head, dozens of fluttering sparks, lighting in the pine trees, drifting back, alarmingly, toward the house, before they burned out. Some pages were nearly whole, and these he caught and balled up and threw back into the fire, but most of the floating sparks were flakes and shards of paper, and they scattered all over the yard.

He finds the pieces still, months later, little white flakes singed around the edges, nestled in the crabgrass by the house or out along the far side of the yard, where the woods begin. Fragments of words and sentences, a man's cursive in blue ink, blurred so much by the weather that most of them he can't make out . . . *sweet breath . . . your flower . . . every night I dream . . .* He leaves them be.

They never went back to Cape May, and they never spoke to each other about their honeymoon. Sometimes, when they fought, he could feel it just under the surface—the knowledge of what they were capable of. "You're no angel either," he once said to her, in an argument he can no longer remember. But that was all. When Anne, planning her own honeymoon, asked them about theirs, Effie said only that the weather had been poor, and that they should have gone to Florida.

How young and foolish he once was. How naïve when, for a brief moment, he imagined running away with a girl he barely knew. He understands now the way desire spreads, like heat—how, when he and Effie discovered it in each other, they awoke to the swollen desirability all around them. He hadn't been able to resist it. Neither had she. If she ever forgave him, he couldn't say, but he could forgive her for Charlie Morrell.

Now he can feel her drifting away, when he looks through their photo albums: he feels the contours softening. The light surrounding them turns more flattering. Henry believes in heaven, as he always has, but lately it no longer comforts him. If it's true that in heaven everyone will be free from sin, then in heaven all the people he has ever loved, though he may recognize their faces, will be strangers to him.

He imagines them all around him, a multitude—Effie beside him, divinely serene and pure.

This is better: they are back at the station in Cape May, boarding the train that will take them back to the rest of their lives. She's ahead of him. He's carrying both of their suitcases, struggling up the steps. He stumbles and she turns back and glares at him. She seizes his wrist. She will never let go.

Acknowledgments

I'm indebted to a great many people for helping me bring this book into the world and for paving the way for me to write it. It's been a long road.

Thank you, first of all, to my amazing agent, Katherine Fausset, who has been and continues to be an incredible advocate and source of reassurance, support, and editorial wisdom. I would trust her with my life (no pressure). I'm immensely grateful as well to all the team at Curtis Brown for their support and belief in this book, especially Holly Frederick, Jonathan Lyons, Sarah Perillo, and Olivia Simkins.

To Deb Futter, my wonderful editor at Celadon Books: you changed my life in a single day. Thank you for believing in this book and for taking a chance on it, and thank you for your guidance and unflagging enthusiasm. I'm indebted to everyone on the Celadon team, whose warmth and support have been overwhelming—especially Rachel Chou and Christine Mykityshyn for their marketing and publicity wisdom; Anne Twomey, for a beautiful cover; Alexis Neuville, for her mastery of schedules and logistics; and Randi Kramer, for clearly and kindly explaining things to me.

Thank you to my fabulous U.K. editor, Federico Andornino, and to all the people on the W&N team—and thank you as well to the editors at Blessing Verlag, Einaudi, Editions Stock, Lumen, and Lindhardt & Ringhof: I am honored to be on your lists.

This book would not exist without the support of my writing

group, the Chunky Monkeys: Jennifer De Leon, Calvin Hennick, Sonya Larson, Alexandria Marzano-Lesnevich, Celeste Ng, Whitney Scharer, Adam Stumacher, Grace Talusan, and Becky Tuch. In addition to being intimidatingly sharp readers, writers, and disciplinarians, they are also some of my closest friends, and I would not have had the guts to see this book through without their encouragement and wildly inappropriate email chains.

Thank you to my teachers—especially Margot Livesey, who is a role model to me; Pamela Painter, my thesis advisor at Emerson College, who worked me to exhaustion; and Frederick Reiken, who among other things opened my eyes to Alice Munro. Thanks also to Andrea Barrett, Maud Casey, Maria Flook, DeWitt Henry, Katia Lief, Randall Kenan, Thomas Mallon, and Jessie Sholl.

I would have been lost at sea after my MFA program without the amazing community of writers, teachers, and students at GrubStreet, the literary arts nonprofit in Boston where I taught fiction and worked on staff for nearly a decade. Thanks, especially, to Christopher Castellani, who has become a mentor over the years, as well as a great friend. Thanks also to Eve Bridburg, whose belief in me and encouragement of my career have been invaluable. And thanks to all my friends from the staff, current and former, whom I love like family—Sonya Larson and Whitney Scharer (again), Alison Murphy, Sean Van Deuren, Rowan Beaird, Sarah Colwill-Brown, Jonathan Escoffery, Dariel Suarez, Lauren Rheaume, and Ian Jude Chio—and to my fellow instructors, who have taught me so much, among them: Alysia Abbott, Howard Axelrod, Jenna Blum, Lisa Borders, Michelle Hoover, Ron MacLean, Ethan Gilsdorf, and many, many more than I can name here, as well as the Grub-adjacent Ryan Scharer, whose home, with Whitney, has been the scene of many sloppy cocktail nights and insufferable discussions of craft. And finally, thank you to all my students at GrubStreet over the years, who inspired me every week and made me a sharper writer and a better person.

I'm deeply indebted to the Bread Loaf Writers' Conference, which changed my writing life and broadened my horizons. Thanks to Michael Collier and Jennifer Grotz, and especially to the calm presence of Noreen Cargill, whom I was fortunate enough to work with in the back office for a couple of years. Thanks also to Mike Scalise and Cara Blue Adams, my beloved head waiters, and to all my fellow waiters of 2011.

Thanks as well to the Tin House Summer Writer's Workshop, the Vermont Studio Center, and the St. Botolph Club Foundation— organizations that each gave me support and encouragement when I needed it—and to Emerson College, for my MFA, and to the New School, where I took my first writing workshops.

My friends are everything to me, and they have supported me and my writing life in more ways than I can count. Thank you to my dear friend Lizzie Stark, whose family's beach house in Cape May inspired the setting for this book, and to George Locke, her husband, who taught me everything I know about noise music and kettlebells; thank you to Cam Terwilliger, who for months met me at six every morning at Diesel Café in Somerville to write; to James Scott and Urban Waite, with whom I wish I were sitting right now around a pit fire, sipping bourbon; to Laura van den Berg and Paul Yoon, magical, otherworldly beings; to John Cotter and Elisa Gabbert, fellow book-club members; to Benjamin Allen and Ashley Peterson, with whom Katie and I will always be tubing down the Deerfield River of our hearts; to Dan Pribble, my DM for life, and to Marianna Hagbloom, who taught me everything I know about whale penises; to Scott Votel (a.k.a. Gregor Hategood) and Moira Mannix, whose calm advice helped Katie and me in our first months of parenthood; to Amanda Dykstra, who needs to keep writing, and to Greg Esposito, whose recipe for haddock has strengthened my marriage; to Sean Lanigan, who also needs to keep writing, and Cami Hennekens, beloved former roommates; to Jaime Clarke and Mary

Cotton, owners of the indispensible Newtonville Books; to Jennifer Olsen, Christen Enos, Kathleen Rooney, and Abby Beckel, who welcomed me at Emerson and have been good friends ever since; to Julia Cadieux, who informed me that balls smell like pancake batter; to Elizabeth Souder, whose sofa allowed me to move to New York many years ago; and to my oldest friends, Iain Campbell, Carlos Chavez, and Vicky Tsai, who have always loved and supported me.

Thank you, Mom and Dad, for raising me right and always encouraging me, even when my decisions haven't seemed sensible, and thank you, Wes, my brother, for being my best friend all my life—and to my sister-in-law, Cindy, and my nephews, K.C. and Ben: I love you all.

Thank you, Aunt Jackie, for more than I can say here.

And thank you, finally and most of all, to Katie Hunt, my wife, my love, and to our baby daughter, Audrey, whose due date provided the deadline I needed to finish this book. My tender sweeties, I love you both so much.

CAPE MAY READING GROUP DISCUSSION QUESTIONS

1. How does the anonymity provided by a mostly empty seaside town contribute to the story?

2. How does the time period inform the characters' interactions and decisions throughout the book?

3. Henry is only twenty years old, and Effie just eighteen. Do their ages change how you feel about them? Why or why not?

4. What role do wealth and status play in the characters' perspectives on life and on one another?

5. Discuss how you feel about Alma.

6. Marriage involves both give and take. What does Henry give? Take? How about Effie? What can this tell us about their relationship from beginning to end?

7. Is it possible to define a "breaking point" for a marriage? What factors have to be considered? Do you think it is possible to truly forgive?

8. Do you think Henry and Effie are sympathetic characters?

9. Would Henry and Effie's marriage have been different if they hadn't gone to Cape May for their honeymoon?

10. Discuss how you feel about the final chapter.

11. How would you feel if an event that took place on your honeymoon defined the course of your entire marriage?

CELADON
BOOKS

Founded in 2017, Celadon Books, a division of
Macmillan Publishers, publishes a highly curated
list of twenty to twenty-five new titles a year. The
list of both fiction and nonfiction is eclectic and
focuses on publishing commercial and literary
books and discovering and nurturing talent.